"I Admire People Who Are Strong Enough to Dream,"

said Rio. His long fingers caressed Hope's face, feeling the warmth of her tears beneath his fingertips. "Like you."

"You're strong," she whispered. "What are your dreams?"

"I don't have any. I stopped dreaming the day I really understood what half-breed meant."

Hope's eyes darkened and she shook her head, silently denying both the pain of Rio's long-ago discovery and her own realization that she had fallen in love with a man who had no dreams.

"I'll dream for you, Rio," she promised in a husky voice.

Dear Reader,

When two people fall in love, the world is suddenly new and exciting, and it's that same excitement we bring to you in Silhouette Intimate Moments. These are stories with scope, with grandeur. These characters lead the lives we all dream of, and everything they do reflects the wonder of being in love.

Longer and more sensuous than most romances, Silhouette Intimate Moments novels take you away from everyday life and let you share the magic of love. Adventure, glamour, drama, even suspense— these are the passwords that let you into a world where love has a power beyond the ordinary, where the best authors in the field today create stories of love and commitment that will stay with you always.

In coming months look for novels by your favorite authors: Maura Seger, Parris Afton Bonds, Elizabeth Lowell and Erin St. Claire, to name just a few. And whenever you buy books, look for all the Silhouette Intimate Moments, love stories *for* today's women *by* today's women.

Leslie J. Wainger
Senior Editor
Silhouette Books

IMRL-7/85

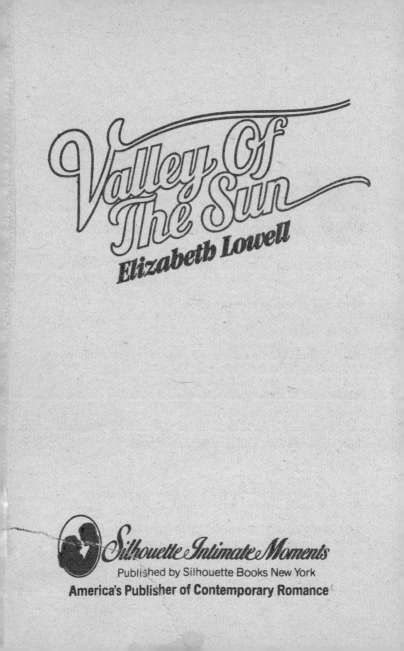

Valley Of The Sun

Elizabeth Lowell

Silhouette Intimate Moments

Published by Silhouette Books New York

America's Publisher of Contemporary Romance

SILHOUETTE BOOKS
300 E. 42nd St., New York, N.Y. 10017

ISBN: 0-373-07109-4

First Silhouette Books printing September, 1985

10 9 8 7 6 5 4 3 2 1

Books by Elizabeth Lowell

Silhouette Desires

Summer Thunder #77

Silhouette Intimate Moments

The Danvers Touch #18
Lover in the Rough #34
Summer Games #57
Forget Me Not #72
A Woman Without Lies #81
Traveling Man #97
Valley of the Sun #109

ELIZABETH LOWELL
lives in California with her husband and their
two children. Her beautiful marriage is
responsible for her strong belief in romantic
love. That belief, combined with her
imaginative power and sorcery with words,
makes her a favorite with romance readers.

For Heather,
daughter, friend, fan

Chapter 1

THE SIERRA PERDIDA RANGE ROSE DARK AND SILENT TO the east of the Valley of the Sun. The mountains were lush with evidence of water—grass valleys and rippling green forests and a few sheltered snowfields like diamonds scintillating high above the desert afternoon. Hope Gardener was too far away to see the snowfields or the water-rich valleys or the forests, but she knew that they were there. They were always there, a dream to tantalize the ranchers who lived with the dry reality of the high desert that lapped around the mountains like a sagebrush sea around green islands. Yet Hope wouldn't have traded a single one of the tawny, thirsty, harsh sections of her ranch for all the Sierra Perdida's easy beauty.

She would not, however, have minded some of the mountains' tumbling wealth of water. She wasn't greedy. She wasn't asking for a deep river that ran year around, or even a stream that ran upside down, concealing its water a few feet beneath the dry river

bed. She wasn't asking for a lake shivering with wind
and trout. A pond, though. Yes, just a pond. Sweet
water that could slake her cattle's endless thirst.
Water to soothe and nourish the tender roots of alfalfa
and oat hay. Just one source of water that would stay
wet no matter how dry the surrounding land became.

"Why not ask for hot and cold running money while
you're at it? If you're going to dream, dream big!"

Hope's mouth turned down in a smile at her own
expense as her muttered question was swallowed by
the road noises rattling around the water truck's dusty
cab. The steering wheel bucked suddenly in her
hands. Automatically she braced her body, hauling
the rented army surplus truck back into the center of
the rutted excuse for a road. Muscles in her arms and
her shoulders knotted in protest. She ignored the
burning aches just as she ignored the exhaustion that
had made her overlook the pothole in the first place.

"Just one more load," she promised herself.

At least, just one more load for today. Tomorrow
was another day, another stretch of Nevada's seam-
less sunshine baking the dry land, another string of
hours when only dust devils moved over the empty
land. *And this battered truck,* she reminded herself
silently. *Don't forget poor Behemoth, lurching over
this lousy road like a dinosaur on the way to extinction.*

Like the Valley of the Sun itself, dying.

Hope set her teeth and forced herself to pay
attention to the washboard road rather than to her
thoughts circling like vultures around the certainty of
the death of her ranch and her dreams. Resolutely she
reminded herself that tomorrow could bring many
things. The price of beef could rise so that the cattle
she couldn't water could be sold at break-even prices.
The bank could decide that the last hydrologist's
report on Silver Rock Basin indicated a good proba-
bility of water and lend her enough money to go after

it. A hydrologist who wasn't a con artist might answer her ad and find the artesian river she believed flowed deep beneath the Valley of the Sun. One of the old wells could begin producing water again, enough water to see a core of her breeding stock through this endless drought.

It could even rain.

Hope leaned forward to peer out the dusty windshield at the Perdidas. A few wisps of water vapor clung to their rakish peaks. Not enough clouds, though. Not nearly enough. Rain might fall in the high country in a day or two or three, but not in the high desert of her ranch, where the land cracked and bled sand and the cattle gathered around dry wells to bawl their thirst.

For an instant Hope's reflection looked back at her from the dusty glass. The western hat concealed everything about her face but the lines of worry and weariness thinning her otherwise generous mouth. Her hazel eyes were just a flash of light within the dark shadow of the hat brim. Her loosely curling, bittersweet-chocolate hair was swept up and hidden from the sun beneath the battered crown of the hat. A few tendrils had escaped to lie along her neck, held there by the moisture that heat and the effort of controlling Behemoth had drawn from her fine-grained skin.

"Oh, boy, if your agent could only see you now," muttered Hope, grimacing at the dusty reflection of herself that faded even as her eyes focused on it, like a mirage shimmering above the empty desert. "It's a good thing your fortune was in your legs, not in a perfect little-girl face. Because you aren't a little girl anymore. What will it be next birthday—twenty-four? And what do you want for your birthday, big girl? A well, you say? A nice, deep, clean, sweet, endless well?"

Hope laughed, a sound that was musical and humorous and sad. Almost twenty-four years ago her father had brought in a well that was nice and deep and clean and sweet. He had named it, and his just-born daughter, Hope. The well hadn't been endless, though. Unless a miracle occurred, it would run dry by her twenty-fourth birthday.

The empty water truck rattled and shook down the steep grade to the Turner ranch boundary. More than miles separated the two ranches. One ranch had water. The other did not. It was as simple and final as that. No fences separated the two ranches. It wasn't necessary. No Turner cattle would wander miles away from water onto dry Gardener land. As for Gardener cattle, there had never been enough to wander anywhere. There had been plans, though, and dreams. Her grandfather's. Her father's. Her own.

And there had been the land, a land Hope loved as she had never loved anything else. Other girls had dreamed of boyfriends and babies, honeymoons and happily-ever-afters. Any inclination Hope might have had to share her girlfriends' dreams had died on her eighteenth birthday. What little trust in men and love that remained to her after that night had been eroded to nothing as she watched her own mother, and Julie, her beautiful older sister. Now Hope put her faith in the land. Its tawny power called out to senses as no man ever had. Life had taught her that the land endured and love did not. Deep inside herself she had always known that she was a woman born for enduring things. She could not walk away from a man she loved as her mother had. Nor could Hope learn to move from man to man, affair to affair, leaving behind pieces of herself until nothing remained but a hollow smile. Like her sister.

With unnecessary force Hope wrenched the steering wheel, holding the lumbering Behemoth to the rutted road. The truck rounded a shoulder of the rugged hills and dropped down into a long, narrow valley. At the lower end of the valley, Turner's windmill rose thinly above the land. There was a startling flash of green around the machinery, sagebrush and willows gone wild, a silent shout signaling the presence of water. The patch of grass was less than ten acres in extent, a ragged emerald saucer surrounding the circular metal cup that was filled to overflowing by the windmill's tireless turning. Hope knew that the windmill's metal straw went more than six hundred feet into the land, sipping up water that was clean and cold and pure. Cattle lay in the lacy shade of huge clumps of sagebrush and desert shrubs, chewing quietly, waiting for the sun to descend. The Herefords' russet hides made a rich contrast to the green and blue oasis.

Hope shouldered open the cranky cab door and jumped lithely to the ground despite her tiredness. A quick look beneath Behemoth's ungainly barrel assured her that the lower valve was closed tightly. She connected the intake hose after a brief struggle with its balky canvas coils. There was another struggle connecting the hose to her jerry-rigged pump. The portable generator that ran the pump was so old that it had to be started with a crank. She had discovered the pump rusting in the barn a month ago. It was then that she had gotten the idea of hauling Turner water to Gardener cattle in the hope of surviving until the rainy season began.

At first it had been a trip every three or four days through the searing September sun to supplement her ranch's overworked wells. But in October the rains still hadn't come, not even to the Sierra Perdida's high country. She had made the trip to Turner's well every two days, then every day. Twice a day. Four times a day. Dawn to dusk and then even longer as the drought continued and the water table fell more and more. She had connected portable generators to three of her windmills when the desultory wind proved not up to the task of drawing water from the depths of the land. Now, in early November, her generators worked around the clock to bring up less and less water. And Hope—Hope worked until she couldn't lift her arms to drag Behemoth around one more bumpy curve. Only then did she sleep, a sleep haunted by the bawling of thirsty cattle.

Hope pulled off her gloves, stuck them into the hip pocket of her jeans, and picked up the battered tin bucket that leaned against the pump. Like the cattle, Behemoth's radiator had a bottomless thirst. A gust of unseasonably hot wind swelled through the narrow valley, making the windmill's arms turn with lazy grace. As she reached to dip the pail into the huge circular trough, she hesitated, caught by the beauty of water welling over the lip of the metal pond. The fluid silver veil fell musically to the ground, creating a rich, dark ribbon of earth that cattle had churned into ankle-deep mud. The mud didn't bother Hope; she would have moved heaven and earth to see mud like that around her own wells. Her stock tanks didn't overflow slowly, turning baked ground into a wealth of earth oozing with promise. Her own wells couldn't even keep up with the searching, dusty muzzles of her cattle.

Balancing on the plank walkway that she had made over the slick mud, Hope braced herself against the tank. Overflowing water was a cool shock against her thighs and a dark stain spreading down her jeans. Suddenly Hope set down the dry bucket, put her hat inside, and thrust her arms elbow-deep into the sweet water. She brought her cupped hands to her face in a silver shower of moisture and laughter that was as musical as the sound of water overflowing.

Deep within one of the nearby thickets a horse moved restively at the sudden sound of laughter. Rio bent his dark head next to the horse's and murmured softly. The animal quieted, returning to its three-legged doze. Rio straightened, then flowed down out of the saddle with the silence of a shadow. He had heard the truck's labored approach and had watched Hope's efforts to set up the awkward hose that would fill the empty truck. He had started to come out of the concealing brush with an offer of help when something about her had stopped him. Though obviously tired, she moved with the grace of a wild thing as she filled the big truck's steaming radiator and coped with the ancient equipment. Slender, determined, she used an instinctive knowledge of leverage when her own strength wasn't enough to handle the awkward machinery. A hip braced here, a shoulder thrust there, a quick twist of her hands, and the ragged canvas hose was coaxed into place.

And then her laughter came, as quicksilver and unexpected as water in a dry land. Now her faded jeans and shirt clung wetly to her, revealing a body as surprisingly lush as the dark tumble of her hair shimmering richly beneath the sun. She was long-legged, elegantly curved, and her breasts were intimately outlined by the wet blouse. Rio couldn't help responding to the picture she made as she stood arched against the sky, totally lost in her sensual response to the sparkling water pouring from her outstretched hands. He wondered if she would come to a man like that, nothing held back, nothing calculated, a quicksilver woman laughing and burning in his arms.

A slight smile softened the otherwise unyielding lines of Rio's face. No wonder John Turner had kept trying to lure Hope into his bed by proposing marriage. If rumor were true, she kept turning him down, had been turning him down since she came back to the ranch two years ago. That was what had brought Rio out to the distant well. He had wanted to see a woman who cared more for a doomed ranch than she did for any man, even a rich white-eyes like Turner. Any other woman Rio had ever met would have given in to the inevitability of sinking water tables and drought-ridden land. Any other woman would have shaken off the Valley of the Sun's brutal demands like a dog coming out of water and would have been happy to curl up at Turner's big feet.

But not this woman. She was out here alone, a battered tin bucket in one hand and her dreams in the other.

Hope put on her hat, filled the bucket, primed the pump, pulled on her gloves with a few practiced motions, and began wrestling with the crank that served to start the generator. The iron handle was long and had been in the direct sunlight for enough time that the rough iron felt warm even through leather gloves. The machine was also stubborn. It took both hands and a lot of determination just to make the crank turn. To make it turn fast enough to start the generator took every bit of strength she had.

With a grimace Hope forced her tired arms to drag the crank around quickly. The generator sputtered and almost caught. Encouraged, she worked harder, thinking of her beautiful black cattle waiting thirstily by their hot, dry trough. Far too hot for November. Far too dry. If it weren't for this wretched generator, she would have been forced to sell off the last of her range cattle and the first of her Angus. The thought gave strength to her aching arms, but not quite enough. The generator coughed and shivered and refused to catch.

"Let me help."

The quiet male voice startled Hope. She let go of

the crank and whirled around. Only Rio's quickness saved her from getting a painful rap as the crank's long iron handle leaped upward, completing the circuit she had begun. He lifted her out of danger with one arm and with the other hand snagged the crank handle. Automatically Hope balanced herself by putting her hands on his shoulders. In the instants before he released her, Hope's senses registered the bunched strength of his arms and the long, resilient muscles of his torso and legs.

"I—thanks," Hope said, finding herself safely on her feet again as suddenly as she had been snatched off them.

Hope watched as he worked the ancient machine with a power and coordination that fascinated her. He was over six feet tall, long-limbed, wide-shouldered. The hair that showed beneath his battered Stetson was thick and straight, as blue-black as a raven winging through the desert sky. His clothes were dusty with the day's ride, but otherwise clean. A shadow of satin-black hair showed in the open front of his faded blue work shirt. His skin was dark, almost mahogany. His boots were like his leather belt— supple, worn, of highest quality. The buckle closing his belt was of smooth silver with an intricate inlay of turquoise, coral, and mother-of-pearl. Hope recognized the Zuni workmanship and the cryptic symbols telling of a shaman calling down rain upon the thirsty land. She realized that the buckle was not an affectation with him. Like his hair and his skin, the symbols were part of his heritage.

The generator surged into life, sucking water from the circular trough. The hose leading to the truck began to swell. Hope watched as the man studied the generator, made an adjustment in the hose coupling, and listened with a cocked head to the engine's racket. In some ways he reminded her of her stallion, Storm

Walker. There was a physical assurance about him
that spoke of horizons explored, tests passed, and a
primal awareness of his life in relation to the land
around him.

The hose became as tight as a sausage. Water shot
out in a fine spray from the coupling Rio had adjusted. There was less water than usual, because he
had tightened the coupling more securely than Hope
had been able to.

"Sorry," she said, laughing and ducking as mist
beaded her face. "I should have warned you about the
connection."

Rio could have evaded the spray. Instead, he swept
off his hat, unbuttoned his shirt, and let the cool water
bathe him as he worked over the coupling. Unlike
most cowboys, he didn't have a line of white skin
beneath the band of his hat. Nor was his chest pale
beneath the open shirt. Despite the desert's harsh
sun, it was obvious that Rio spent at least part of his
time hatless and bare to the waist. It was also obvious
that he was a man fully alive to all of his senses. His
naked appreciation of the water struck a primitive
chord within Hope.

Rio's hands both coaxed and coerced the metal
threads of the coupling into a tighter mating. As he
worked, water drops beaded brightly over the tanned
skin and smoothly coiling muscles of his arms and
back. Slowly the spray diminished into little more
than a sheen of moisture trickling from the corroded
brass and sun-bleached canvas.

"Sometimes," said Rio as he shook back a thick
wedge of hair from his forehead and replaced his hat,
"the best part of life is an accident that goes right."
His voice was quiet, calm, subtly gentled by a south-
western drawl.

With a brief touch he led her away from the noisy

generator into the lacy shade of a clump of brush. Using quick glances, he checked the fat hose and the generator and the well.

"You can't be a cowboy," she said in a low voice, thinking aloud as she watched him.

Rio looked at her suddenly. She saw that his eyes were navy blue, clear, almost shocking in their intensity. They were also as aloof and private as a winter sky.

"Cowboys have white foreheads and chests," explained Hope, feeling more than a little foolish.

Rio's smile took Hope by surprise. At first glance she had simply thought of him as another range rider—taller than most, yes, and stronger, but still just one more cowhand. Then he had opened himself to the diamond spray of water and smiled, and his words had revealed the humor and intelligence beneath his tanned face.

"Hope Gardener," she said, taking off her work glove and holding out her right hand.

"Rio."

His larger hand enveloped hers. She had a distinct sensation of warmth and strength, then his hand released hers and vanished within his worn leather work glove once again. Like his voice and his eyes and his coordination, his hand was unexpected. Long fingers tapering to well-kept nails, fingers hard and yet gentle with her softer flesh, the hand of a musician or a surgeon. But there were scars across his knuckles, and a quickness that could either comfort or threaten.

The realization made uneasiness streak through Hope as she remembered another man with scarred knuckles. Turner had not had any comfort in him at all. Yet Rio did. There was gentleness and warmth in his smile, and reassurance in his way of being close to her without crowding her.

Sighing unconsciously, Hope relaxed with Rio as she had relaxed with few men since her eighteenth birthday.

"Rio," she murmured. Her hazel eyes shifted focus, turning inward. She had heard that name before. Just Rio. No first or last or middle name. Spanish for river. Was it Mason who had mentioned the name Rio? "I keep thinking I've heard that name before."

"Maps," offered Rio laconically, his smile lurking just on the point of release. "Rio Bravo. Rio Colorado. Rio—"

"—Verde and Amarillo and Grande," finished Hope, smiling openly, realizing that he wasn't going to say any more about himself. "And a whole lot of other *rios* I've never even heard of, I'd bet."

"You'd win," agreed Rio. "The Indians were here first, but the Spanish knew how to write. And since white men couldn't wrap their tongues around Indian words—" He shrugged, not finishing his sentence. The maps spoke for themselves: Spanish rather than Indian names. Without bothering to button his shirt he tucked it into his jeans with a few swift motions. "Hear you're looking for water."

Hope barely heard Rio's words. His quickness fascinated her, as did his grace. She decided then that he was more like a mountain cat than a stallion. Or maybe he was some of both, a legend born out of its time, trapped in a century that had neither appreciation nor use for myth. Nor, she admitted, for Indians themselves. It must have been difficult for a man of Rio's intelligence to suffer the casual abuse of bigots.

Then the meaning of Rio's near-question penetrated her mind. "Er, yes," she said. "I ran several ads for a hydrologist."

" 'Willing to take risks,' " quoted Rio softly. "Like you. You're a gambler, aren't you," he said. It was a statement rather than a query. "You're a dreamer, too. And I'm a man who finds water."

Hope's smile slipped. Rio had obviously read her ad and thought little of her chances of finding water. She waited patiently, withdrawing into herself, disappointed that he was just one more con man come to see how many dollars he could wring from her dreams. And even if he weren't a con man, what made him think that he could find water where better-trained men had failed? What vast store of experience gave him the right to comment on her and her hope of saving her ranch? Because that was what he was doing. He was offering to work for her and at the same time he seemed to be saying that it was useless. *Gambler. Dreamer.*

"No," she said, her voice as cool and impersonal as water flowing over the steel lip of the trough. "I'm neither a gambler nor a fool. I believe there is a fighting chance of finding artesian water beneath the Valley of the Sun. That's all I ask. A fighting chance."

Rio's eyes narrowed, measuring the change in the woman who stood before him. Now he could believe that this slender, lonely young woman had refused John Turner and every other prowling male in Nevada's Basin and Range country. The Hope who was speaking now was someone who counted no unhatched chicks, asked no favors, and took no prisoners. She knew what she wanted, and what she wanted was the land. Rio could understand that. It was what he had always wanted, the only thing that he had taken from life. The West, all of it, rich and wild; and he was the wind moving unhindered over the face of that land.

But all he said to her was "Dreamer doesn't mean fool."

Hope said nothing. She had watched her sister's dreams, and her mother's. Perhaps all dreamers weren't fools, but some dreamers died young, disillusioned, crying for men who never loved in return. Hope couldn't control other people's dreams, but she could control her own. She could ask only for what was possible. Artesian water, not a dream of love. Water that would give back to her the one enduring thing in her life—the Valley of the Sun. It had been there long before drought and men who didn't love enough; it would be there long after all men were less than dust lifting on a dry wind.

"Ask Mason," said Rio quietly. "Then decide."

He turned and walked back into the sagebrush clump. He emerged a moment later, riding a *grulla* mare that moved as though she had been born in the wild and only recently tamed. Yet the mare was no more an average slab-sided mustang than Rio was an average tongue-tied cowhand. The mare might have been raised wild, but Arab blood ran hot in her veins and intelligence glowed in her wide dark eyes.

"She's beautiful," breathed Hope, thinking of Storm Walker and the incredible foals that might come of such a mating. "If you ever want to breed her, bring her to—"

"Storm Walker," interrupted Rio quietly, reining the mare around Hope. He rode as he had walked, with economy and grace and power. A tiny gesture of his left hand lifted the mare into a long lope, and he merged his body with the mare's supple movements as though he were part of her.

"Yes. Storm Walker," said Hope after a few bemused moments.

She was talking to herself. Only a faint hint of dust in the air remained to tell her that for a time she hadn't been alone. There was no sound but that of water falling into the rapidly filling barrel of the truck. The windmill turned slowly, bringing up more water. The level in the tank kept dropping, though, liquid wealth transferred into Behemoth's steel belly, Turner water on its way to thirsty Gardener cattle.

The thought didn't bother Hope. She would have done the same for any neighbor had she been the one with abundant water and had her neighbor's animals bawled with thirst. John Turner had more than enough water. At one time her father had seen Turner's interest in her as the salvation of the Valley of the Sun—money and water piped in from the Turner ranch. But her father had been wrong. Turner had wanted only Hope's body, not a woman to marry; and he had tried to take by force what she had not wanted to give.

From old habit Hope's mind shied away from the terrifying night of her eighteenth birthday. She uncoupled the hose, yanked it into place on the truck's rack, fastened the clamp down, and swung into the cab. If she hurried she might catch Mason before he had to drive out to the wells and refuel the generators. Mason would know about Rio. Mason knew about everyone who had ever left a mark in the West. And somehow Hope was sure that Rio had.

The thought of finding out more about Rio made Hope impatient with the road, the heavy truck, and her own insufficient strength. Skill, technique, and finesse could only accomplish so much. If she had had Rio's easy strength, she could have gone twice as fast and not worried about losing control on the corners or in a rut.

By the time Hope pulled into the ranch yard she was hot and tired all over again. Even in the late afternoon, the sun had not lost all of its intensity. Sweat had replaced cool well water on her skin.

"Mason!" cried Hope, spotting him just as he climbed into the pickup truck that was the ranch's only other transportation.

Hope leaped down out of the high cab as Mason

turned and faced her. Even across the dusty yard she could see a smile crease his leathery face.

"You're back early," he called. "I left you some lemonade."

"How about ice?" she said, smiling, knowing that the old man loved ice—and hated refilling ice trays the way a cat hates mud. When she was gone all day she usually returned to an empty freezer, a jumble of ice trays in the sink, and a chagrined smile on Mason's face.

Mason tried to look offended and failed entirely. He chuckled. "You know me too good, gal."

"After all these years, I should hope so!" she retorted.

Hope slipped her arm through his and led him into the relative coolness of the kitchen. Two years ago, when she had come back to the ranch to live full-time, she had taken some of the money she had earned modeling hosiery and had transformed the worn kitchen into a bright center of ranch life. In the winter when the long winds blew from the north, she and Mason played cribbage on the old oak table while she listened to stories of his father and uncles, grandfathers and great-uncles and great-grandfathers, and the women they married, the children who died young and the children who survived, the people who built and the people who destroyed.

It was a fascinating living history revealed to her in the gravelly, wry words of a man more than twice her age, a man whose ancestors had known the best and the worst the West could deliver. It was her own history, too, for Mason's family had worked alongside her mother's family in the Valley of the Sun for more than a hundred years. Her mother hadn't felt that way about history and the ranch, though. She had hated the Valley of the Sun, had cursed its tawny heights and shadowed canyons with a depth of emotion that had once terrified Hope.

"Have you ever heard of a man called Rio?" asked Hope quickly, not wanting to remember her mother, who had loved and hated as deeply as anyone Hope had ever known.

"Big man, easy moving, Indian look to him?"

"Ummm," agreed Hope. "With a smile that makes you believe in life everlasting."

Mason shot her a sideways glance. "Musta took a liking to you. Rio don't smile much."

"He was probably laughing at me," she said, remembering Rio's comments about dreamers and gamblers.

"Doubt it."

"He don't laugh much?" suggested Hope, imitating Mason's ungrammatical drawl.

"Good thing you got them pigtails cut, or I'd pull 'em sure as hell." Mason's smile faded as he reversed a kitchen chair and braced his arms across the back of it. "Rio don't laugh at nobody but fools. You may be stubborn as flint, but you ain't no fool."

Hope squeezed the old man's shoulder affectionately. He felt like a handful of rawhide braid beneath her fingers. Age hadn't stooped him, nor even slowed him very much except for the occasional arthritis in his hands. He was still nearly six feet of "hard times and bad water," as her father had once described his foreman and best friend.

"What does Rio do?" she asked, bringing her iceless glass of lemonade to the table and sitting down.

"Breaks horses."

"Is that all?" asked Hope, trying to match Mason's laconic description to the more complex reality of Rio.

"If you're Rio, it's a good plenty. He's part horse hisself. Swear to it. Ride anything that grows hair. Gentle about it, too," added Mason, stretching his arms over his head with a force that made bones shift and pop quietly. "Never knew him to bloody a horse, and he's rode more than one that had it coming."

Hope took a sip of the fresh tart drink and sighed. "He said he was a man who found water. He said to ask you and then decide."

Though Hope wasn't looking, she sensed Mason's sudden and complete attention. Faded green eyes fastened on her with an intensity that somehow reminded her of Rio.

"He liked something about you," said Mason flatly. Then, seeing her quick glance, he added, "Nope, not like that. Oh, you're plenty of woman and he's sure enough a man, but that won't saddle no broncs for Rio. If he said he'd look for water, it's because you did something he liked."

"He was at Turner's well. All I did was wrestle with that damned generator."

Mason looked at the woman who sat before him. The coltish girl of his memories had grown into a woman as beautiful as her mother had been. But unlike her mother, Hope didn't hate the ranch. She was part of it, as deeply rooted in the land as the plants that tapped hidden water far below the desert floor. Like her older sister, Hope had tousled dark hair and a generous smile that set men to dreaming. She didn't see it, though, or the men. All she saw was the land, and she was willing to work for what she saw. Her sister hadn't been. Julie had been as pretty as a butterfly—and as useless when there was work to be done.

"Rio liked your grit," said Mason, nodding. "That's the only thing Rio respects. Grit."

"Well, I've plenty of that," Hope said, deliberately

misunderstanding as she wiped her dusty face with the back of her equally dusty arm. "Can he do it?"

Mason's eyes narrowed and looked inward. "Honey, if there's water anywhere on the ranch, Rio will find it."

"How?"

The old man shrugged. "I heard it said he's a water witcher, a dowser, grandson of a Zuni shaman. I heard he was a soldier and a mapmaker. I heard he was raised in Houston and on an Indian reservation beyond the Perdidas."

"How much of that do you believe?" asked Hope curiously.

Mason lifted his battered Stetson and settled it more firmly on his head. "All of it. And I'll tell you this," he added, pinning Hope with a shrewd green glance. "Rio's smart and quiet and faster than any rattler God ever made. He's half-Indian and all man. He don't push worth a damn, and he's pure hell in a fight. Once I saw him take apart three yahoos in less time than I could pour a cup of coffee."

"You make him sound—brutal."

"Like Turner?" said Mason, eyeing Hope's lemonade. He looked up, sensing her sudden worry about Rio. "Not a chance. Turner's bone-deep mean. He likes hurting people."

With difficulty Hope concealed a shudder. She knew that aspect of Turner all too well.

"Rio's easygoing when easy gets it done, and no meaner than he has to be the rest of the time." Mason rubbed his aching knuckles and looked at Hope. "Honey, two of those three men Rio whipped had knives. There was a lot of loose talk about how they was going to skin out the breed that thought he was good enough to drink with white folks. Whatever those men got they had coming."

Hope turned her head quickly, catching the hard

look on Mason's face. "You really like Rio, don't you?" she asked.

"If God had seen fit to give Hazel and me kids," said Mason evenly, "I'd have died proud to sire a son like Rio."

For an instant Hope could think of nothing to say. She had never heard Mason talk about anyone as he did Rio, not even the near-mythical figures out of the Mason family's past.

"Where did you meet Rio?" she asked.

Mason hesitated. He lifted his hat again, settled it with a jerk, and said, "It's Hazel's story, really, but she wouldn't mind me telling you. Her sister's kids was in trouble, never mind what kind. Rio sorted it out."

Hope thought quickly, remembering what she knew about Mason's dead wife. Hazel's sister had married a half-Indian drifter. The man had vanished after a few years, leaving four children behind. Part-Indian children. It shouldn't have mattered—but there were still a lot of places where it did.

And Rio had "taken apart" three men who hated Indians.

"I see," murmured Hope. Then, quietly, "I hope those men learned a lesson."

"Doubt it," said Mason. "Can't teach a snake to sing. But you can set your watch by this," he added with grim satisfaction, "those three don't beat up on kids no more."

Hope decided that she knew all she needed to about the man called Rio. Whether or not he could find water, at least he wasn't a con artist hoping to pick clean her dreams.

"Thanks, Mason," she said, standing up suddenly and kissing his gray-stubbled cheek.

"You gonna do it?"

"Yes." She started for the phone, then stopped. "I don't even know how to get hold of him!"

"Don't worry," said Mason, smiling. "You turn around, he'll be there."

"But how will he know I want to hire him?"

"Same way the wind knows to blow."

Hope made an impatient sound.

Mason looked up, green eyes calm and certain. "He's Rio. He'll know."

Chapter 2

HOPE MADE AN EXASPERATED SOUND. " 'HE'LL KNOW,' "
she quoted in disgust. "Mason, if you had pigtails, I'd
pull them right off your stubborn head. I don't have
time to wait for Rio to mysteriously 'know' I want to
hire him. I need water and I need it now!"

"You always were a headlong sort of gal," agreed
Mason, smiling to himself. "I might be able to find
him, for a price."

"What price?" groaned Hope, thinking of the list of
chores that had to be done—chores that she and
Mason both disliked doing.

"Ice cubes for a week," he said promptly.

"Done." She smiled wickedly. "You're slipping,
Mason. I always do the ice cubes."

"Yeah, but now I won't feel bad about it."

Hope laughed and shook her head, making light
burn darkly among her loose curls.

"He's breaking horses for Turner."

"Oh." Hope frowned. She didn't want to call the

Turner ranch. Since she had come back to the Valley
of the Sun to live, John Turner had pursued her
relentlessly. The more often she refused him, the
more he was determined to have her. Though she had
outgrown her terror of him, she still hated him for his
casual brutality. Just being in the same room with him
was intolerable to Hope. She tried to disguise her
feelings because she knew that they would only make
him more insistent.

"He been bothering you again?" asked Mason, his
voice rough.

Hope shrugged. "Ever since his aunt's bank gave
me a second mortgage on Valley of the Sun, John
seems to think he owns me."

"I may be near seventy," said Mason coldly, "but
so help me God I'll pistol-whip that son of a bitch if he
ever touches you again."

Hope put her hand on Mason's arm, both restraining and reassuring him. Even while her father was
alive, Mason had protected her as though she were his
own daughter. In many ways he was an old-fashioned
Western man. He believed that if a woman said *no,*
she meant it, and that was the end of the matter. It
was a belief that John Turner did not share. Like a
spoiled child, he was obsessed by whatever he could
not have. His father had prevented him from taking
Hope six years ago; but Big Jase Turner had died last
winter, leaving no one to put a leash on his only son.

With an ease that came from many years of prac-
tice, Hope buried the thought of the Turners and her
father's futile dreams of a "good" marriage for his
younger daughter. It had all happened a lifetime ago.
Both fathers were dead, her mother was dead, her
sister was dead. Hope was alive, and she had learned
the difference between a man's easy promises and the
terrifying reality of his lust.

But even more important than yesterday and lies

and a young girl's screams, today Hope was a woman
whose ranch was dying beneath her feet. Next to that
fact nothing mattered, certainly not the irretrievable
past.

She picked up the receiver and dialed quickly. "Hi,
Sally, this is Hope," she said to the housekeeper, who
answered the phone. "I'd like to leave a message for
one of your hands."

"I'll get John," said Sally quickly.

"No, there's no need to—"

It was useless. Sally was gone. Hope closed her eyes
and waited for the lord and master of the Turner
empire to come to the phone.

Mason's eyes narrowed as he watched a mask settle
over Hope's face. It had almost broken his heart when
he had seen her dropped off by Jase Turner nearly six
years ago. Her face had been pale, bruised, far too
old to belong to a laughing girl who had just turned
eighteen.

Mason sighed and rubbed his neck wearily. Thinking about the past always made him feel old and futile.
The only good things about those years were Hazel,
and Hope's father, Wayne, and they were both dead
now. And Hope, of course. She had come out of the
past and she was alive. To hear her laughter on a
winter morning made everything worth it. He would
do whatever he had to in order to ensure that she
would never again forget how to laugh.

"Hello, John," said Hope coolly. "I told Sally not
to bother you."

"It's never a bother talking to you."

"I'd like to leave a message for one of your hands.
A man called Rio."

There was a fractional pause. When Turner spoke
again, his voice wasn't nearly so intimate. "What do
you want with him?"

Hope waited for a long moment, letting the rude

question echo. "Sorry to disturb you," she said crisply. "Good-bye, John."

"Wait, babe. Don't be so stiff-necked. I'm just looking out for your interests."

Hope said nothing.

"This Rio is a drifter and a—well, he's kind of a hand with the ladies, if you get what I mean."

Hope did. "Thank you, John," she said dryly. "I can take care of myself."

Now.

Neither of them said the word, but it was there between them. Hope hadn't been able to hold her own with a man when she was eighteen, but she could now. For that, she could thank John Turner. For that, she once had wished him and herself dead. The thought almost made her smile now. It was hard to believe that she had ever been so young and foolish.

"I thought you and Mason broke all your horses on your own. The ones you have left, that is. If you'd just give me the word, babe, I'd have you three deep in the best horses money can buy. And if it's Storm Walker that's giving you trouble, I'll be glad to put the spurs to him myself. He's too damn much horse for a woman."

With a grimace Hope schooled her voice to show nothing. When she spoke, she ignored the oft-repeated proposal to become the second Mrs. John Turner. She also ignored his casual reminder that she had only five horses left, one of which was a stallion who was a double handful of thunder to ride.

"If you see Rio, tell him I called," she said quietly.

"He won't be in for several hours, maybe not for days. He's an independent bastard. You better tell me what you have in mind. He'll want to know if—"

"He already does," Hope said, cutting Turner off.

"Wait. Are you coming to the barbeque tomorrow?"

It was an effort to keep her voice civil, but she managed. She needed his water too badly to give way to her temper. "Sorry. There's just too much to do here."

"You're working yourself right into the ground, babe. You don't have to. I'll take care of you. I want to. You can keep your ranch. Hell, I'll even pipe water over for you. It'd be my wedding present to—"

"Thanks for passing on my message," Hope said firmly, stopping the flow of unwanted words.

Turner laughed. "All right, babe. But you're going to say yes one of these days. I know it."

Hope hung up and turned to face Mason's knowing eyes.

"Still after you, huh?" asked the old man.

"It's just a game with him. If I said yes, he'd take off like a chaparral cock."

Mason shook his head slowly. "Don't you believe it."

Hope's smile was small and tight. "I don't. But in a way, it's true all the same. If he had me, he wouldn't want me for more than a week or two. That's just the way he is. He's always been that way. He'll die like that."

"Yeah," retorted Mason, "and he'll die considerable before his time if he tries more than sweet-talking you."

"I don't know what I'd have done without you," she whispered, hugging Mason. "I love you."

Mason's large-knuckled hand smoothed Hope's hair as he returned her hug. "You'd been buried in ice cubes, that's what," he said. Almost too softly for her to hear, he added, "I love you, honey." Then he turned her in his arms, swatted her paternally on her rump, and said, "Now, you git before them cows dry up and blow clean to the Perdidas."

"If Rio calls—"

VALLEY OF THE SUN

"Gal, you ain't been listenin' to me," said Mason patiently. "Rio will find you. He don't need no help from me, and he sure don't need no yellow-bellied son of a bitch like Turner to point out the trail."

Hope gave up. She gulped a fast swallow of lemonade, then left Mason to enjoy the spoils of her hasty exit. He took the glass, emptied it, and called after her from the porch, "Beans and beef at sundown."

"And salad," she yelled as she got into Behemoth's dusty cab. "There's lettuce, tomatoes, green onions, and mushrooms in the refrigerator."

"Rabbit food! You expect me to fix rab—"

The rest of Mason's outraged words were lost in the roar of Behemoth's engine. It was no accident. Hope knew that while Mason might occasionally eat, and enjoy, "rabbit food," he felt it was beneath him actually to prepare it. He would do it, though, cursing every crisp leaf. And he would enjoy it, both the crisp leaves and the cursing. The ride to town was long, which meant that fresh vegetables were rare at the ranch house.

Smiling, Hope drove past the home pasture where her breeding cattle clustered around the trough, their black coats dulled by dust. Alongside the dirt road ran a narrow pipeline pitted by sand and sun. The well that had formerly supplied the ranch house's needs had gone dry more than a quarter of a century ago. Her father had drilled the well deeper, until he struck bedrock, where earthquakes had taken water-permeable rock strata and shifted them beneath impermeable slate. Another well had been dug several miles away, on the far side of the buried fault.

That was the well that shared Hope's name. It was the Hope's water that had been piped down to the ranch house and its outbuildings. Another well had once irrigated the nearby pastures and filled the cattle troughs to overflowing. No more, though. The fields were dead and the windmill-driven pump that had once brought up water was disconnected, motionless. The water that came out wasn't enough to keep the prime on the pump, much less supply the needs of the black Angus and the crop lands.

It was not quite so bad with the well her father had once named Hope, but that well could not produce enough for a normal number of range cattle and the ranch house, too. So she had capped the pipe leading from the Hope to the ranch house, sold off some of the range cattle at a loss, and started hauling water to troughs both at the ranch and farther away. When even that proved insufficient, she had gotten rid of more range cattle, selling off pieces of her future in order to survive the endless dry months.

The crop lands and ranch-house lawns were long dead, as were all but the oldest, most deeply rooted trees surrounding the buildings. She had been forced to let the vegetable gardens beyond the kitchen die, for she could not feed the plants' thirst and that of her cattle, too. Water needed for the ranch house was hauled from Turner wells and fed into the cistern buried beneath the ranch yard. And still it wasn't enough. Each day the Hope pumped a little less water up to the thirsty surface of the ground. Each day the cattle needed a little bit more to drink. Each day dawned hot and bright in a sky that might never have known the moist caress of clouds.

But it would rain soon. It must. Every drought had an end. All she had to do was survive until the rains came and the temporary waterholes filled and the groundwater rose to meet the thirsty wells. Then grass would be renewed, cattle would breed and fatten and grow in number and size, and the Valley of the Sun would live again.

With the money Hope had saved from modeling, she could manage for another year; with luck, even longer. She could meet the balloon payment on the second mortgage, which was due in three months. She could keep the ranch solvent even longer if she took the money she had set aside for drilling a new well and used that to meet the ranch's monthly expenses. If she used up the well money that way, though, the ranch itself almost certainly was doomed in the long run. The rains did not come as they had a century ago, fifty years ago, even thirty years ago. Without a new well, a new source of year-round water, in time the land would be virtually worthless for ranching.

Hope looked at the tawny country flexed against the endless fall of sunlight. Big sage lifted its shaggy gray limbs overhead, making graceful, enigmatic patterns against the cerulean bowl of the sky. Shadow creases of ravines outlined the muscular land as it rose to meet the heights of the Perdidas to the east. Plants in shades of subdued green and brown grew on the broad alluvial fans that swept out from the base of the mountains. When intermittent streams ran down into the low basins, they filled with temporary lakes where birds abounded and wary desert animals left delicate, braided trails along the soft shorelines. In the winter the alluvial fans were green with grass and new growth, and bright with the tumble of water in streams that ran dry during the hot weeks of summer. And, increasingly, those same streams ran dry longer each year until ravines and pools that had once watered range cattle no longer even grew grass. That was when wells had to be heavily depended upon.

And that was when wells failed.

The resinous, tangy smell of the high desert poured through the truck's open window. Hope breathed in deeply, letting the pungent scent of the land revive her. It was hot, though not nearly as hot as it had been two months ago. But even then, even when the land burned beneath a brutal sun, Hope loved it. The searing days only made the brief twilight more silky, and the night was like drinking dark wine from an immense crystal chalice.

She turned off the ranch road onto a track that was little more than twin ruts. In the rainy season the ruts would soften and run like sticky wax and then, for a short time, freeze in the cold northern winds. But by then it wouldn't matter if the road was impassable. In the season of winter rains and ice she wouldn't have to haul water to the well.

Behemoth lurched and pulled sideways like a stubborn horse wanting to go back to the barn. She yanked the wheel and hung on until the truck was lined up with the road again. She knew that it was going to be all she could do to drag down the heavy canvas hose, connect it, and pull it to the dry steel trough through the milling, thrusting, thirsty cattle.

Under her relentless grip the truck bounced over the top of a small rise and toward Hope's namesake. Rio was there, standing motionlessly next to his tough *grulla* mare.

Hope braked in a turmoil of dust and crept toward the empty trough as bawling cattle, scenting water, swarmed around the truck. Rio swung into the saddle and went to work on the cattle, herding them aside. His *grulla* worked neatly, precisely, gracefully, spinning on her haunches, turning cattle away from the truck with a well-trained cowpony's lack of fuss. Rio rode the swiftly pivoting animal as though he were part of her, balancing his weight to ease the mare's work, letting the horse's momentum sweep through him, swaying to her motions with supple movements of his spine.

Hope parked the truck right alongside the empty circular tank. It was big, the size of a backyard swimming pool. She peered into the trough. The generator wasn't working; either it had broken down

or the cutoff switch had been tripped by a lack of
water moving through the pump. The windmill was
turning though, sending a narrow rivulet of water
from its cast iron pipe into the trough. As soon as the
water fell it was sucked up by the thirsty cattle.

Hope watched, and knew that the well was almost
dead.

The tiredness she had been holding at bay closed
over her. She shut her eyes for a few seconds as fear
squeezed her heart. *She could not lose the ranch.*
Determination rose in her, pushing away fear. The
cab door rattled and slammed as she leaped down to
the ground on the side away from the empty tank. She
avoided the milling cattle easily. They wanted the
trough, not her. She glanced at the herd, checking
their condition with an experienced eye.

The Herefords were lean and hard. Too lean. Too
hard. They should have been sleek and placid, like
Turner's cattle. But her cattle had to forage several
miles beyond the tank for food, and then walk back to
the tank for water. Each day they had to go a bit
farther to satisfy their hunger, and then a bit farther
back to satisfy their thirst.

Hope knelt under Behemoth's metal belly, swear-
ing silently as she fought to connect the slightly
warped, definitely corroded coupling to the valve.
Her arms shook, silently telling of her exhaustion. She
felt a slight movement, a brush of fabric along her
thigh, and then Rio's hands lifted the hose from hers.
She dropped her arms gratefully and watched him
wrestle with the mulish coupling.

"One of the threads is bent," said Hope as Rio tried
to find a way to screw the hose on. "There's a trick to
it. If you can hold the hose up for me—"

Rio moved the hose so that its brass coupling was
just short of the valve's dark mouth. Hope reached
through his arms and tried to make the threads of

valve and hose match. Without the weight of the wet
hose dragging the end down, it was much easier.
After a few false starts she succeeded in screwing the
hose on enough so that she didn't have to hold the
brass in place with one hand and turn with the other.
Unconsciously she took a deep breath, bracing herself
for the job of tightening the stubborn coupling so that
it wouldn't blow apart with the first weight of water
rushing down.

Rio sensed Hope's deep breath in the stir of her
breasts against his arm. He glanced aside at her, only
to realize that she wasn't aware of what she had done.
She was focused on the stubborn coupling with the
kind of intensity that came only from exhaustion or
fear. He saw the marks that sweat had made on her
face, the patina of dust and heat, and the fine-grained
skin beneath. Tendrils of hair licked down from her
hat and swayed across her face like dark flames. Her
hazel eyes showed almost none of the green that had
been visible in the pouring sun by Turner's well. Now
her eyes were dark, too dark, just as her lips were too
pale against her sun-flushed cheeks. Rio realized then
how tired she was, and wondered how many times she
had made the trip from Turner's well to her own dry
land.

Gently Rio covered Hope's hands with his. He
eased her fingers aside and began tightening the
coupling. He was surprised at how difficult it was to
keep the threads turning delicately and at the same
time keep the weight of the hose from jamming the
two pieces of brass. The thought of Hope trying and
failing and trying again and again to make the coupling work brought a grim line to Rio's mouth. *Where
the hell was Mason? How long had she been making
water runs alone?*

"Thanks. I'll get the wrench," said Hope, pulling
herself out from under the truck.

She returned quickly, carrying a plumber's wrench as long as her arm and a lot heavier. Rio took the wrench from her, lifting it with an ease that she envied and he took for granted. She watched as his shirt strained rhythmically across his shoulders and biceps while he tightened the coupling with smooth, powerful motions of his arms.

"Stay put," he said when Hope began to tug at the hose, straightening it for the rush of water that would come soon. "I'll take care of it."

Hope watched the dark man crouched so close to her, enjoying the complex play of muscle and tendon as he worked. She sighed and sat down, resting her head against Behemoth's curved metal belly. "Thanks. I owe you one."

Rio shook his head slowly, remembering Hope's beauty as she arched against the sky while her hands sprayed liquid diamonds over her beautifully curved body. It was an image he could not get out of his mind. She had been as vivid and unexpected as a desert rainbow. And like a rainbow, she had given pleasure and asked nothing in return.

"No," he said quietly, "you don't owe me a thing."

She turned her head toward him but he didn't look up, concentrating solely on the coupling. When he was finished he slid out from beneath the truck, propped the wrench against a tire, and began dragging the hose off its rack and into the trough.

"Ready," he called.

Rio's voice was pitched to carry over the bawling, shoving cattle crowding around the water tank. They couldn't quite wedge themselves between the truck and the trough. Neither Rio nor Hope was in danger of getting stepped on as long as they kept to Behemoth's bulky shelter.

When Hope didn't answer, Rio glanced over his shoulder. He saw her propped against the truck, eyes closed, soaking in every instant of rest like dry land absorbing water. Contrasted with the truck's bulk she looked very small, almost fragile.

"Hope?"

She opened her eyes and smiled up at him. With a grace that belied her tired appearance, she retrieved the heavy wrench and applied it to the valve. Water swelled in the hose and rushed over the lip of the tank to fall hard and fast into the nearly dry tank. Cattle bawled and crowded closer, jostling the truck. Rio abandoned his position and slipped back under the ancient army vehicle next to Hope.

"Eager little devils," he commented, watching the forest of dusty legs milling beyond the truck's shelter.

After a time the cattle which had been first at the water tank allowed themselves to be pushed aside by the animals which had yet to drink. The animals that had drunk earlier in the day waited on the fringes or grazed invisibly among the big sage and scattered piñon that grew over the gently folded land. Those were the animals that would be most eager tomorrow, the ones up in front shoving and bawling for their first taste of water.

Rio and Hope didn't try to talk over the noise of the cows. With a half-apologetic smile to him, she lay on her back in the dust, her head on her hat, her eyes closed, all but groaning with the pleasure of stretching muscles cramped from the day's demands. This was one of the moments she waited for, when the hardest of the work had been done and all that remained was uncoupling the hose, racking it, and driving Behemoth back home. Sometimes before she left she would take off her clothes and immerse herself in the trough. She would paddle quietly for a time and then rest her arms along the rim and float motionlessly, watching as glittering stars bloomed in the indigo depths of evening.

With an odd smile Rio watched Hope as she lay unselfconsciously near him. He didn't know whether she was too tired for the usual flirtations or forthright advances of the women he had known, or whether she simply wasn't interested in him because he was a half-breed. Then he remembered the times he had turned and found her watching him, approval clear in her expression.

He was tempted to stretch out next to her, sharing the truck's bluntly curving shelter and resting his body at the same time. His day had begun well before dawn, when he had caught Dusk, his tough *grulla,* and rounded up some of Turner's skittish horses. The Thoroughbreds were as elegant as cats, and even less useful for working cattle.

It was Turner's quarterhorses that Rio truly enjoyed. They were muscular and quick, perfectly suited to working cattle. By the time Rio was done, John Turner would have some of the best cow horses in Nevada. And then Turner would ruin them trying to win flashy buckles in rodeos. Turner had no more sense of how to treat a horse than he did how to treat women or the land. He took and did not give back. He did not even know that he should.

Rio slouched down farther, propped his head against a dusty tire, and drew his feet out of the way of the importunate cattle. He could have slept, but didn't. He savored the peace of the moment, the cattle's thirst being slaked, the woman resting only inches from his thigh, the tactile memory of her breasts brushing against his arm. With a silent curse he told himself what kind of fool he was even to look at a woman like Hope.

She's not a woman for bed today and good-bye tomorrow. So stop thinking about the way she looked outlined against the sky with her blouse shaping her the way you'd like to. Even if she came to you, asking for

*you, you'd only hurt her. Is that what you want? You
want to give her a hand when she's down and needs
you and then drag her off to bed like she's just one
more Saturday night? Hell, you outgrew that kind of
screwing before you were old enough to drink.*

Grimly Rio listened to his thoughts, approving
them with his intelligence and disapproving them with
every one of his fully alive senses. Yet he made no
move toward Hope, neither word nor gesture. Instinctively he knew beyond doubt or argument that she
would not give herself casually to any man. And he
knew that he did not give himself at all to any woman,
not really. In the last thirty-three years he had learned
many things about himself. One of them was that
Brother-to-the-wind was more than an Indian name.
It was his fate, and he had finally accepted it. He had
spent his life searching for something that was more
powerful, more enduring, more beautiful, more compelling than the endless sweep of the western lands.
He had found no place, no person, capable of holding
him when his brother the wind called to him, whispering of secret springs and shaded canyons where men
never walked.

The other thing that he had learned about himself
was that while he was born white, raised white until he
was twelve, and educated white, white women didn't
want him. Not all of him. They didn't want his silences
or his hybrid insights into life and the land.

Most of all, white women didn't want a part-Indian
kid.

Rio pulled his hat down over his eyes, shutting out
the sight of Hope's vulnerable body within easy reach
of his hungry fingertips. He subdued his desire with
the same iron discipline that had kept his raging
temper under wraps when he was growing up and
people had baited him, calling him *breed* and *blankethead*. He had fought his tormentors with icy ferocity,

but he hadn't killed any of them. And he could have. When he was grown, most of the men who had backed him into a corner had depended on numbers or the simple presence of weapons to make them strong. Rio had learned never to depend on anyone or anything but himself. It gave him an advantage in sheer ruthlessness that at first surprised and then finally overwhelmed his opponents. It also made him very much a man alone. He had accepted that, too. *Brother-to-the-wind.*

Cattle milled and shoved, raising a dust that turned the air into a shimmering brass color. Water rushed out of Behemoth, thundering into the tank with a cool sound. The smells of cattle and water and dust merged with that of sunlight and piñon and sage. The mixture of odors was soothing to Hope, familiar, reassuring. She sighed and relaxed even more. Tiredness washed over her in waves, making her feel lightheaded. She realized that she was on the edge of falling asleep miles from home while a strange man half-lay so close to her that she could sense each stirring of his body.

The thought didn't disturb Hope. Since she had been eighteen, she had learned about people in general and men in particular. Rio didn't give out any of the signals of a man who would leap upon the first woman he found alone and unprotected. He had looked at her with veiled male appreciation, but had not crowded her in any way.

And even if she hadn't been sure of her own instincts, there was the fact that a man Mason Graves would be proud to claim for a son would not be the kind of man to take advantage of anyone—man or woman. In fact, Hope's only regret about the present situation was that she didn't know Rio well enough to use his shoulder as a pillow rather than the dry, unforgiving ground. The thought made her smile. She was still smiling when she fell deeply asleep.

Rio watched Hope for a long time, repeating to himself all the ways he was wrong for her and she was wrong for him. Then he lay down beside her and eased her head off the hard ground and onto his shoulder. She stirred vaguely but did not pull away. She moved even closer, sighed, and relaxed against his body with a trust that made him want to wake her and tell her what fools they both were being.

He lay very still, trying not to think, caught in the gentle, bittersweet pleasure of holding a woman in his arms who trusted him more than he trusted himself.

Chapter 3

THE SUN WAS BALANCED IN CRIMSON GLORY ON THE edge of a distant ridge. Long shadows reached under the battered truck, dark forerunners of night. The stock tank stood more than half full, its clean water reflecting the last blazing light of day. The Herefords grazing the rumpled land looked like garnet statues carved and set among the nearly black flames of piñon trees. The little *grulla* mare dozed three-legged next to a clump of sage that gleamed a ghostly silver in the rich light. The mare's reins trailed loosely, for she was tied in place by immaterial bonds of training and her affection for the man who lay quietly beneath the old water truck.

Rio looked from the thick, dark lashes lying along Hope's cheek to the stunning transformations of sunset in a wild land. He had known many such times, days inevitably changed by condensing darkness, cool scented winds sweeping down from water-rich heights. Yet he had never known a sunset just like

45

this one. In the past he had been alone with the land, and now a woman lay in his arms as quietly as sunlight in a hollow. It was a strange sensation to hold Hope, pleasure laced with uneasiness, as though he were a trespasser in an intriguing, forbidden land. He wondered if his Swedish grandmother had felt this way when she lay with her Indian lover, a Zuni shaman whose very existence was an affront to the Christianity that she had come to teach on the reservation.

The *grulla* snorted and stamped her front foot, discouraging a persistent fly. Rio felt the cool velvet shadows lapping over his feet and reluctantly admitted that it was past time for him to awaken the woman sleeping in his arms. Gently he shifted Hope's head back onto her hat. She made an inarticulate, protesting sound. He brushed his lips over her hair and then leaned against the dusty tire once more, no longer touching her.

"Hope," he said softly, letting his hand smooth over her shoulder. Then, more firmly, "Hope."

She woke in a rush, disoriented. He had been expecting it. He held her shoulder so that she couldn't sit up. It was all that saved her from cracking her head on Behemoth's metal belly in the first heedless instant of waking. Her eyes were dark amber, as clear and pure as the evening itself. For a moment she was self-conscious, then she smiled crookedly, accepting the fact that she had fallen asleep on the most interesting man she had met in her life.

"Hope my snoring didn't keep you awake," she said.

Rio had seen both the instant of unease and her humorous acceptance of reality. His smile transformed his face the way moonrise transforms night. Lines that had been harsh became gentle, and angles that had been forbidding became merely strong.

"Sorry to disappoint you," he said, "but you didn't snore even once."

"Must have been your lucky day," said Hope, stretching luxuriously. "God, I didn't know the ground could be such a grand mattress."

"It was," said Rio cryptically, responding to her first comment about luck. "It isn't," he added, referring to the ground.

Hope blinked and shook her head. Before she could ask for an explanation, Rio stood and went over to his horse. He led the mare to the tank and watched as she plunged her muzzle into the clean water. Hope came to stand beside Rio, dusting off her jeans with her palms. She would have given a great deal to be able to peel off her clothes and float for just a few moments in the crimson water. With a small sigh she turned away from the tempting liquid.

"The only water this tank will ever see is Turner water," said Rio quietly, watching the *grulla* drink. Then he turned quickly, catching the despair on Hope's face as his words sank in. "If you want me to drill here, forget it. It would be a waste of my time, your money, and your cows' lives."

Hope said nothing. She counted the rings expanding through the water as the *grulla* drank. It wasn't that Rio's words were untrue or even unexpected. They were so final, though, the end of the Hope spoken in a stranger's deep, certain voice. She wanted to protest, to ask Rio how he could be so sure, but she did not. In some still, deep center of herself she did not doubt him. She sensed that he knew the land in a way that neither could be described nor wholly understood. She could trust his knowledge, though, the same way she trusted the sun to rise in the morning.

Hope fought against the futile tears closing her throat. She felt defenseless, neither truly asleep nor yet awake, suspended between the end of one dream and the beginning of an unwelcome awakening. She had enough money to drill her namesake well deeper, but not enough to find and drill an entirely new, probably much deeper well from scratch. She didn't realize how much she had secretly counted on being able to revive the Hope until now, when she finally and fully accepted the fact that the well was dead. The desolation was numbing.

"Hope—"

"It's all right," she said huskily, interrupting, sensing that Rio hadn't wanted to hurt her with his blunt assessment of her dream. "I understand."

Do you? he asked silently, cursing himself for his unforgiving summary of the well's chances. But so long as Hope held on to an unrealistic dream, there would be no opportunity to replace it with one that had at least a fighting chance of coming true.

"I'd hoped that if I just drilled farther down, through the bedrock, I'd strike artesian water," Hope continued in a low voice. Then, slipping through the restraints she had imposed on herself, came the last cries of her dream. "Are you sure? How can you be so sure?"

Rio said nothing, merely watched her with eyes as deep and clear as the water she had hoped to find. He was sure. But he couldn't explain it to Hope. It was a combination of instinct and education and long experience in dry lands.

"Well," said Hope, her voice steady despite its unusual huskiness, "thanks for being honest with me. You could have cleaned out my drilling account and then walked away."

"Is that what you heard about me?" he asked, his tone aloof, hard.

She shook her head, making her hair shift and shimmer darkly in the dying light. "No. And even if I had," she added, meeting Rio's eyes directly, "I wouldn't have believed it after being with you. You aren't a liar or a thief."

For a long moment they looked at each other, silently accepting. She trusted him not to lie to her. He trusted her to believe him without any proof other than his word.

"If there's water on your land, I'll find it for you," said Rio. His voice was as soft and certain as when he had told her that the Hope was dead.

She smiled sadly. "Unless the water you find is close to the surface, I can't afford to go after it."

"First, let's find the water. Then we'll worry about getting to it. I'll work nights and weekends here until I'm finished with Turner's horses. Then I'll work full-time. My pay will be room and board for me and my horse."

"That's not enough," objected Hope, only to subside as Rio continued talking.

"I saw some old drilling equipment in your barn. We'll salvage what we can. I've got some equipment of my own that I'll have shipped in. Between us we'll put a drilling rig together that won't cost you much. Your biggest expense will be pipe and fuel."

"And your fee," said Hope firmly. "It isn't fair that you work only for room and board."

Rio's smile gleamed briefly in the dying light. His eyes were even darker now, as mysterious and radiant as the twilight expanding throughout the land. "It isn't fair that you have to do the work of two men just to hang on to your ranch."

Hope shrugged. There was no help for it, so there was no point in complaining about it.

"You're going to work until rain falls—or you do," continued Rio. "Right?"

His choice of words made her smile. "I'm no different from anyone else," said Hope. "I do what I can for as long as I can, and hope to God that it will be enough.''

Rio thought of the men and women he had met who had worked as little as they could for as short a time as possible, and bitched every step of the way about bad luck and bad people and the unfairness of a world that didn't give them everything they had ever wanted. Those were the people Rio avoided. The other people —the ones like Hope, who worked their hearts out for a dream and didn't whine when the going got rough— those were the people Rio was drawn to as inevitably as rain was drawn to the thirsty ground. Those were the people he helped, sharing their dreams, giving what he could, taking only what they could afford in return. And when the dreams were changed or realized, he moved on like his brother the wind, speaking only in the wild silences of the land, searching for something that neither he nor the wind could name.

"I'll help you,'' said Rio softly, "and hope to God that it's enough. I don't want money as payment. If I bring in a well, I'll leave ten mares to be bred to Storm Walker. You'll treat the mares and their foals as your own, no better and no worse. From time to time I'll come to the Valley of the Sun, take the horses I want, and leave the mares to be bred to your best stallion. For as long as the water in my well flows.'' He waited, looking deeply into her eyes. "And Hope—none of my wells have ever gone dry.''

She closed her eyes but still she could see Rio, his skin like mahogany, his eyes deep and clear. Echoes of his velvet voice moved like a caress over her skin. "Yes,'' she said, her voice as calm as his eyes. "Ten mares. Storm Walker. And more, Rio, if you want. Horses, cattle, whatever. I have a lot of land and no water. Yet.''

Rio watched Hope's expression, felt her truth and

her trust in him, and knew both pleasure and uneasiness. He had taken one dream from her and given her another: water unending, sweet water reviving the dusty land. But he could not guarantee that the second dream would be any more possible than the first. "Sometimes there's no water to be found," he said in a voice that was both quiet and rough.

She smiled wearily. "Yes, I know. In any case, your mares will be bred and the foals cared for until I no longer own the Valley of the Sun."

"No well, no payment."

"Your mares will be bred," repeated Hope, her voice firm. "Ship them in anytime." With a wry twist to her mouth she added, "Storm Walker will thank you for it. This last year I've had to use my four mares for working cattle rather than for breeding."

Rio's smile gleamed in the gathering darkness. He held out his hand. She took it without hesitation, letting the warmth of him seep into her as the last of the sun's crimson light fled the sky. His touch was a flesh and blood reality that gave substance to all hopes, all possibilities, everything. Eyes shining, heart beating rapidly, Hope allowed herself to dream again.

"For as long as the water flows," she said softly, pressing her hand against his, both clinging to and giving back his touch.

The echo of his own words went through Rio like a wild wind, shaking everything. He wanted to tell Hope not to trust him so much, not to believe in him. Yet that wasn't what he wanted to say, not really. Her dream of water she could trust him with. Her heart was a different matter. And it was her heart that accelerated at his touch, making her pulse beat visibly beneath the soft skin of her inner wrist. She wasn't aware of it, though. He could see that as clearly as he had seen her courage and determination as she worked to save her cattle and her ranch from drought. She thought it was the new dream that was exciting her. He knew that it was not, not entirely, for the same sensual hunger stirred in his own blood as the heat of her skin slid over his.

Rio could not draw back from Hope. Her dream was as deep and compelling as she was. That was why he wanted to—why he *must*—help her. He had stopped dreaming long ago, and the emptiness that had come with the end of dreams was a void that even the wind could not fill.

"When can you start?" asked Hope, feeling oddly breathless, suspended between Rio's male warmth and the intimacy of desert twilight.

"I already have."

"You have?"

"I looked at all your wells."

"Oh." Hope said no more. Neither did Rio. There was nothing more to say. The Valley of the Sun's wells were dead. She drew in a deep breath. "I see. Well, then, it's past time for me to make good on my promise of room and board. Mason will have dinner waiting by the time we get back. Nothing fancy. Beef, beans, bread, and salad."

Rio's black eyebrows rose. "Salad?"

"Don't tell me," groaned Hope. "You're another one of those cowboys who can't stand rabbit food."

Rio's soft laughter curled around her like a caress, like his voice when he finally spoke. "No problem. I get real hungry for fresh vegetables."

"Good. We'll gang up on Mason and demand our rabbit rights."

Still smiling, Rio pulled the cold hose out of the stock tank and began wrapping the canvas coils around the rack bolted to the end of the truck. Hope helped as much as she could, feeding coils to him. By the time the hose was stowed away they were both wet and more than a little muddy.

"Feel free to take a dip in the tank before you ride in for dinner," said Hope, grimacing as she wiped her muddy hands on her jeans. "I usually do. It's more fun than a basin bath at the ranch. And until I can take time out from watering cows to make another run to Turner's well, that's all there will be at home—a washrag and a basin of water. But," she said, smiling crookedly at Rio, "the washrag is of the highest quality."

Rio frowned as he realized that the water shortage at the ranch house was little short of desperate. Hope could not continue to supply the house and the scattered range cattle, too. There simply were not enough hours in the day or strength in her body to do what must be done. He turned toward the *grulla* and whistled. Though not shrill, the sound carried as cleanly as a hawk's cry through the silence. The mare's head came up. She walked over to Rio. He took the reins and handed them to Hope.

"Give her a few seconds to get used to your lighter weight," said Rio. "She's the best night horse you'll ever ride. I'll take the truck. Don't wait dinner for me. I'll be a while."

Hope's fingers closed automatically over the reins. She hesitated, then decided not to ask the obvious question. She either trusted Rio or she didn't. In any case, she wasn't the kind of employer who needed to keep her men under her thumb at all times.

"Reverse gear is really dicey. Avoid it if you can. If you get into reverse, you have the devil's own time getting out," she said. "Keys are in the ignition. Oh—don't trust the fuel gauge. It always registers half full. If you're going more than fifty miles, drop by the ranch. Diesel is in the blue tank to the left of the barn."

Rio nodded, turned away, then turned back with an odd expression on his face. "Are you always this trusting with strangers?"

"No," said Hope evenly. She looked but could not see more than a flash of light where Rio's eyes were. "I don't trust strangers at all." She smiled wryly, though she knew that her expression would be all but invisible to him. "And I don't sleep under trucks with them, either. What about you, Rio? Do you let strangers ride off with your horse?"

"Never."

The quiet word told Hope more than she had teasingly asked. She sensed that no one but Rio had ever ridden the *grulla*. Before she could say anything more, he came to her, laced his hands together to make a stirrup, and lifted her onto Dusk. The mare minced restlessly for a moment before she arched her neck around and sniffed Hope's muddy boot. Hope murmured calm words and stroked the mare's warm, ghostly-gray neck. At a gentle pressure on the reins, the horse's ears came up and she stepped eagerly into the gathering darkness.

"See you at home," said Hope, knowing the words would carry back to the man who stood without moving, watching her vanish into the night.

"There's a jacket in the saddlebag," called Rio softly.

By the time Hope rode into the ranch yard, she was glad to be wearing Rio's jacket. She was also glad to have ridden Dusk. Rio had been right about the mare; she was the best night horse Hope would ever ride. Most horses were balky or skittish to the point of wildness at being ridden alone into darkness. Not Dusk. She had moved quietly, confidently, cleanly, like the man who had trained her. Even the sudden *swoosh* of an owl's wings hadn't made her shy. As for the eerie harmonies of coyotes, Dusk had simply cocked her ears and moved on, unruffled.

A rectangle of yellow light spilled out to meet Hope. Mason stood in the center of it, silhouetted against the doorway.

"Nice pony," said Mason, satisfaction in every syllable. "Rio's?"

"Yep," said Hope, imitating Mason's laconic speech.

He waited, but no more information was forthcoming. "Truck break down?"

"Nope."

Mason waited. Nothing. "You lookin' for trouble, gal?" he asked in exasperation.

Smiling, she reined the *grulla* toward the barn. "Nope. Just dinner."

The old man muttered something fully suited to the barnyard and went back inside, banging the screen door behind him.

"Set an extra place," called Hope.

The door slammed open again. "He's gonna do it? He's gonna find water for you?"

"He's going to try."

Mason's whoop of triumph made the mare shy suddenly. Hope had expected it. Even so, she nearly ended up in the dust. The *grulla* was very fast. Hope dismounted, led the mare into a stall, and rubbed her down thoroughly despite the fact that her arms cramped every time she lifted them above her shoulders. She put several flakes of hay in the manger, poured grain in on one side, and hauled water for the stall trough from a spigot on the side of the house. When she was certain that the mare was content in her unfamiliar surroundings, Hope shut the stall door and walked slowly toward the ranch house. She was so tired that she felt as though she were wading through mud. The thought of a long, hot, deep bath made her want to groan.

"Then don't think about it," she muttered to herself. "There's enough water for drinking and for spit baths and not one drop more."

There was a basin of warm water waiting for her in her bedroom. She peeled off her clothes, washed carefully, rinsed, and resolutely refused to think about the bathtub across the hall. She brushed her hair and went downstairs, realizing for the first time how hungry she was.

"Dinner?" she said hopefully, walking into the kitchen.

"Light and set," said Mason automatically, gesturing toward the table.

His hands hesitated as he reached for the gallon-sized bottle of salad oil. It was slippery and his hands hadn't been very cooperative for the last few days. He paused over the ingredients, frowning as he tried to remember the ratio of vinegar to oil and salt to pepper for the salad dressing.

"I'll do it," Hope said. She could tell by the careful way Mason moved his fingers that the arthritis in his knuckles had flared up again. His pride, too, was in full flare. "You always use too much oil," she added, as though she hadn't noticed his difficulty making his fingers move with their former suppleness. It was hard enough on Mason's temper when he couldn't handle the truck and the hose. Not to be able to handle kitchen work would be the final indignity.

"Rabbit food," said Mason, his voice rich with disgust as he turned his back on the heavy, treacherous bottle of oil. "When's Rio coming?"

"He said not to wait dinner."

"Then I'll just put the *real* food on the table."

Smiling, Hope said nothing.

"Price of beef went down half-cent a pound," said Mason.

Hope's smile slipped.

"Feed's up in cost."

She sighed. "Even if it's a mild winter, we'll be buying feed before spring."

"Nope."

Hope paused in her vigorous stirring of the vinaigrette. "Why not?"

"Won't have no cows to eat it." Mason's faded green eyes looked squarely into hers. "Gonna have to sell some more range cows. You know it. I know it. Gotta be done."

"Not yet," said Hope stubbornly. "I can still water them for a while longer. Maybe it will rain soon."

He started to argue, then shrugged. As he'd said before, she was stubborn but no fool. "Don't kill yourself, honey. Nothing's worth that. Longer you wait to sell, less them cows is gonna weigh. Natural feed's about gone and nothing's coming up to take its place. No rain."

Mason's succinct summary angered Hope. Not because he was wrong, but because he was right. "Then I'll haul feed," she snapped.

He shook his head and said nothing more. Even if the two of them worked around the clock, they couldn't haul water and food to all the cattle. Too many cattle. Not enough hours in the day. Not enough muscle between the two of them. But Hope was young. She'd have to find her own limits. He had found his long ago, and the older he got the more those limits shrank in on him. He looked at the swollen knuckles of his hands and cursed softly. Not for himself, but for her. For her he would have endured the agonies of being young again, just to have the strength to help her build her dream. She was the daughter he had never had. He would have moved mountains for her if he could.

But he could not.

Silently Mason went to the stove, threw a hunk of butter into a hot cast-iron frying pan, and began cooking Hope's steak. She put beans and salad on the table, helping herself to both. Then she opened the oven door hopefully. The tantalizing aroma of garlic came out. Though at first Mason had maintained that garlic bread was a foreign sacrilege that never should be allowed to mop up good American beef juices, he had eventually become hooked on the pungent stuff.

"Get it while it's hot," he said a short time later, putting the sizzling beef in front of her.

Hope poked the steak dubiously. "Did you hear that?"

"What?"

"It mooed at me."

Mason started to say something indignant, then saw the laughter lurking beneath Hope's words. He smiled unwillingly, ruffled her just-brushed hair, and went back to the stove. A low, sweetly rendered *mooooo* followed him. He looked back quickly. An angelic Hope was cutting into her steak with every evidence of satisfaction.

"Mmmmmm," said Hope, chewing slowly. "Mason, nobody can do a steak like you."

Smiling, singing off-key, a pleased Mason fried his own beef. It took even less time than hers. Soon the only sounds to be heard were those made by silver against earthenware plates, the occasional creak of oak chairs as weight was shifted forward or back, and the rapidly accelerating perk of the coffeepot as the liquid inside darkened in color and fragrance.

When she could eat no more, Hope took pity on the patient Mason and told him about the agreement that she and Rio had made. Mason listened quietly, nodded at appropriate moments, and smiled with satisfaction when she was finished.

"Well, better open the pipe to the water heater," said Mason, wiping his mouth with a paper napkin and pushing his chair back from the table.

Hope looked at him as though he had suggested frying one of the oak chairs for dessert. "What?"

"Don't you want a bath, gal?"

"Well, of course, but—"

"Then don't keep me here jawing with you when water could be heating."

"Mason," she said slowly, carefully, as though he were deaf or slightly crazy or both, "if I take a bath, there won't be any drinking water for tomorrow."

"Sure there will. Whole truckload. What do you think Rio's doing out there on an empty belly—driving that heavy rig around in the dark for the hell of it?"

Hope's mouth opened, then closed. "Do you really think—?" she began wistfully, longing for a bath with every aching muscle in her body.

"Why don't you ask him yourself?" retorted Mason.

The noise of the old water truck rattling into the ranch yard sounded loud in the sudden silence.

"Fast trip," commented Mason.

Hope said nothing, too astonished for words. She hurried out into the front yard.

"Where do you want it?" asked Rio.

"Around back," said Hope. She stepped onto the truck's running board and reached for the cab door. "I'll take care of it. You must be starved. Go in and eat."

Surprised, he looked at her for a moment, unused to that kind of consideration from anyone, much less a woman as tired as he knew Hope must be. He smiled gently. "Thanks, but it won't take long. Hang on."

Hope clung to the cab door as Rio eased the heavy truck around the house and up to the spot that had once been lawn but now was little more than two tire tracks ground through a crust of dead grass. The pipe that had formerly brought water from the Hope had been cut and the stump threaded to permit the canvas hose to be coupled to it. Hope took a flashlight from the truck, bathing Rio's hands in light as he made the connection between the water truck and the buried cistern that served the ranch house. While water fattened the hose and fell into the nearly empty tank, muted thunder rose from beneath their feet.

"How big is the tank?"

"It will hold half a truckload. Go in and eat, Rio, I'll watch here."

Rio might have argued, but Mason stuck his head out of the back door and yelled, "Come and git it 'fore I feed it to the pigs."

"Do you have pigs?" whispered Rio to Hope.

"No, but I haven't had the heart to tell Mason."

"Too soft, huh?"

"For some people," agreed Hope. Her smile was quick, but Rio caught its gleam. "Mason is one of them."

"Is Turner?" asked Rio, not knowing why.

Hope gave him a level glance. "I make sure I'm not around Turner long enough for it to matter either way."

"Sorry. None of my business."

She shrugged. "Everybody in a hundred miles has made it their business at one time or another. Why should you be different?"

Rio started to speak, then obviously thought better of it.

"Go ahead," sighed Hope. "But please be original. Don't tell me that he's a bastard, because I already know it. Don't tell me that he's rich, because I don't care."

"Is he crowding you?"

Something in Rio's voice made Hope wish that it were daylight and she could see his expression clearly. "Nothing I can't handle."

"If that changes, let me know."

"You'll have to get in line after Mason," said Hope dryly.

"It would be a pleasure."

Hope had the distinct feeling that Rio meant every word. Apparently he and John Turner didn't get along very well. Which wasn't surprising. Anyone with a minimum of self-respect had a hard time getting along with Turner. His arrogance had to be experienced to be believed.

"Rio, this here dinner of yours ain't getting any hotter," called Mason. "Gal, you git on back in here and set. That danged hose ain't going nowhere and you know it."

After a moment's hesitation Hope played the light once more over the coupling, saw that it was tight, and put the flashlight back in the cab. Rio waited for her, walking by her side toward the pouring yellow light where Mason stood impatiently. Rio said nothing to her, simply moved quietly, his long-sleeved shirt brushing against hers in a tactile companionship that needed no words. For an instant Hope forgot that she was tired and that tomorrow would be worse, not better. An absurd feeling of well-being swept through her, as unexpected as Rio's gentle smile. She wanted to laugh and hold her arms up to the brilliant stars and feel their billion bright possibilities cascading through her.

"Mason," said Rio, holding out his hand, "it's been a long time."

"Too long," Mason said, taking Rio's hand in his own gnarled grasp.

Only Hope noticed the tiny instant of hesitation when Rio saw Mason's swollen knuckles. Rio shook hands firmly but very gently, sparing the older man's arthritic hand. The feeling of warmth that suffused Hope increased. Knowing that Rio cared enough about Mason to discreetly spare his pride made her certain that she had been right to trust Rio.

"Judy sends her love," Rio said, "and the kids want to know if you'll be up for Thanksgiving. They're having a three-state wingding from the sound of it."

Mason's glance slid to Hope, then away. "Maybe," he said, promising nothing.

Rio nodded, understanding that Mason wouldn't leave Hope alone on the family holiday.

Hope understood, too, and wanted to protest. Judy was Mason's sister-in-law, the last connection he had to the dead wife he had loved for forty-seven years. But Hope said nothing. She and Mason had argued on that subject before. He wouldn't go without her, and the ranch couldn't be left untended that long.

"Water's warm," said Mason, gesturing toward the basin and towel waiting just inside the service porch.

With the quick, efficient motions Hope had come to expect from Rio, he swept off his hat, rolled up his sleeves, and washed as much skin as he could reach. When he was finished he picked up the basin and flipped its contents on the ground, where a wilted lilac bush struggled to survive in the lee of the porch.

While Rio ate, Hope enjoyed the rare luxury of sitting and doing nothing more strenuous than drinking a cup of Mason's potent coffee. She let her mind drift, dreaming lazily of a time when the ground would be green rather than granite-hard, and her cattle wouldn't have to walk themselves thin to get from food to water. Rio's deep voice and Mason's

age-roughened tones wove in and out of her dreams.
She didn't really listen until the men began discussing
beef and water.

"How many cows are you going to sell?" asked Rio
as he forked a succulent chunk of steak into his
mouth.

"Not a one."

Rio looked up quickly. In the artificial light his eyes
were like indigo crystal, startling against the tanned
planes of his face and the thick rim of jet black lashes.

"Boss don't want to sell," explained Mason, gesturing toward Hope with the stem of the ghastly old pipe
he loved and she refused to let him smoke indoors.

Rio went back to eating without another word.

"Aren't you going to tell me that the price of beef
will only get lower and the cattle thinner?" asked
Hope, her voice tight with the echoes of old arguments and refusals.

"Waste of time," said Rio. "You know your choices
better than anyone here."

For a moment Hope's new dream slid away from
her, leaving her suspended in a cold present that had
few choices, none of them pleasant.

"When you decide to cull the herd," continued Rio
matter-of-factly, "use the *grulla* if I'm not here to
help. She'll cut your work in half."

Hope nodded, unable to speak for the tears and the
sudden fear squeezing her throat. The more cattle she
sold, the closer she came to the moment when she
would have to auction off her beautiful Angus herd.
They were the very core of her dream of a new ranch,
a new life, a future that held fat black cattle instead of
the knife-lean Herefords of her nightmares. Maybe in
the water-rich future of her dream, the house would
ring with people and laughter again. Maybe then she
could dare to dream beyond the enrichment of the
herds to the enrichment of her own life; maybe then

she could dream of finding a man who would love her, of having children who would grow up tall and straight on the land. . . .

Hope's mug of coffee hit the table with a solid thump as she stood up hurriedly, slamming the door on her thoughts. Not since she was eighteen had she allowed herself to dream of love and children. There was no point in dreaming now. She had other dreams, attainable dreams, dreams that depended only upon her own will and determination rather than on the unknowable, undependable currents of a man's needs. In her lifetime she had found few men to respect. She had found none whose children she wanted to have.

"Think the water's hot yet?" asked Hope.

"Not likely," said Mason. "The buckets on the stove are, though. I'll haul them up for you."

"Don't bother," Hope said quickly, heading for the huge ranch stove. Two big buckets of water simmered over the hot flames.

Hope picked two potholders off a nail and reached for the buckets' wire handles. The potholders were plucked from her hands by long dark fingers that were becoming increasingly familiar to her. With the easy strength that she admired, Rio lifted the full buckets off the flames and turned toward her.

"After you, ma'am," he drawled.

"Thank you," she whispered too softly for Mason to hear.

Rio nodded slightly, understanding her desire to protect the old man's pride. As Rio followed her up the stairs he could not help admiring the womanly swing of her hips and the long, graceful lines of her legs. The thought of sharing her bath crossed his mind, only to be shunted aside ruthlessly. He waited while she bent over and put the plug in the big, old-fashioned bathtub's drain. The line of Hope's back and breasts was even more alluring than her walk had been. Beneath the frosted glass globes of the bathroom lights her hair was a rich satin sheen that fairly demanded to be tangled in a man's fingers. She looked over her shoulder at him with gold-flecked eyes and a generous mouth made for giving and receiving kisses.

"Ready?" asked Hope, wondering why Rio was watching her so intently.

Heat spread out from the center of Rio's body, tightening it in a rush of sensation that made his pulse beat heavily. His lips flattened into a line of self-disgust. He was acting like a kid with his first party girl—and God knew that he was no kid and Hope was no party girl.

Without a word Rio emptied the buckets of scalding water into the tub, turned, and left the steamy room and the woman who watched him with dreams in her eyes.

Chapter 4

THE ADVANCING SEASON WAS REVEALED IN THE PRE-dawn chill. Hope's breath came out in a pale gust that was absorbed almost instantly by the dry air, as though even the sky itself was thirsty for any bit of moisture. The stars had a brittle brilliance that came only with an atmosphere that was almost totally devoid of humidity. A breeze stirred fitfully, bringing with it a bite that foreshadowed the winter waiting to sweep down out of the north, riding on the back of the long, icy wind.

Hope pulled her denim jacket closer around her body and hurried into the barn. A rooster crowed rustily, then with greater force, although only an optimist would have said that dawn was imminent. Hens clucked and muttered as though resenting the rooster's strident summons to another day of pecking the dust and each other. Hope scattered food for the fowl, then checked the nests for eggs while the hens were busying their sharp little beaks on grain. The drought hadn't inconvenienced the chickens in the least. Fifteen eggs waited within straw nests like pearls within amorphous golden shells.

She didn't realize that Rio had already been up and in the barn until she saw that the *grulla* had been fed and the stall raked out. For a moment Hope wondered if Rio had gotten any sleep at all. She had fallen asleep in the hot bath, only to be startled awake by the sound of the water truck being driven through the front yard and into the pasture opposite the house. The Angus had lowed uneasily, then accepted the wheeled intruder as Rio filled the stock trough beneath the moon's thin, cold smile.

By the time Hope had washed her hair, dried it, and dressed in clean clothes again, Rio had driven off into the night. She knew without asking that he was going for more water. Mason had already gone to the bunkhouse that he and Hazel had converted into a home. Since the death of his wife, Mason's housekeeping had been minimal. Nor would he let Hope help. Much of the bunkhouse hadn't been touched since the day Hazel had unexpectedly died. Hope knew that Mason very much preferred it that way. If Rio were to stay at the Valley of the Sun, it would have to be in the second bunkhouse or in the main house.

It was too late to make the second bunkhouse habitable for that night. Rio would have to use either the remaining upstairs bedroom or the day bed on the screened porch. Hope had made up both beds, left Rio a note telling him to take his pick, and gone to her own bedroom. The sound of the truck pulling into the yard had awakened her. She heard the downstairs shower run very briefly, then the creak of the door leading from the kitchen to the screened-in porch that

ran along the back of the house. She had heard
nothing more until her own alarm went off in the
small hours of the morning.

Carrying the fresh eggs in a paper bag, Hope
hurried across the dusty, gravel-strewn yard between
the barn and the back of the ranch house. She
hesitated at the back porch door. A quick glance told
her what she had already suspected—Rio was gone,
leaving no sign that he had ever been there. The day
bed was made with military crispness, the braided rag
rug was smoothly in place on the floor, and the
washbasin was empty and wiped clean. It was as
though she had dreamed yesterday afternoon, the
unexpected luxury of a hot bath, and the tall man with
night-black hair and gentle hands.

Hope checked the side yard. The dusty pickup
truck that she and Mason used was gone. Not that it
mattered. She had no errands to run in town. What
did matter, and what she reluctantly faced, was that
she had been looking forward to seeing Rio this
morning, to sharing coffee and eggs and conversation
with the dark stranger who seemed more familiar to
her than many people she had known for years.

Mason wasn't waiting in the kitchen as Hope had
expected him to be. Instead, she found a note explaining that he had taken Rio to the Turner ranch and
would be back sometime before noon. Hope ate
quickly, hardly taking the time to admire the color
and freshness of the eggs. She poured the rest of the
coffee into a large Thermos, tucked it under her arm,
and hurried toward the water truck. She had three
other stock tanks to fill, some of them even larger
than the Hope's. She wouldn't get them all completely
full, of course. There wasn't enough time. All she
could do was keep them full enough to prevent the
cattle from drifting off into wild country in a futile
search for water.

With a deep, unconscious sigh Hope opened the noisy truck door and swung into the cab. The truck grumbled and coughed and grumbled some more, but finally started. She let in the clutch, turned the wheel—and discovered that the truck's tank was already brim-full of water. Rio had not only filled the trough in the Angus pasture, he had driven all the way back to the Turner well, filled up again, and driven all the way home just to help her out. Hope blinked rapidly, feeling an absurd impulse to burst into tears at this fresh evidence of Rio's thoughtfulness.

"Oh, great," she muttered to herself, swallowing hard, "you stand to lose everything you ever had or wanted and you don't snivel one bit. But let somebody be kind to you and you spring a leak."

Hope had to blink several times before she could see well enough to steer the awkward rig out of the yard and onto the dirt road. She drove as quickly as she could to the nearest well, an old one hidden in an unexpected hollow of the land. The windmill was motionless when she got there, for it was too early in the day for the wind to blow. It wasn't too early for the cattle to be thirsty, though. Yet none were pressed around the trough waiting for a drink.

Fear squeezed Hope's heart, making it beat harshly. *Why weren't the cattle crowding around to drink? Were they lost? Stolen? Dead of thirst?*

Finally she caught the gunmetal gleam of water brimming in the trough and understood what had happened. This time she couldn't stop the tears from spilling down her cheeks. Rio had filled this trough, let the cattle drink, and filled it again, waiting until the cattle were done, all thirst slaked. He had emptied the last of the truck's water into the trough, gone to the Turner well and filled up once more, working long hours while she relaxed in a hot bath and slept more soundly than she had in months.

And he had done it without being asked, because he knew she was too stubborn—and too afraid—to admit that she had to cull her herd again, selling off range cattle she didn't have the time or strength to haul water to.

"Damn you, Rio," she whispered, tasting her own tears on her lips. "You're not fighting fair."

Then she realized that he wasn't fighting at all. He was simply doing what had to be done if she wanted to keep what remained of her range cattle.

"He worked most of the night to give you half a day's start on your dream," Hope said to her reflection in the dusty windshield. "Are you going to use it or are you going to sit here and cry?"

Hope wiped her eyes, took a fresh grip on Behemoth's wheel, and drove toward a more distant well. She was half afraid to look, not knowing what she would do if Rio had somehow managed to be there before her. He had not. Cattle were gathered around the useless windmill and its nearly empty tank. Hope drove the truck in close, wrestled the hose into place, and sat in the cab while the trough filled and the sun climbed out of night's deep well. She loved the pale tremors of peach and rose that preceded dawn, and the incandescent orange and scarlet that silently shouted the arrival of yet another miraculous day.

For despite the drought, despite her deep fear of losing everything, despite the exhaustion that would come before sunset, Hope counted each day spent on the ranch she loved to be a miracle. She rolled down the window of the cab and listened to water rushing into the tank. Cattle bawled and shoved and thrust their dusty white faces eye-deep in the water, drinking lustily. Smiling, Hope settled back into Behemoth's rump-sprung seat and dozed to the rich sounds of water pouring.

All too soon it was time to get more water. The

drive to the Turner well was both long and tiring. Behemoth had nothing so modern as power steering, automatic shift, or power brakes. Driving the truck was a test of will and muscle that left Hope aching. She looked forward to the moments of relative quiet while water was being pumped into the truck. Then she would rest again, hoarding her strength for the drive back to the Valley of the Sun with a truck that was three times as awkward fully loaded as it was empty.

As soon as Hope turned down into the little valley where the Turner well was, she knew that there would be no peace and quiet for her while the truck filled with water. John Turner's carefully polished Jeep was parked just beyond the windmill.

Hope's hands tightened on the wheel in silent dismay. She eased the truck into place by the generator, shut off the ignition and hopped out with a lightness she was far from feeling. The sight of Turner's six foot three inches of thick-shouldered body did not do anything at all for her except make her wish that she were somewhere else. Since the drought and the second mortgage on the ranch, Turner had been around her like a vulture circling a downed antelope, waiting for it to admit the vulture's inevitable supremacy and die.

"Morning, John. You're up early," said Hope as she walked by him to get to the hose rack at the back of the truck.

"Where's Mason?"

Hope glanced quickly at Turner. As she spoke she wrestled a few coils of the stiff canvas hose off the rack and scrambled across the top of the tank, dragging a section of hose behind. "I don't know. Do you need him for something?"

"No, but you sure as hell do. Look at you, driving a truck and dragging that ratty old hose around like a

hired hand. If Mason can't haul his own weight, fire
him. Only a fool would pay an old man's wages and
then turn around and do his work for him, too."

Hope pushed the hose into the tank far enough to
ensure that the coils wouldn't leap out and flail around
when water coursed through their canvas length. She
took an extra amount of time about her work, too,
trying to control her rising anger at Turner's arrogance. She climbed down the narrow metal ladder to
the ground, caught up the end of the hose that would
be coupled to the generator-driven pump, and
dragged the hose into place near the machine.

"Well?" demanded Turner, following Hope.

"Well what?" she asked, trying to brace the hose so
that its weight wouldn't drag the brass coupling apart
while she struggled to bring the warped threads into
alignment.

"I asked you a question!"

"I answered it. I don't know where Mason is."

"That's not what I meant and you know it," Turner
said irritably, jerking off his hat and snapping it
against his thigh.

Out of the corner of her eye Hope saw his curly
chestnut hair gleam in the sun. At one time the sight
of that hair had made her young heart beat faster. But
she was no longer young. His hair meant less to her
than the dusty russet hides of her range cattle. A lot
less.

The threads slipped and jammed. Hope set her
teeth, unscrewed the coupling, tugged the heavy hose
back into alignment, and again tried to make the
threads mesh. This time she succeeded. She turned
the brass ring carefully, making sure that the threads
stayed aligned. Holding her breath, she coaxed the
coupling into a good mate.

"Hope," said Turner in a threatening tone, "answer
me!"

She reminded herself that she was using Turner's water. It was all that kept her from ignoring him completely. She got up, dusted off her hands, and went back to the truck for the big wrench.

"All I heard was a lecture on my stupidity. If you had a question, you'll have to repeat it," she said evenly, manipulating the jaws of the wrench until they fitted over the brass ring on the hose.

"What the hell was Rio doing at your ranch last night?"

Anger swelled in Hope as silently as the sunlight slanting thickly across the land. "He works for me part-time," she said, her voice so carefully controlled that it had no tone at all.

"I thought I told you not to hire him."

The wrench clanged against the ring. Hope readjusted the jaws, took a better grip, and tightened the coupling with a vicious downward yank.

"Well, Hope? Didn't I tell you?"

"Do I tell you how to run your ranch?" she asked quietly, shifting her grip for another yank.

"I'm a man."

"The day you run your ranch using nothing but your gonads is the day I'll accept that argument," said Hope coldly. "Until then, I'll run my ranch like any normal person would—with my *head* and my *hands*."

She yanked down again. The coupling was so tight that it all but sang with tension. She loosened the wrench, removed it, and propped it against the generator. She grabbed the bucket she would use to prime the pump and went to the trough. Turner watched her without moving or saying anything. His face was unusually ruddy, though. She could tell by his color and by the set of his jaw and shoulders that he was angry. His normally brown eyes were almost black beneath his hat brim.

"Fire Rio," snapped Turner.

"No."

Hope worked over pump and generator, finally getting the crank to turn hard and fast enough to start the balky engine. The pump sputtered, the hose shuddered, and water began sliding through its canvas length into the empty truck.

"You like using my water?" he asked harshly.

The fear that leaped inside Hope didn't show in her face. "Are you saying that if I don't fire Rio, you'll shut off the water?" she asked with outward calm.

Turner hesitated. Put that baldly, it didn't sound either reasonable or even particularly rational. As far as he was concerned, Hope's struggle to keep the Valley of the Sun alive was both irritating and laughable, but it had attracted more than a little sympathy in the closed circle of cattle ranchers to which Turner belonged. When it became known that he had refused to give her water—water that he himself didn't need—simply because she had hired a drifter to find a well, Turner would find himself the butt of hostile jokes and contempt among the other ranchers.

"No decent woman would be alone with Rio," said Turner finally.

"Why?" asked Hope with deceptive calm. She was tired and furious, a combination that loosened her tongue. "Does Rio promise to marry a naive girl, give her birthday champagne, and paw her until she's bruised and screaming? Then does Rio shove a hundred-dollar bill into the girl's hand and tell her he's engaged, but he'll be around later to collect what's owed him?" Hope faced Turner with hazel eyes that were harder and less feeling than glass. "And then does Rio's father drive the girl home, lecturing her the whole way on how she can't expect to marry above herself?"

Turner made a wide gesture with his right hand,

sweeping aside her arguments. "Rio's no damn good. He's got women all over the West."

"Are they complaining about the arrangement?"

Turner shrugged impatiently.

"If the women like it and Rio likes it," said Hope blandly, "what's the problem?"

"They aren't my women. You are."

"No," she said curtly.

"Bull. You're mine. You want me. You just don't want to admit it."

Hope said a single, succinct word.

Turner flushed. "Listen, babe. I've had enough of your high-and-mighty act. Your mother was a drunk and your father was a loser. Hell, even your grandparents weren't much more than dirt farmers," added Turner. "You should be glad I'm offering you more than a hundred dollars a throw."

"But I," said Hope clearly, spacing each word with extreme care, "don't want *you.*"

Turner smiled and shook his head, his confidence unruffled by her words. He reached for her. "Sure you do, babe. But like I said, you just don't want to admit it. I'll show you."

Hope blocked Turner by lifting the heavy wrench and putting it between her body and his much larger one. He laughed and made another grab for her.

"That's it, babe," he said, his voice thickening with excitement. "Fight me. It turns me on when a woman fights me. Remember?"

Hope remembered. With a lithe twist of her body she dropped the wrench, evaded Turner's hands, and leaped into the cab, locking the door behind her. He laughed and reached for the wrench. Before his fingers closed around the heavy iron handle, he heard the sound of a vehicle descending into the valley at a speed too fast for the road. Still smiling, Turner

straightened and faced toward the road, assuming that
it was one of his own men coming to check on the
well.

Hope felt a wave of relief when she spotted her own
beat-up tan truck coming into view with Mason
behind the wheel. Only then did she admit that
Turner's persistence had frightened her. With an
effort of will she forced her breathing to slow until her
body relaxed and her hands stopped trembling. She
was safe. Mason was here. Mason would take care of
her.

And then she realized that she couldn't tell Mason
that Turner had made a grab for her. If Mason knew,
he would lose his temper and try to fight Turner. She
couldn't let that happen. Mason would be badly
beaten. For she had learned that about Turner. He
liked using his huge strength on weaker people,
hitting and hurting them with his thick hands.

"Well, old man," said Turner as Mason got out of
the truck, "I see you finally got here. I thought I was
going to have to do all the work myself."

Mason's eyes were so narrow that they showed
almost no color as he gave Turner a contemptuous
glance. Mason saw the wrench lying in the dust and
Hope inside the water truck with the window rolled
up nearly all the way.

"I'm here," said Mason. His body language said
that he was staying here, too.

Turner smiled genially. "Then I guess I can get back
to the ranch." He looked up at Hope. "See you, babe.
I'm looking forward to it."

"Good-bye, Turner." Hope's voice was like her
face, without expression.

Hope didn't move until Turner's Jeep was accelerating out of the tiny valley. Then she swung down from
the cab and smiled at Mason.

"Glad you stopped by," she said, her voice casual.

"It gets real boring just talking to a bunch of cows while the truck fills with water."

"Did he lay a hand on you?"

"Nope," she said honestly. What she didn't say was that all that had prevented it was her own speed.

Mason stared at her, suspecting that he was getting only a part of the truth. He started to say something, then bit it off. His lips flattened into a colorless line. "I'll do the water hauling from now on."

"No," she said, her voice smooth, leaving no possibility of argument. "But if you'd like to ride shotgun," she added, smiling at him, "I'd love the company. Like I said, talking to the cows isn't very stimulating."

He looked at her for another long moment. She was smiling her familiar, heart-warming smile, but her skin was too pale. He knew then that Turner had tried something. It was what Mason had feared since the moment he had dropped Rio off at Turner's corral and had learned from one of the hands that for once the boss had gotten up before noon and gone to check on one of the wells. Mason hadn't stayed around to chat after that. He'd gotten in the truck and driven recklessly until he had reached the well where he knew Hope would be getting water.

And worst of all, Mason knew that Hope wouldn't say anything to him for the same reason that she had taken over the water runs—she knew that his hands were too bad right now to handle the heavy truck and the stubborn couplings, much less to handle a man less than half his age and nearly twice his weight. Quietly, secretly, Mason cursed the fate that had let him live long enough to lose his beloved wife and then grow too old to defend the woman who meant as much to him as any blood daughter could have.

"I'll ride with you from now on," he said quietly.

Hope didn't argue. She was relieved to know that

she wouldn't have to face Turner alone again. The man simply didn't understand the word *no*. To him, *no* was a coy prelude to a wrestling match. Maybe that was how his other women liked it, but not Hope. The thought of fighting Turner both frightened and repelled her.

Mason went back to the pickup truck and lifted a rifle from the rack that stretched across the rear window. He checked the load, eased the firing pin back into place, and pulled a box of shells out of the glove compartment before he returned to Hope. He smiled at her. There was something in the smile that made her very glad to be his friend rather than his enemy.

"Snake gun," said Mason, his voice rough with age and the anger that still turned deeply inside his gut at the thought of Turner lying in wait for Hope like a coyote at a water hole. "Drought like this, you git snakes at the wells." Then he stopped smiling and looked at Hope unflinchingly. "If I ain't around and you gotta go to a well, you be damn sure you got a snake gun with you. And you keep it real close to hand. Hear me?"

Hope tried to smile but could not. She hugged Mason quickly. "I hear you."

He nodded curtly. "I'll watch the pump. You go over that little rise and run a few rounds through this here rifle. Been a long time since we done any shooting together."

There was no point in arguing. Hope took the gun and the shells and walked over the rise, where there would be no chance of a ricochet hitting any of the cattle. She found a particularly ugly clump of big sage growing against one bank of a dry ravine, mentally labeled the bush *Turner,* and began trimming it down to size one twig at a time.

When Hope had shot enough rounds to soothe

Mason and herself, she walked back over the rise to the well. Mason was tinkering with the generator. Whatever he was doing had an immediate effect; the sound of the engine decreased by about half. As he stood up again she saw the long-spouted oil can in his hand.

"You're incredible, Mason," said Hope, half exasperated, half pleased. "I greased that blasted machine two days ago and it didn't get a bit less noisy."

He smiled, pleased that there was something he could still do right despite his aching hands. "You done fine, honey, but you don't like this generator and she knows it. Takes a gentle hand to keep her happy."

"Not to mention gas and oil," muttered Hope, reaching out to unscrew the fuel reservoir cap and check the contents.

"Already checked it," said Mason. "It'll do 'til tomorrow."

Hope hesitated, then said quietly, "I'm calling up Hawthorne when I get back to the ranch."

Mason took off his hat, rubbed his forehead, and then settled his hat back into place with a quick tug. "How many you selling?"

She closed her eyes, trying not to think of her range cattle burning like garnets against a sunset ridgeline where piñon grew in ragged lines of black flame. "I—I don't know. Half." She swallowed. "Yes, half. That should stretch the natural feed, too."

"Hawthorne gonna use his own men for the cows?" asked Mason.

"He did the last time," said Hope, shrugging. "If not, I'll hire the Johnston boys. They love a roundup."

Mason smiled. "Yeah. Good kids. A mite young, but we all was once."

Hope remembered her own teenage years and smiled a bittersweet smile. "Yeah. Real young." She

sighed unconsciously and looked around the land. "I
spent most of my time after I was fourteen missing the
ranch. I hated L.A. Julie and Mom loved it, though."
Hope fell silent. If her father hadn't had to pay for
two homes, he might have had enough cash to look
for more wells. But her mother had insisted on having
her daughters go to high school in a "civilized place."
So her father had taken the ranch's small profits and
mailed them to L.A., and he had prayed that the
Hope would continue to run sweet and pure until he
had money to dig a deeper well. "Poor Dad." She
sighed, not realizing that she had spoken aloud.

Mason put his arm around Hope's shoulder. "Don't
go feeling sorry for him. He done what he wanted and
let hell take the rest."

"But he worked so hard," she whispered, her
throat aching with unshed tears.

"He didn't grudge a bit of it. He lived for the
summers when you and your ma came home." Mason
didn't mention Julie. Hope's sister had always been a
beautiful butterfly child, hardly able to stand up to the
heat of a simple summer day much less to the hard
work and isolation of the Valley of the Sun. Not
Hope, though. She had loved the heat and silence and
the sight of cattle moving through the piñon. She had
been born for this land in a way that her mother had
never understood. "Having you following him around
with bright eyes and bushels of questions made him
feel taller than God and smarter than Satan."

Hope smiled sadly. She had loved her father very
much. So had her mother, a fact that Hope hadn't
realized until her mother was dead and Hope found
the letters that her parents had written while they
were separated. "Mom loved him."

Mason sighed. "Your ma's passions ran deep. Hate.
Love. Deeper than the wells we never drilled. You're
like her in that, honey, when you let yourself be. You

got your dad's grit, though. His and then some. You musta got Julie's, too." Mason shook his head at the memories welling up from the past like a clear, unexpected spring. "She was pretty as a Christmas calf, and just as sure to die young."

The familiar tightness settled in Hope's throat. She had loved her older but not wiser sister, had held her hand through foolish affairs and brutal rejections. Hope had tried to talk with her, to help her sister understand and cope with a world that simply did not care whether one Julie Gardener received champagne and roses or vinegar and skunkweed. Julie had never understood that basic reality. Her self-absorption had been both innocent and bone-deep. After their mother died, Julie discovered drugs. She was dead within two years.

"Don't look so down in the mouth, honey," said Mason, tugging gently on a handful of Hope's dark curls. "Julie just wasn't made for this world. It happens that way, time to time. So you bury the ones that couldn't make it and you wipe your eyes and you get on with living. Because you was made for this world, Hope. No mistake about it. You're strong and straight and giving. You was made to love a good man and raise tall sons and laughing daughters. You and your children will heal the Valley of the Sun. And then the past will all be worth it, all the dying and the tears and the pain."

Hope looked at Mason's seamed face and clear eyes. She felt his certainty like a benediction. She stood on tiptoe and kissed his cheek. "You're a good man, Mason," she whispered, her voice catching. "The best."

Mason smiled gently at Hope and handed her a faded scarlet bandanna to catch the tears that were welling silently from her wide hazel eyes.

"Thanks." She laughed oddly as she wiped her

eyes. "Lately I seem to have more water than my namesake."

"You're tired, honey. You're doing the work of two men."

Hope's only answer was a long, ragged sigh. "Not of two men like Rio. Did he get any sleep at all last night?"

"He's a tough son," said Mason, approval warming the laconic words.

"But it isn't fair for him to—"

"Fair don't water no cows," interrupted Mason bluntly. "You git to worryin' about fair and you won't have no time left to smile. Take my word for it, gal. I been there."

"The least I can do is fix up the other bunkhouse for him to use."

"Don't bother. Rio liked the porch just fine. If it gits too cold," added Mason matter-of-factly, "he can take one of the upstairs bedrooms."

Hope looked at Mason, her surprise clear.

"Something wrong?" he asked.

"As long as I've been at the ranch, you've been standing over cowhands with a shotgun if they so much as said hello to me. But Rio—Rio moves into the house with me and you don't turn a hair!"

"He's different." Mason looked at Hope with eyes that were faded by age and made wise by experience. "Rio won't touch you, honey. Oh, you might tempt him sure enough. He ain't blind. But he won't let nothing happen."

"Why?" she asked, her voice tight with the surprising pain she felt.

"He got too much respect for you—and for hisself —to bite off something he ain't got no intention of chewing."

"What do you mean?"

"Rio knows you're a permanent sort of woman.

And Rio . . ." Mason shrugged. "Rio's a temporary sort of man."

Hope said nothing for the simple reason that her throat was closed tight. She didn't doubt the truth of what Mason was saying. In the deepest part of her mind she knew that he was absolutely right.

And in the deepest part of her heart she wished that he was absolutely wrong.

Chapter 5

HOPE CLIMBED SLOWLY DOWN FROM THE CAB OF THE water truck and stretched, loosening arm muscles cramped by steering the heavy vehicle out of ruts and around tight curves. Even with only half the range cattle she had had before, there were still barely enough hours in the day to make the necessary runs. In the days since Hawthorne's men had trucked away her cattle, she had been working constantly while dry winds churned dust devils out of an empty sky.

She looked almost eagerly toward the Perdidas rising tall and hard from the dry land. Thin clouds shimmered and swirled around the rocky peaks. Other patches of clouds floated randomly in the cerulean sky. The temperature had dropped into the low sixties for several days, with the nights getting down into the forties. Rain had been predicted yesterday and the day before, part of a northern storm front sweeping down from Alaska and Canada.

Rain hadn't fallen in the high desert yet, though the

air was no longer so dry that it burned against Hope's skin. Clouds had condensed, piled up against the Perdidas, and thickened into a black veil stitched with glittering threads of lightning. Some of the intermittent creeks draining the Perdidas had small amounts of water in them again, enough so that the most venturesome cattle could spread out from the wells, easing the demands made on the natural feed around the troughs. Already the tiny pools in the creek beds and ravines were drying up, though. The land was sucking up water much faster than it could be replenished by mountain runoff. If it didn't rain again soon, and hard, there would be no more surface water around than there had been a week ago.

If it didn't rain soon, Hope would have to begin hauling feed as well as water to her range cattle. They were on the edge of overgrazing the land around the wells, damaging it beyond repair or recovery.

"Hope, you're borrowing trouble again," she said to herself. "No need to do that. God knows you have enough without going looking for more."

Nearby an Angus lowed and walked with odd grace toward Hope. The cow's eyes were huge, dark, and had lashes as long as Hope's little finger. The animal's coat was thick, slightly curly, and of a black satin richness that begged to be stroked. With a gentle butt against Hope's arm the cow demanded to be petted.

"Hello, Sweetheart," said Hope, smiling. She rubbed her palms vigorously over the cow's long, solid back as she looked for any cuts or scratches that might need a swipe from the bottle of gentian violet that she always kept in the truck. "Where's your Sweet Midnight?"

Sweetheart snuffled.

"Out running around again, huh?" she said sympathetically, scratching the base of the cow's ears. "Well, what do you expect of a half-grown bull calf?"

Sweetheart butted Hope a good deal less gently, knowing that there was a handful of grain somewhere nearby. Laughing, Hope shoved against the cow's muscular neck. She might as well have pushed on the Perdidas. Sweetheart stood pat on her four strong legs, demanding her due as Hope's first and most favored Angus.

"Sweetheart, if I'd known eight years ago that such a cute little 'kivver' would grow into twelve hundred immovable pounds of bovine assurance, I'd have sold you for steaks."

The cow blinked her incredibly long-lashed eyelids. Her moist muzzle prodded Hope's stomach. Hope gave up and returned to the cab for a shallow cake pan full of grain. Sweetheart cleaned the pan with more thoroughness than manners. When Hope began to pull hose off the back of the truck and drag the ragged canvas toward the well, the cow backed up a bit and watched with what could have been interest, bemusement, or disdain.

None of the more than thirty black cattle crowded in around the trough as Hope filled it. She had been careful not to let the water get so low that there were shoving matches and trampling hooves around the big tank. It wasn't just that the Angus were considerably more valuable than the Hereford range cattle. The Angus were the very core of her dream of building the Valley of the Sun into a productive ranch. For that— and for their massive beauty—Hope loved the Angus.

Sweetheart was more of a pet than the elusive cats who kept the barn from being overrun with mice. Four of Sweetheart's calves were a part of the breeding herd, including Sweet Midnight, the most recent of the offspring. Already Hope had had offers for the robust yearling. She had turned down every one of them. Sweet Midnight was going to be the father of many future Angus on the Valley of the Sun. The cows he would breed were as carefully selected and nurtured as Sweetheart had been. Their bloodlines were of the first rank. It showed in their ponderous grace and surprisingly gentle temperaments, and in their vigorous, muscular offspring.

Slowly Hope relaxed as she leaned against Sweetheart's massive warmth and listened to her cattle suck cool water from the trough she had filled. Other cows came up and snuffled over Hope's shirt as though to say hello, then moved off to bury their noses in the fragrant hay that Mason had brought to the pasture earlier in the day. Hope watched each cow, each calf, knowing them individually. She was alert for any signs of disease or injury, no matter how small. There were none. With a wry smile Hope acknowledged that the cattle were in better shape than she was.

Sweetheart turned and looked beyond the truck, her blunt, furry ears cocked forward. Hope glanced over her shoulder and saw Rio walking toward her. Sweetheart mooed softly as she wandered over to the tall man. Hope could see the sudden flash of Rio's smile as he ran his hand down the cow's neck. Sweetheart's long tongue curled out, swiped across his extended palm, and vanished.

"What's your secret?" said Hope as Rio walked up to her, Sweetheart in tow.

"Salt," he admitted, grinning. He shoved hard on the persistent cow's neck. She heaved a barn-sized sigh and ambled back to join the other Angus.

Hope smiled. "Must be time to put out another salt lick."

Rio looked over the cattle as thoroughly as Hope had. "Good herd," he said simply. "One of the best I've ever seen."

"Thank you," she said, knowing she sounded proud of the cattle she had chosen and unable to hide it. "They're my gift to the Valley of the Sun."

"Your family didn't raise Angus?"

She pushed off her hat, letting it hang from its rawhide thong down her back. "No," she said, shaking out her hair and running her fingers through it, loving the feel of the wind lifting the heavy mass of hair away from her face. "Dad always wanted to. The first thing I bought him with my modeling money was Sweetheart. He didn't live to see her bred."

"You were a model?"

Hope thought of the picture she must make—dirty boots and blue work shirt, faded jeans and a beat-up hat. She smiled crookedly. "Long ago, far away, in another country."

Rio's glance took in the purity of Hope's profile, her shining hair, the womanly lift of her breasts, and the long, achingly lovely line of her legs. He had known more beautiful women in his wanderings, women who could make most men stop and stare in hunger and disbelief; but he had never known a woman who called to his mind and senses as Hope did. He wanted to talk with her, laugh with her, help her, protect her, stand close to the shimmering radiance of her dream.

And he wanted to touch her, to discover the hot, secret textures of her body, to know the sweet demands of her mouth and the heat of her response, to hear her cry out his name as the pleasure he brought to her consumed her.

Grimly Rio called himself several kinds of fool. Hope wasn't for him. His mind knew it, but his body was fighting that knowledge every bit of the way. Hope had only to breathe and he wanted her with a force that was unlike anything he had ever known with another woman. He would not take Hope, though. He had nothing to give her but the well he wanted to find for her, for her dream. When he found it, when the dream was truth, then the wind would call to him and he would leave.

Hope deserved better than that.

"I'll bet you were good at it," he said quietly, turning his glance and his thoughts away from what he could not have.

"Modeling?" Hope shrugged. "I made a lot of money, but I wasn't an international cover girl, if that's what you mean."

"Did you want to be?"

"No."

"Why not?"

"All I ever wanted was the Valley of the Sun. After Mom and Julie died, I was free to come back home."

"You don't model anymore?"

Hope gave Rio a sideways glance out of hazel eyes that were touched with shadows and flecks of gold. "No. When I'm in L.A.—" She shrugged. "I'm not a city girl. I can do it, but I don't like it. And I thought I had enough money to keep the ranch alive after I paid inheritance taxes, enough to keep going until I could build up the herds and put the ranch on a paying basis." She shrugged again and gave Rio a bittersweet smile. "I was as green as grass. I didn't know that there's no such animal as 'enough money' when you're talking about a desert ranch."

"Could you go back to modeling?"

"Could you live in a city?" she asked quietly.

"I have."

"And now you don't." Hope looked out at her beautiful black cattle and the brilliant currents of water welling silently up from the hose at the bottom of the tank. "I could exist in the city," she said slowly, trying to make Rio understand what she could barely articulate herself. "I can only *live* here. This is my past, my present, my future. The Valley of the Sun is the only home I'll ever have, no matter where I live. I've always felt that way. I always will. This land is part of me."

Rio wanted to put his arms around Hope, to fold her gently against his body and hold her, promising her that he would give her the well that would allow her to live forever on the land she loved. But he could not do that, neither the holding nor the promising. He had learned as a child that promises were only words, and that the promise implicit in a comforting hug could be the biggest lie of all. Not that his parents had meant to be cruel. It just had turned out that way. They had been more interested in fleeing the Indian part of their heritage than they had been in anything else, even their black-haired son.

In silence Hope and Rio watched the cattle glisten blackly beneath the clear light of morning. The fact that it was Friday morning—and early morning at that—suddenly registered on Hope. Rio shouldn't have been here at all.

"Did you finish with Turner's horses?" she asked.

"After a fashion."

Hope turned and looked at Rio. "What does that mean?"

He smiled sardonically, remembering. "Turner gave me a choice—work for him at triple my present wages, or work for you full-time." Rio's drawl deepened. "I allowed as how I'd rather dig wells with a toothpick than work for him."

"Damn his arrogance!" hissed Hope, suddenly furious. "I'll make it up to you somehow, Rio."

"Like hell you will," he said coolly, no drawl left. "Any problems I have with Turner are mine, not yours."

"Not in this case. Turner doesn't want you working for me. He threatened to cut off the water unless I fired you."

Rio said something beneath his breath that Hope was just as glad not to hear. "When did this happen?" he demanded.

"A couple of weeks ago. It was just a bluff."

He nodded. "And then Turner found twenty hours a day of work for me to do at his ranch."

Hope said nothing. It explained why Rio hadn't had time to do much toward finding a well.

"He's saying that you're engaged to him," added Rio matter-of-factly.

Anger sent scarlet rising in Hope's cheeks. "He's lying."

Rio measured the truth and fury in her quiet statement and nodded. "Is that why you're carrying a rifle in the water truck these days?"

"Mason said there were a lot of snakes around the wells," said Hope with a careful, casual shrug.

"Smart man," said Rio dryly. Then with deadly quietness he asked, "Did Turner make a try for you at his well?"

Hope looked at Rio's eyes and saw the promise of violence in their cold blue depths. She looked away and said nothing, not wanting to lie to Rio.

"Hope?" asked Rio softly.

"It wasn't anything serious," she said finally. "It just takes a while for the word *no* to sink into Turner's thick skull."

"Try using that wrench to drive home your point," offered Rio, hooking a thumb toward the cast-iron tool that was propped against the truck's rear tire.

"The thought had occurred to me," she said wryly.

He glanced sideways, saw that she meant it, and smiled slightly. All the same, he promised himself that he would make sure that Hope was never alone if she left the ranch.

Then Rio remembered that he wouldn't always be around to protect her.

Hope saw Rio's sudden frown. She didn't know why he had responded so deeply to Turner's actions, but she had no doubt that Rio was almost as protective of her as Mason was. Quickly she changed the subject. "I have enough money to pay you. Not as much as Turner, but—"

"No," said Rio, interrupting her. "Our deal hasn't changed. Room and board for me, range and a stud for my mares."

"For as long as the water flows."

"I have to find the damn stuff first," said Rio sardonically, raking his hat from his head with a long-fingered hand, holding on to the Stetson's dusty black curves.

Hope watched as Rio squinted toward the Perdidas, weighing them on some inner, instinctive scale. He nodded slightly before he smoothed the Stetson back into place and turned toward her again.

"Rain by tonight," he said, his voice deep and certain. "A good rain. Not enough to bring up the water table much, but it should fill some of the natural holes and revive a few of the shallow seeps. For a week or so we'll have to haul water only once a day, twice at most. We'll have to start hauling feed, though."

"I'll do the hauling," Hope protested quietly. "I didn't hire you as a ranch hand."

"That's right," agreed Rio. "I volunteered."

"I can't let you—"

Rio cut off her words with a dark blue glance that told her he was every bit as determined as she was. He was bigger, too, and he knew it. But that wasn't the determining factor, as it would have been with John Turner.

"If we share the water-hauling, you'll have time to ride the land with me," Rio continued, surprising himself even while he heard his own words echo in his mind.

As he spoke he knew that this was part of the reason he had offered to find a new well for the Valley of the Sun. The thought of riding the land with Hope had flowed deeply beneath his offer like artesian water beneath a stratum of unyielding slate. He could not have her but he could share her dream for a time, filling the emptiness that had come to him long ago, when he had stopped believing in his own dreams.

"I'll bet there are parts of the Valley of the Sun that you've never seen," Rio said softly. "It's your land, Hope, your future, your dream. You should know every beautiful, hard inch of it."

She looked at his eyes, as deeply blue as twilight condensing into night. She sensed the isolation in him, the darkness that lay beneath his smile, the long times of silence when he saw no one and spoke only in the depths of his mind. Like the land she loved, Rio could be harsh and beguiling by turns. She wondered what secrets were hidden in his depths, what riches and sweet waters were concealed by hard surface barriers that no one had ever breached.

And because she wasn't a fool, she also wondered what dangers were waiting beneath his rugged surface, if there were fault lines where reality could shift suddenly, crushing the unwary.

Yet danger, too, was part of the reason that Hope loved the land. The Valley of the Sun accepted few people, and none of them easily. The children of the land knew how to survive. They also knew how to *live*, how to take a single moment and make of it an incandescent joy that few people ever found. The incredible, silken coolness of water in the midst of drought. The shimmering flash of light as the sun sank behind a stark, blue-black ridge. The piñon-scented breeze that flowed out of canyon mouths when everywhere else the air was still. The terrible power and beauty of an eagle swooping down on its prey. The lush, secret perfume of a night-blooming cactus. And the land itself, a silent symphony in every tone of gold and brown. These were just a few of the moments of intense pleasure, soul-deep awareness, that the Valley of the Sun gave to those who understood her.

Did Rio know those moments? Had he found others he could share with her?

"Yes," said Hope quietly. "I'd like to ride the land with you."

His eyes examined her face, seeing both the darkness and the gold in her hazel glance. He nodded briefly. "I'll unload my gear at the house. I'll take the east bedroom upstairs, if that's all right. That way you and Mason won't feel like you have to tiptoe through my territory every time you use the back porch."

"Good," said Hope quickly, stifling the fugitive flash of sensual awareness that came at the thought of Rio sleeping in the room next to hers. She acknowledged ruefully to herself that Rio could sleep right in the same room and she wouldn't need to worry about him making a pass at her. Not by so much as a gesture had he indicated any real interest in her sexually. He liked her, though. She was sure of it. Even Mason had commented that he had never seen Rio smile so much as he did when Hope was around.

"You going to the Hope next?" asked Rio.

"Yes."

"I'll be ready."

"Have you eaten yet?" she asked.

Rio shrugged.

Hope looked at the level of the tank. Not quite full. "I'll be finished in about twenty minutes. Breakfast in thirty-five."

"You don't have to make—"

"Better hustle," she said, cutting across his objection. "If your boots aren't under the table when the eggs are finished, I'll feed every bit to the nonexistent pigs. That would be a terrible waste of fresh eggs."

His smile flashed quickly, a hard curve of white against his dark face. He touched his hat brim in a brief salute. "Yes, *ma'am*," he drawled deeply, his tone of voice both soft and suitably awed.

She tried not to smile in return, failed, and laughed aloud. Rio's actions were those of a polite, slightly backward boy, yet he radiated a seasoned masculinity that was unmistakable. It was impossible not to be amused by the difference between the diffident words and the confident reality of the man.

Rio saw Hope's struggle not to smile, heard her laughter, and winked conspiratorially just as he turned to go back to the house. He didn't know who was more surprised by the wink, Hope or himself. He couldn't remember the last time he had felt so lighthearted, as though the day ahead were packed with new places and possibilities to explore. There was something indefinably exciting about being in the presence of Hope, whether it was the woman or the simple fact of hope itself.

The memory of Rio's teasing kept Hope's sense of humor intact even when the brass coupling on the hose proved unusually stubborn. She subdued it with the heavy wrench, stowed everything in its proper place, and drove the truck out of the pasture, stopping only long enough to unlock and carefully lock the gate. After she had washed up outside, she let herself into the kitchen through the back porch. Immediately she saw that Rio hadn't taken any chances on missing breakfast. His place was set with plate, silver, coffee mug, napkin—and a pair of his boots had been tucked neatly under the table.

Hope laughed aloud, feeling like a teenager again.

She had expected many things after hearing Mason's description of Rio, but Rio's droll sense of the ridiculous wasn't one of them. Still smiling, she quickly lit the oven, turned it as low as it would go, and put Rio's plate and a big platter inside. Then she took thick slices of bacon out of the refrigerator and draped them in a heavy cast-iron pan to cook. While the bacon sizzled she cut up potatoes into another black pan. As soon as the bacon and potatoes were crisp and ready, she moved them onto the platter and tucked it into the oven again. Four slices of bread disappeared into the toaster. They emerged shortly, transformed into crunchy brown squares. She buttered the toast and stashed it in the oven to stay warm.

When she heard Rio's soft footsteps on the stairs, she reached up to the open cupboard shelf where she kept fresh eggs in an unglazed pottery bowl. As she brought it down to eye level, she stopped in surprise. Nestled amid the smooth white curves of the eggs was a scattering of tiny golden blossoms, wildflowers that bloomed out of season in the wake of desert rains. The flowers' fragrance was like a delicate caress, a silent promise of life renewing itself despite the harshest drought. She closed her eyes and breathed deeply, filling herself with both the fragrance and the promise.

When Hope opened her eyes Rio was there, watching her with an expression that was close to hunger and even closer to regret. She smiled at him, wishing that he weren't a temporary kind of man, wanting him despite that, wanting him even as she accepted that he wouldn't take her. She didn't know that her smile was an echo of his own expression, hunger and regret mingling.

"Thank you," she said simply.

"My grandmother called them rain flowers," said Rio, seeing Hope's fingertip touch a soft petal, wishing that it were his skin rather than the flower that

Hope was caressing. "She said that they were the only gold that mattered in this land."

"What did your grandfather call them?" asked Hope, remembering Mason's words to the effect that Rio's grandfather had been a Zuni shaman.

Rio's eyes narrowed as he tried to remember rituals from deep in his past. The soft golden blossoms were medicine flowers, revered for their endurance in the face of the harshest conditions. Slowly some of the memories condensed, returning part of his childhood to him. He spoke in phrases that had odd rhythms, ritual intonations, sacred sounds from a time and a place and a culture to which he no longer belonged. He did not translate the words into English for Hope, for there was no translation that anyone would understand. His grandfather's beliefs had been a synthesis of Zuni and Navajo, Apache and missionary Christian rituals, an attempt to integrate the ageless animism of Indian heritage with the invincible reality of European man. It had worked for his grandfather in ways that Rio understood but could not articulate.

"There's no real translation," said Rio. Then, softly, he added, "I've always called these flowers *hope,* for they bloom at times and in places where nothing else can survive."

Silence stretched between Hope and Rio, a silence that was taut with unspoken words and needs. As she looked away from the blue depths of his eyes, she realized that for the first time in her life she wanted a man, truly wanted him. The thought of not having Rio, of never having him, was a pain so intense she had to fight back a cry of protest.

Hope's hands trembled as she filled a shallow earthenware saucer with a thin layer of water. Carefully she picked out the small blossoms and floated them on the transparent shimmer of liquid. She placed the saucer gently on the table between her place and Rio's. The blossoms shivered with each movement of the water, as though they were alive and taking quick, tiny breaths.

"How do you like your eggs?" asked Hope, her voice vibrant with the emotions that she was suppressing.

"Over easy," said Rio.

He reached past Hope and picked up the huge black coffeepot on the back of the stove. Inadvertently his arm brushed over hers. The brief sliding contact sent warmth rushing through him as he remembered the instant weeks ago when her breasts had pressed against him while she wrestled with the stubborn coupling on the canvas hose. The tactile memory was as clear and as hot as the flame burning beneath the cast-iron pan. The intensity of his response to a memory and a casual touch both surprised and disturbed him. Nothing of his emotions showed in his face as he poured himself a cup of strong coffee. He had learned long ago to school his features to show no more expression than that of an eagle arrowing out of the sky to claim its prey.

As Rio replaced the coffeepot, Hope reached for an egg. Her hand bumped into his arm. There was a sensation of resilience, heat, and strength as his biceps shifted beneath her fingers. She was appalled at how hard it was to draw back from the touch. The temptation to extend the contact by running her palm over his arm was almost overwhelming.

"Excuse me," she said, snatching back her hand as though she had touched fire rather than flesh. Then, quickly, "How many eggs do you want?"

"Four," said Rio, noticing the very fine trembling of her fingers as she blindly reached for an egg.

The knowledge that his closeness affected her to such an extent set off a soundless explosion of hunger that he could neither control nor deny. He watched her over the rim of his steaming coffee mug. A lock of bittersweet-chocolate hair crept free of the clip she had put on. The tendril of hair swept forward to curl softly against her neck. He wanted to capture the dark curl in his fingers, to lift it to his lips, and then to kiss the golden skin where the lock had lain. He didn't know how deeply he wanted that until he saw his own hand reaching for the satin curl of hair. Cursing silently, he turned away from Hope's endless, inadvertent temptations.

Rio sat down at the table, saw his boots beneath, and remembered the delicious laughter that had floated up the stairway when Hope had discovered them. Grimly he kicked his stocking feet into the boots and adjusted his pant legs. "I've been looking over the papers that your last hydrologist left. Educated man, no doubt about it. But he didn't know a hell of a lot about this country on a firsthand basis," Rio added dryly, sipping at his hot coffee again.

"He was just out of school," said Hope, turning the eggs expertly. "City boy through and through. Nice kid. Earnest and real sorry that there wasn't any water on my ranch."

She slid the eggs onto Rio's warm plate, retrieved the platter with its load of bacon, potatoes, and toast, and put it all in front of him. Silently she added honey and a jar of cherry preserves to the table. After pouring herself a cup of coffee, she began making sandwiches for a snack lunch. Between sips of coffee she deftly assembled slices of beef and slabs of yeasty homemade bread. Several apples, plus a tin of oatmeal and raisin cookies, completed the lunch.

When it was all tightly wrapped and ready to go, she poured herself some more coffee and sat opposite Rio, not at all bothered by his silence. She had grown up around ranch men. The appetite raised by hard work left little desire for conversation until hunger had been appeased. Then the men would lean back and talk until their dinners settled or their consciences got the better of them and prodded them back to work once more.

Rio sensed Hope's relaxation and relaxed himself, grateful for her acceptance of silence. It left him free to savor each bite of the crisp fried potatoes, country bacon, homemade bread, and perfectly cooked eggs. He ate every bit, mopped his plate neatly with a last crust of toast, and sighed contentedly.

"I'll take my wages in your cooking any day," he said, meaning every word.

She shrugged and smiled slightly. She had been raised cooking. She had always loved it, the colors and the textures and the smells, the pure sensual rewards of creating a good meal. "Thanks. It's hard to go wrong with breakfast when you have fresh eggs in the cupboard and your neighbor's best pig in the freezer."

Rio made a sound of disgust. "Tell that to the hundred or so bunkhouse cooks I've known."

Hope smiled. "That's how I learned. The hands threw the cook in the corral trough and threatened to quit. I was only ten, but I'd been cooking since I was seven. Mom hated to cook."

"Did you spend much time in the trough?" Rio asked, his mouth curling upward in a smile.

"Just once. I made chocolate cake, but I mixed up the sugar and the salt. It was so awful even the dog wouldn't eat it."

Rio threw back his head and laughed. The deep sound was as much a reward to Hope as his appreciation of breakfast had been. She laughed softly, shaking her head at the memory of her culinary gaffe.

"Even today when I make a chocolate cake Mason takes a very tiny first bite," she admitted. "Nothing obvious, mind you. Just a cautious little taste to make sure that the sugar and the salt didn't get swapped around."

"I'll remember that," promised Rio.

He drained his coffee cup with a long swallow, then stood up with a smooth determination that Hope remembered from her childhood: Man of the house, fed and ready to go back to work. The thought of what it would be like to have Rio as the man of her house flashed in Hope's mind, only to be shunted aside almost instantly. She had neither the strength nor the emotion to spare for futile dreams. Rio was as rootless as the wind keening across the land, searching for something, never finding it, always moving on. She didn't need Mason to tell her that. It was there in Rio's eyes, in his silences, in his memories of countless bunkhouse cooks.

Rio saw sadness veil the humor that had made Hope's eyes brilliant just a moment before. He wondered what memory or fear had come to her, stealing her laughter. His long fingers tightened around the coffee mug. Suddenly, fiercely, he wanted to know what haunted her, wanted to smooth the downward curve of regret from her mouth with his own lips. But if he did, in the end they both would have more regrets, more sadness, the unending bitterness of betrayal.

Brother-to-the-wind.

Chapter 6

"WHERE DO YOU WANT TO START?" ASKED HOPE, WALK-ing beside Rio to the horse pasture just beyond the barn.

"We'll ride the boundaries first," said Rio, settling the saddlebags he was carrying over his shoulder. "Starting up there at the northern end of the ranch," he added, gesturing toward the Perdidas rising ruggedly above the rumpled land.

"Better take a tough horse. The Valley of the Sun goes as low as two thousand feet here in the south and as high as seven up along the northern boundaries."

"You have timberland?" he asked, surprise clear in his voice.

She gave him a wry, sideways glance. "Are you kidding? If it's a tree, it's on government-lease land. The part of the ranch that's above seven thousand feet is all on northwest-facing slopes. Big sage, mountain mahogany, piñon, and juniper. Not a decent board foot in the lot."

Rio's mouth turned down in a sardonic curl. "It's the same way all over Nevada. The best land is government, the worst is Indian, and the rest of the Basin and Range country belongs to anyone strong and smart enough to hammer a living out of it."

"It's a beautiful land, though," said Hope.

"Most people don't think so," Rio said in a dry voice. "They look at the sagebrush and the naked mountains and they can't drive through the state fast enough. Maybe you have to be born here to appreciate it."

"My mother was born here. She hated it."

"So did mine," admitted Rio. "Being raised on a reservation was no treat for a girl. She couldn't get out fast enough."

"Did your father like it?"

Rio made a sound that could have been laughter, but was too hard. "He hated this land more than she did. He was part Athabascan, born to northern forests and lakes. He hated them, too. But most of all he hated being called Indian when his father was a renegade Scotsman and his mother was half Dutch." Rio moved his wide shoulders in a casual shrug that was belied by the dark memories in his eyes. "My father never grew up. He never accepted the fact that there's no such thing as part white. People look at you and see only *not* white."

There was a sophisticated cynicism in Rio's appraisal that made Hope ache. "When I look at you," she said quietly, "I see a man. Period."

Rio glanced quickly aside at Hope. He started to say something, but a drumroll of approaching hooves cut him off. He turned in time to see Storm Walker canter up to the fence from the center of the pasture where the Appaloosa stallion held court with two of Hope's four remaining mares. Black except for a white stocking and the black-spotted white "blanket"

that covered his powerful rump, Storm Walker made
an arresting picture as he came toward them. The
stallion moved with a muscular grace that made Rio
want to climb on the black back and ride. He watched
with a horseman's knowing, appreciative eye as the
stud minced up to the fence and nickered a greeting.

Quietly Rio stroked the horse's warm, glossy neck.
Neither the man nor the stallion was wary of the
other. They had made friends the first time Rio had
leaned against the fence and talked Storm Walker
over to him in low, soothing tones. Since then Rio had
come to the horse pasture at least once a day, bringing
a reassuring touch, a sprinkle of salt, and an admira-
tion that grew every time the stallion moved over the
ground with long, liquid strides.

Storm Walker blew on Rio's hat and shirt collar.
Smiling, he pushed away the velvety, impertinent
muzzle. "You're an old softie, aren't you," he said
beneath his breath.

Hope heard and retorted dryly, "Only until you get
in the saddle. Then he'll shake the change right out of
your pockets."

"Rough-gaited?" asked Rio, sounding surprised.
"Sure as hell doesn't look it."

"Oh, once he settles down he's as smooth as deep
water." She paused, then added dryly, "Settling him
down is a bone-shaking proposition, kind of like
riding a landslide. He needs a lot more exercise than
he's gotten lately."

"You don't have the time," said Rio, understanding.

"Even if I did, I can't afford to risk that he'll throw
me. If I break an arm or a leg trying to ride Storm
Walker, I either have to sell my cattle or let them die
of thirst." She shrugged. "Storm Walker will just have
to wait until the rains come. Then I'll ride his spotted
rump right into the ground."

Rio's smile faded quickly at the thought of Hope climbing up on the big stud and being bucked off into a corral fence. Not that he thought she was a bad rider—when he had put her up on Dusk, Hope had been as graceful and confident in the saddle as she was on the ground. Storm Walker, however, was big, hard, and had a stallion's aggressive temperament.

"Is he a good rough country horse?" asked Rio.

"He was born in the foothills east of here and ran free for the first three years of his life."

"Like Dusk. She lived wild until two years ago."

"Did you catch her?"

He nodded. "She led me one hell of a chase, too." Rio's eyes focused on an inner distance as he remembered. "Her mama was a ranch horse gone wild, an Arab-mustang mix that was tougher than an old boot. Her daddy was part Morgan, part quarterhorse, and ninety percent cougar, near as I could tell."

"How did you catch her? Airplane?" asked Hope, remembering how her father had hated it when the wild herds had bred beyond the land's ability to nourish them. Then the meat hunters would come, flushing the wild horses with airplanes and driving them lathered and terrified into funnel-shaped corrals concealed by brush. It had been necessary in order to cull the herds back from the brink of starvation and to return feral horses to their owners—but it had been a brutal process just the same.

"I used the oldest method," said Rio, "the one the Indians invented a few hundred years ago when the horse was so new to America that the Cheyenne called it 'big dog.' I walked her down."

Hope turned and stared at Rio. Mason had told her of men walking down wild horses more than a century ago. They followed the wild herds from waterhole to waterhole, never allowing them to rest. At first the horses ran at the sight and smell of man. Then they cantered. Then they trotted. Then they walked. And finally they were too tired to move at all. It, too, could be a brutal method of capture; but at least it was almost as hard on the men as it was on the horses.

"It wasn't that bad," said Rio, accurately reading the expression on Hope's face. "I wore out Dusk's flight response as much as her feet. I just hung around the fringes, leaving bits of salt and grain, following the horses everywhere until I kind of grew on her. By the time I walked up to her with a rope, she simply wasn't afraid of me anymore. I was a member of the herd." Rio grinned suddenly. "A strange, slow, small, awkward kind of horse, but one of the herd just the same."

"How long did it take you?"

He shrugged. "Eight weeks. Ten. Maybe more. I lost track of time. This country's good for that."

"Losing track of time?"

Rio nodded absently. His attention was once again on the glossy Appaloosa stallion. "Mind if I ride him today?"

"Only if you break something," said Hope wryly.

"I wouldn't hurt a hair on his spotted hide."

"It wasn't Storm Walker's hide I was worried about," she retorted. "He's been ridden only a few times in the last year." Then she remembered that Rio made his living as a horse trainer when he wasn't drilling wells for dreamers. "I'd appreciate your riding him," she said frankly. "The longer he goes, the harder he'll be for me to handle."

Rio didn't waste any more time discussing it. He flipped the saddlebags he was carrying over the rail and went after Storm Walker. He had the stallion caught, curried, bridled, saddled, and inside a corral before Hope could change her mind. She held the stallion still with one hand wrapped around the bridle just above the bit. Rio gathered the reins tightly and sprang into the saddle with catlike ease. His right foot went unerringly into the stirrup even as Storm Walker's body bunched into a hard knot of protest.

"Turn him loose," said Rio softly.

Hope let go of the bridle and climbed the corral fence in two seconds flat, expecting Storm Walker to come unglued behind her. Rio didn't allow that. He held the stallion's head up and let him fight a useless skirmish with the bit. The horse's powerful hindquarters rippled as he alternately lashed out with his heels and spun on his hocks, trying to unseat his rider in the only way left to him short of scraping Rio off on the fence or rolling over on him—and Storm Walker was basically too good-tempered to resort to those tactics.

Smiling slightly, Hope watched the man and the horse test each other, probing for weaknesses. Storm Walker backed up incessantly, as though to say if he couldn't buck, he wasn't going to go forward, either. Rio's long, powerful legs closed around the stud's black barrel, urging him forward with relentless pressure. Rio could have used the small, blunt spurs he always wore on his boots, but he didn't.

After a few backward circuits of the corral, Storm Walker stood still and chewed the bit resentfully.

"Round one to you," said Hope.

Rio glanced sideways swiftly, catching Hope's anticipatory smile. "Something tells me I can either let this son buck here or I can let him buck out there when my mind is on something else," he said dryly.

"You've got it. Storm Walker just won't settle down until he's had his fun."

"Yeah, I was afraid of that. Had a horse like him once."

"What did you do with it?"

"Swapped it for a dog and shot the dog," drawled Rio sardonically. "Course," he added, "it was a gelding and ugly as sin."

Hope laughed, not believing a word of it.

With a sigh Rio tugged his hat down hard, eased his grip on the reins, and touched Storm Walker lightly with his spurs. The stud's head shot down, his heels shot up, and for the next few minutes he did his best to turn inside out. Rio rode the whirlwind with a skill that made it look easy. Hope wasn't fooled by appearances. She had been there. She knew that there was nothing easy about Storm Walker working off a head of steam.

After the first few moments she let out her breath slowly, confident that neither horse nor man would be hurt. She relaxed on the top railing, hooked her feet around the next railing down, and simply enjoyed the picture the man and the stallion made as they tore up the corral, two healthy animals perfectly matched, subtly enjoying each other's power and skill.

Without warning Storm Walker's head came up. He snorted deeply, then pricked his ears and looked over his shoulder at the man who hadn't come unstuck.

"Finished?" drawled Rio.

Storm Walker rubbed his nose on Rio's boot and then stood as placidly as a cow, waiting for instructions from his rider.

"That's it," said Hope, jumping down from the fence. "He won't buck again this ride."

"Thank God for small favors," muttered Rio, stretching his back and shoulders, feeling the stallion's power in every muscle of his body. He looked at Hope's slender body and wondered how she had managed to stay on top of Storm Walker. "You must be one hell of a rider."

"I've eaten my share of dirt," she said ruefully. "And that spotted stud had fed me most of it."

Rio laughed softly and shook his head, enjoying her matter-of-fact acceptance of getting thrown. At the same time he quietly promised himself that if Storm

Walker threw anyone for a while, it would be him.
"Want to ride Dusk, or does one of your mares need
work?"

"I'll take Aces. She's Storm Walker's favorite. He'll
be less anxious to get home if she's along."

Rio moved to dismount, then stopped and looked
dubiously at Storm Walker.

"Don't worry," said Hope, hiding her smile.
"You're okay as long as you don't take off the saddle.
That's how Storm Walker knows a ride is finished—
when the saddle comes off."

"One bucking session per saddling, huh?"

"That's it."

"Makes a man consider the joys of sleeping in the
saddle," muttered Rio.

Hope stopped trying not to laugh. She leaned
against Storm Walker and let the laughter bubble up
like pure spring water. It had been a long time since
she had simply given herself to any emotion except
determination. When the last laughter finally rippled
into silence, she took a deep breath and looked up at
Rio.

"You're good for me," she said, her lips still
curving in a deep smile.

"Keep you from breaking your neck?" he guessed
dryly.

"No. You teach me to laugh again. I'd almost
forgotten how."

Her words sank into Rio like water into thirsty
land, renewing him. Without stopping to think he
smiled gently and touched her cheek with his fingertips. "It's you who teach me," he said, his voice warm
and deep.

"What?" she whispered.

"Beautiful dreamer," he said softly. "You don't
know, do you? You don't know what your dreams do
to me. And your laughter." He closed his eyes,

shutting out the green and gold eyes that watched him, eyes luminous with dreams, deep with promises that shouldn't be made and couldn't be kept. The fingers that had touched her so gently retreated and clenched into a fist on his thigh. "I wish to Christ I were a different kind of man, Hope."

"I don't," she said, trembling from Rio's brief touch and from the savage emotions that had made his voice harsh. "I wouldn't change you any more than I would trade the Valley of the Sun for the green Perdidas. I was made for this land, Rio." *And I'm afraid I was made for you, too.*

She didn't say the words aloud. She didn't have to. He heard them clearly in his own mind, as clearly as though he had spoken them himself.

And then he was afraid that he had.

When Rio opened his eyes again Hope was gone. He heard the whicker of a horse from the pasture and felt Storm Walker swell as he whinnied in response. Hope walked into the corral leading a gray mare, using nothing more than her fingers twisted lightly into the slate-colored mane. The mare was big, clean-limbed, powerful. She moved with the calm assurance of a domestic animal that had never been mistreated. Hope shut the corral gate behind Aces and went into the barn. She returned almost immediately, carrying saddle, blanket, bridle, and a bucket of grooming tools.

Rio dismounted. With one hand he took the saddle from Hope and flipped it expertly over the top rail of the corral. The blanket followed. Together they brushed down the mare. Rio checked her steel shoes carefully, knowing they would be going over some rough country. He checked the cinch with equal care. Then he saddled Aces with the same automatic ease that he had done everything else. He had spent his life around horses, and it showed in every motion he made.

When Aces was ready Rio pulled his oversized saddlebags off the corral rail and tied them in place behind Storm Walker's saddle. He stepped into the stirrup and mounted in a single flowing motion. The stallion turned eagerly toward the corral gate.

"How did the last hydrologist get around?" asked Rio as he opened and then refastened the corral gate without dismounting.

"Truck," said Hope succinctly, glancing aside at Rio. The harsh lines on his face had relaxed and his voice was calm, neutral, wholly controlled. It was as though he had never touched her, never regretted the kind of man he was, never heard her response.

"Must have missed a lot of your land," said Rio, following Hope as she turned Aces onto a dirt ranch road that went a short way into the foothills.

"He had a fistful of survey maps."

"Good thing, maps," drawled Rio. "Save a man a lot of saddle and boot leather. Not worth much for finding wells, though."

She let out a long breath. "That's what I'd hoped," she admitted. "I just don't see how he could spread out a piece of paper on the kitchen table and then tell me that if there was any artesian water on my ranch, it was three miles down and hotter than hell."

Rio's mouth turned in a sardonic curve that was a long way from his earlier smiles. "He was half right. Three miles down it is hotter than hell."

With a light touch of the spur Rio lifted Storm Walker into a lope on the dirt road. He held that pace until the horses began to breathe deeply and their coats took on a satin sheen that was just short of sweat. He alternated then between a trot and a lope, eating up the miles. When he reined Storm Walker back down to a walk, Aces was still alongside, her gunmetal legs keeping pace with the more powerful stallion. Rio glanced over at Hope.

"According to my map," he said, "the road ends two miles up from here. Is there a trail to the ranch boundary?"

"The road ends a mile up," corrected Hope. "Landslide."

Rio grimaced. "That's the problem with maps. The land keeps changing."

"There's a trail to Piñon Camp. Dad used to hunt deer there. That's only a few hundred yards from our boundary, I think." She shrugged. "It's hard to tell without a full-blown formal survey."

"Or even with one," said Rio dryly. "Sometimes it seems like each new surveyor has a new opinion. Besides, a surprising amount of the Basin and Range country has never been surveyed. Hell, it's hardly even been settled. Two or three cities and a whole lot of sagebrush."

There hadn't been enough rain to wipe out the tracks of the last vehicle to pass over the road. Tire marks were still visible in places protected from the wind. Rio glanced down and noted that the tread patterns weren't those of either ranch truck.

"Hunters?" he asked, gesturing toward the tire tracks.

"The hydrologist. He came up here to get an overview of the whole ranch."

"Well, at least he wasn't entirely a fool," said Rio. "That's one of the things we're going to do."

The tracks went up to the landslide, stopped, crossed over themselves, and headed back down the mountain. Rio guided Storm Walker carefully, looking for boot tracks or any indication that the hydrologist had gotten out of the truck and walked around. There were no tracks. He turned in the saddle and looked back over the trail. The road had climbed steeply in the last mile. There was a clear view of the tiny buildings, the low desert beyond, and the next mountain range beyond that.

"This was as far as he went," said Hope. "I told him that Piñon Camp had a better view. He said he could see more than enough from here."

Hope looked beyond the landslide to the Perdidas rising darkly above the dry foothills. Then she turned as Rio had, toward the west. The ranch boundaries sprawled invisibly along the rugged foothills like a carelessly thrown blanket. The basin between the Perdidas and the next mountain range fifteen miles to the west was low desert, a place of alkali flats in the summer and temporary, brackish lakes during the season of winter rain and mountain runoff. The foothills were rugged, but not as steep as the east-facing foothills on the Perdidas. Small valleys thick with grass lay in the creases of the hills, guarded by rocky ridges where big sage and piñon and mahogany grew nearly twenty feet tall. They were shrubs rather than true trees, but shrubs so big they often were called forests.

The endless changes of elevation fascinated Hope, the basins alternating with mountain ranges like tawny velvet waves frozen forever in the moment of breaking. A thin silver haze of heat shimmered above the basins, blending invisibly with blue haze of extreme distance. There was nothing to stop the eye but range after range of mountains falling away to the far curve of the earth.

"How much do you know about the geological history of this land?" asked Rio quietly.

"Very little," admitted Hope. "Not much more than the name 'Basin and Range'—and that's self-explanatory," she added, gesturing toward the view.

Rio's clear eyes narrowed slightly, focusing on the distant horizon. "You live in a rare place, Hope. It's almost unique on earth. Its closest analogs are the Baikal region of Siberia and the African Rift Valley. Those are places where the crust of the earth is being stretched by the force of molten basalt pressing up from below. The crust thins and breaks apart under the pressure in a process called rifting. In Africa it has gone so far that parts of the rift are below sea level, waiting only for the south end of the rift to split the edge of the African continent and let in the ocean. Then a new sea will be born. Like the Red Sea, where the Arabian peninsula has slowly split away from Africa and salt water has bled into the gap, concealing the rift."

He watched the horizon for a moment longer, but his eyes saw only the compelling, massive, surpassingly slow movements of continental plates and spans of time so immense that they could only be named, not understood.

"A similar kind of crustal spreading is happening all the way down the center of the Atlantic Ocean," said Rio, his words vibrant with a subtle excitement, his voice that of a man who saw things few other people could, a man who was intellectually and sensually alive to the world around him. "I'll show you maps of it tonight. It's really something to see, all the frozen ridges of basalt and the flat intermediary basins being pushed east and west from a great central seam at the bottom of the sea." He blinked, returning his focus to the rugged land in front of him. "The Basin and Range country is pulling itself apart, too. Basalt wells up deep below the surface, forcing the crust to fracture in thousands of fault zones. Some of the land rises along the faults, some drops, and huge blocks of land tilt up and back like a dog getting up onto its haunches after sleeping in the sun.

"That's what makes our mountain ranges. The tilting." Rio glanced from the Perdidas to the distant basin shimmering with heat. "That's why the west side of the mountains isn't as steep as the east side. The uplift is sharper on the east face of the blocks. If you look with your mind as well as your eyes, you can see the blocks of land shearing apart, rocking back, rising, mountains growing up into the sky. And the higher the mountains go, the less rain falls on the eastern side, the dry side."

Rio looked at Hope with eyes that saw through the surface of reality to the shifting forces beneath—shaman's eyes, darker than twilight, as hypnotic as his voice sinking into her, wrapping her in visions of an earth that she had never seen before.

"That's where part of your water problem comes from," said Rio. "The Basin and Range country is in the rain shadow of the Sierra Nevada mountains. Young mountains, vigorous, tall and growing taller. They block the clouds coming off the ocean, milk them, let very little rain escape." He shifted slightly in the saddle, putting his palm flat on the saddlehorn.

"The other part of your problem," continued Rio quietly, "is that there just isn't as much water in the atmosphere as there used to be. We're in a dry cycle. And I don't mean only the last few decades or generations. A hundred thousand years ago we would have seen water, not sagebrush, if we looked over the Basin and Range country. A lot of little lakes and two big ones covered this land. One of the lakes was nearly nine thousand square miles of water. The other was twenty thousand square miles.

"And they were deep lakes, too," he said, and his eyes looked inward as though he were remembering. "Hundreds of feet deep. They filled the rift where the crust was being pulled apart. The runoff from the

Sierras was much greater then, a year-round torrent flowing down into the crustal rift. There was less heat, less evaporation. The water that came to the Great Basin stayed, creating lakes. Men lived along the lakes, fished there, saw island mountain peaks covered with pine and glaciers, hunted animals that are now extinct, and saw vast fields of wild flowers bloom."

Hope listened without moving, enthralled by the words and the man who spoke them. While Rio talked she saw her land change before her eyes—and she saw him change, too, as the country drawl was overlaid with words and phrases and concepts that should have been utterly alien to a drifting cowhand.

"But the last ice age ended, the weather changed, and the big rains didn't come to this land anymore," Rio said in a low, intense voice, seeing today's drought foreshadowed in the climatic shifts of fifteen thousand years ago. "The vast lakes began to evaporate. They shrank and shrank and shrank until nothing is left today but what we call Great Salt Lake and Pyramid Lake on the California-Nevada border." He closed his eyes for a moment, seeing it happen, vast lakes becoming a desert. "All that immensity of water. Gone."

His eyes opened and he saw again the land of today, a dry land embedded with fossil life forms from long-dead lakes. "Today almost no water flows out of the Basin and Range country to any sea," he continued softly. "Think of it, Hope. Thousands upon thousands of square miles of land whose rivers run into the desert and vanish. Mountain runoff goes down to the *playas,* the sinks, the basins between the ranges. And there the water stays. There are no networks of ponds and lakes, no rills and creeks and rivers running down to a waiting sea. There is only a blazing sun and an empty sky. And the wind, always the wind, blowing over the changing face of the land, touching all of its secrets."

For a moment Rio said nothing more. Hope heard both the silence and the sibilant whisper of a dry wind blowing over the Valley of the Sun. She had a thousand questions to ask Rio, a lifetime of questions aching for answers, but she was afraid to speak because she wanted Rio to keep talking, wanted to see the world as he saw it: an endless procession of change and renewal, seas and mountains rising and falling, continents shifting, and through it all were rivers and clouds heavy with rain, the recurring miracle of water.

As though he sensed her silent plea, he began to speak again.

"In the rare cases where there's enough runoff to keep a low spot covered with water year round," Rio continued softly, "the lakes evaporate at a fantastic rate, up to one hundred fifty inches a year, sending fresh water into the air and leaving tiny amounts of salt behind. Each year the fresh water goes and the salt remains." The saddle creaked when he moved slightly, as though he would try to hold back the inevitable flight of water from the dry land. "What's left becomes a salt lake, useless to man or plants. It's that way from the Sierra Nevada to western Utah and even beyond. All that land. All that water being stolen by the sun and the thirsty sky."

Hope waited, watching Rio with an intensity that made her eyes almost dark, wanting him to tell her . . . what? What was she waiting to hear?

"Not all of the water evaporates, though. Some of it slides down into the land itself. It gathers between fist-sized rocks and pebbles no bigger than my thumb. It hides between grains of sand and oozes between particles of silt so fine you have to use a microscope to see them. It sinks down into some of the rock layers of the mountains themselves, limestone and sandstone and shale. And it stays there, Hope," Rio said, turning suddenly, pinning her with a vivid blue glance. "There's water all through this country. Some of it is old water, fossil water, rains that fell when man hunted mammoths by the shores of ancient lakes."

Hope looked at her ranch with new eyes, seeing beyond the dryness of today to the water of a million yesterdays. Wind like a long exhalation from the past moved over her skin, stirring it in a primal response. She turned toward Rio, radiant with the vision he had shared.

Rio saw the clarity of her eyes, green and gold and brown, a mixture of colors that changed with each shift of light. And he saw his own vision of time and the country reflected in her eyes and in the primal shiver of awareness that rippled through her. She had understood his words as few people would have, or could. She had *listened* with her mind and her soul, and she had seen time and the great land as he had seen them, sharing his vision in an intimacy that he had never known with anyone. At that moment he wanted nothing more than to lift her from the saddle and let her flow over his skin and he over hers like a water-sweetened wind, touching all the secret places, bringing a passionate rain, sharing his body with her as deeply as he had shared his mind.

Silently cursing his unruly thoughts, Rio reined Storm Walker around the landslide. After a moment he heard the long-legged gray mare follow, her hoof making a distinctive sound as steel rang on a stone buried just beneath the surface of the landslide. When Aces moved alongside the stallion, Rio didn't look at Hope. He couldn't. He was afraid that she would read the hunger in his eyes, afraid that her eyes would be hungry, too. Then he would reach for her, lift her into his arms, know her as deeply as he knew the land. And in time the wind would blow and he would leave her as surely as water had left the land.

Rio rode on without speaking, wondering if the Great Basin's long-vanished rains hated themselves for leaving a hungry, hurting land behind.

Chapter 7

THEY RODE IN SILENCE UNTIL RIO COULD LOOK AT THE rugged mountains without seeing a far more gentle flesh, could focus his thoughts on the slabs of differing rock strata broken and canted up to the sky instead of on the hunger that clawed through both his body and his mind. The passionate needs of his body he could deal with. But the passionate hunger of his mind for Hope was new to him, as deeply disturbing to him as the inexorable upwelling of molten basalt was to the thick crust of the earth.

"Most of the boundaries marked on my map of the ranch go something like 'one hundred and twenty paces on a Montana horse' or 'twelve degrees northwest of Black Rock Wash,'" said Rio after a long silence. He knew that the silence, like the shared vision before it, had contained an intimacy that he could neither describe nor deny. But now he was in control of himself again. His voice was practical, empty of visions, offering no more than the dictionary meaning of his words. "Homesteaders' measurements," he continued. "Horseback estimates. Not a hell of a lot of use when you're trying to figure out how to avoid drilling a well on someone else's land. When was the most recent survey of your ranch done?"

"About 1865, shortly after Nevada became a state. That was when one of Mom's great-greats decided to file on land that we'd been squatting on for twenty years," added Hope with a small curve of a smile.

Rio sighed and tugged his hat into place. "That explains it," he drawled. "Some rawhide ancestor of yours took a notion and filed on about thirty square miles of sagebrush and foothills. Damn shame he didn't take a cut of the high country watershed while he was at it."

"Oh, he tried, but we could only show improvements in the foothills—spreader dams we'd built to slow the flow of the intermittent streams, waterholes expanded and cleaned out, wells dug, that sort of thing. Because we didn't need anything like that in the high country, we didn't make any improvements. So the government kept the high country and we kept as much of the foothills as we could. Plus all the government land we could sneak cows onto," added Hope in wry tones. "We've never been real big on fences here in Nevada."

Rio smiled slightly. "How deep were the wells in those days?"

Hope shrugged. "It's hard to say. You know how it is—the 'good old days' were always better. The truth is they had droughts then, too." She hesitated, then added tonelessly, "It's also true that the water table is dropping gradually, and has been for years. Some of the problem is caused by too much pumping for irrigation. And some of it is the simple fact that less rain is falling. This is a dry land and it seems to be getting drier every year."

Rio heard the bleakness in Hope's voice and asked no more questions. Side by side they rode in silence until the dirt track dwindled to a trail winding up toward a ridgeline covered with piñon and juniper. Farther up, far beyond the point where foothills blended imperceptibly into the mountains themselves, stands of aspens touched by frost blazed like golden embers burning against a green-and-gray backdrop of pine and sage. Saddles creaked and the horses began to breathe deeply as they leaned into the steep trail that led to Piñon Camp.

Finally the trail took them to a gently sloping piece of land where piñon and pine grew in thick profusion. A sun-cured meadow contrasted with the black rocks of the mountainside and the dense green of the piñon. To one side of the trail there was a fire-blackened ring of stones, a rack for hanging game, and faint old footpaths leading from the camp to the meadow. Overhead a hawk soared in transparent circles, watching for movement below. Ravens and scrub jays called from nearby perches, warning other animals of the intruders that had appeared from the dry lands below.

Rio took in everything with the comprehensive glance of a man who has spent most of his life in wild country. Then he looked again, seeing beyond the superficial clothing of plants and animals to the geological history beneath. The meadow and the camp were part of a bench, a small block of land that a minor fault zone had caused to break away from the larger mountainblock. The mountain had continued to rise on the far side of the local fault, while on this side the bench had continued to rise, too, but more slowly. The result was a sloping land surface that was higher than the surrounding foothills but lower than the mountain from which it had sheared off.

Under Rio's guidance Storm Walker trotted across the open land toward the place where the mountain rose suddenly, its side bare of all but the most tenacious sagebrush. The steeply tilted layers of rock that made up part of the mountain were revealed in the changing colors and textures of the cliff. Though eroded by time and weather, twisted and broken by the movements of the earth, the strata told a great deal to anyone who could read them. Some of the strata were relatively young sedimentary rocks. But the majority of the strata were old, dense, so darkened and deformed by time and the movements of the earth that they were all but impervious to weather.

Somewhere, tilted at a steep angle and buried from sight, Rio believed there would be at least one thick layer of limestone, legacy of a great sea that had covered the land long, long ago, forty million years in the past, when the Basin and Range country lay beneath a wealth of water that could hardly be comprehended now. Since then, continental plates had oozed over the earth's surface, their passage lubricated by molten rock, changing everything, making mountains rise and dragging other lands down beneath the surface of the earth until they melted into nothing.

"What are you looking for?" asked Hope.

"Potential aquifers," said Rio, his eyes intent on the mountainside as he traced various strata. "Layers of rock that can absorb water."

Hope looked at the mountainside and then at Rio. From the corner of his eye he caught the movement of her head.

"It's hard to believe," he acknowledged, reaching back into his saddlebag without taking his eyes off the mountain, "but some kinds of rock strata are nothing but big stone sponges. Given time and the right conditions, those strata will soak up incredible amounts of water."

As he spoke, he pulled out a worn map and a pencil. "Sandstone is like that. So is limestone. Buried alluvial fans make great sponges. Most of your wells are drawing on buried beds of sand and gravel washed down from the mountains million of years ago." Still talking, he sketched quickly on the map. "The water your wells brought up came from recent rains, this year's water and the last, water soaking into the land and renewing the wells with every season."

Rio tipped his hat back on his head. A forelock of hair as straight and black as night fell over his forehead. He didn't notice, for his attention was on the tiny symbols he was adding to the worn map.

"In most places on earth," he said, squinting up at the mountain, "the groundwater would just ooze slowly downhill until it reached a river or a lake or the sea itself. But this isn't most places. Here the water just sinks down and down until it reaches a layer of rock it can't penetrate or until the heat of the basalt welling up transforms water to steam and sends it pushing back to the surface as hot springs and geysers." He paused, then added with quiet intensity. "Most people think of this land as desolate, sterile, uninteresting. It isn't. In many ways it's the richest, most exciting, and rarest of all the lands on earth."

Hope heard the emotion in Rio's voice and felt even more drawn to him. She, too, loved this lean and difficult land. She, too, had learned the subtle, sweet, extraordinary rewards that the land gave to those who understood it. Her mother had never found those rewards. Her father had, and had given up his wife and family rather than leave them.

A quick movement of Rio's head caught Hope's attention, but it was the mountain he looked toward, not her. She remembered his words, watched his confidence as he reduced his observations to cryptic symbols. And then she wondered who Rio really was, and how someone of his obvious education had become a man who drifted through the country like the wind, leaving little to mark his passage but enigmatic symbols made upon the softer surfaces of the land.

What had set him to living with the wind? What would it take to hold him in one place?

Hope heard her silent questions and smiled a bittersweet smile. Nothing held the wind. Nothing. Certainly not a woman's dreams.

"What we're looking for," said Rio, wedging the notebook under his thigh and reaching back into the saddlebag again, "is a layer of sandstone or limestone that's sandwiched between strata of rock that won't let water leak away. Sort of like a solid river flowing between waterproof banks."

"How would the water get into the limestone if it's sandwiched between waterproof layers of rock?"

Rio glanced aside and smiled, enjoying the quickness of Hope's mind. Other people he had helped had listened to him without understanding him. They had been focused on only one thing. Water. Hope, too, wanted water. Yet she was able to see the land as something more than a way to make a living. She saw that in some deep, indescribable way the land was alive, growing and changing with its own rhythms, its own inexorable movements, its own awesome beauty. And you could share that life if you had enough room in your soul for the sound of a coyote calling to a moon he had always known and would never understand, and for the sheen of a rainbow stretching between drought and water, and for the tiny, ephemeral perfection of a medicine flower blooming against rocks a billion years old.

But Rio said nothing of this to Hope. He didn't

have to. He knew that she had room in her soul for all that and more, much more, things he had always hungered for and never touched. Did she know his hunger? With an odd feeling of sadness he turned his mind to the question she had asked, for that was the only one that he would allow himself to answer.

"If the sandwich is flat," said Rio, demonstrating with his hands, "the rain will just roll off the top, the waterproof layer. But if you break the sandwich in several places and tilt the pieces up toward the sky, the aquifer—the center of the sandwich—will be open to the rain. Most of what falls will still vanish as runoff in mountain streams. Not all of it, though. Some of that water will sink into the aquifer itself. Pulled by gravity and pushed by the pressure of each new rain sinking in, the water percolates down through the aquifer."

For a moment Rio was quiet. Then he dismounted, rummaged in his saddlebags, and pulled out a hinged black box no larger than a pack of cigarettes. He handled it with the same ease that he handled reins or boots, silently telling Hope that the box was very familiar to him. When he opened it she caught a glimpse of a mirror on one side and what appeared to be a complex compass on the other. She watched with growing curiosity as Rio held the box in front of himself, tilted it until it roughly matched the line of the stratum that interested him, fiddled with a small lever on the back of the box, and then wrote something on the map. He repeated the process several times, using different strata of rock.

Sensing Hope's curiosity, Rio looked up from his latest entry. "It's called a Brunton compass," he said, showing the instrument to her. "The built-in clinometer measures the dip of a rock stratum. Of course," he said, smiling crookedly, "you're supposed to lay it right on the stratum you're working with." He glanced toward the rugged, nearly vertical rise of the mountain in front of him. "Since I left my mountain goat at the ranch, I'm doing it the easy way. For now, a guesstimate is good enough."

"What did you learn?"

"That the dip of the strata is steep, but not enough to put an aquifer totally out of reach. Assuming that there's an aquifer in that broken mess," he added, tilting his head toward the rugged mountains. "And assuming that the aquifer runs beneath the mountain all the way down to your ranch without being interrupted by fault zones."

"What happens if it's faulted?"

Rio mounted Storm Walker in an easy motion. "Sometimes the water leaks away at the fault zones. Sometimes the aquifer is offset so much by faults that you can't find it again. Sometimes it just slips down so far that you can't get to it."

"Is there an aquifer?" asked Hope, gesturing toward the steep mountain slope Rio had been measuring.

"No. The sandstone is dry, or there would be a seep right here, maybe even a spring."

It was absurd to feel disappointed, but she felt it just the same. "Oh."

Rio replaced the Brunton compass in his saddlebag. "This is just one small piece of the mountain, Hope. Not even a representative part. It's a transition between Turner land and your own. The mountains near his place are almost entirely made of pre-Cambrian rock a billion and a half years old, stone so hard it rings when you hit it with a steel hammer. There's no way for water to sink into that kind of rock. Everything runs off in streams or gathers on the surface in lakes. Even where little pieces of the mountain have washed down to the plains and built up rough soil, the groundwater stays close to the surface because of the impermeable roots of the mountain beneath."

"That's why Turner has so much water, isn't it?" murmured Hope, visualizing a relatively thin layer of sand and gravel covering the much more solid rock layer beneath. "The water can't sink down and get away from his wells. It's all there, waiting to be tapped."

"For a while, yes. If he doubles his crop land, he'll be living off the future. Sooner or later he'll suck it all dry."

"But my mountains are different?"

"North of here," said Rio, looking at the mountain, "the rocks are much younger, more porous. They erode much more quickly. That's why your mountains are lower than his, despite the fact that they're part of the same block fault. Your alluvial plains are thick and water soaks down quickly into them. There are places where you could go down a thousand feet and then keep on going for thousands more and get nothing but dry gravel."

Hope looked away and took a ragged breath at the thought of drilling that far down and finding no water, a dry well draining away her slender reserves of money, turning her dreams to dust. Rio saw the fear darkening her eyes and cursed his thoughtless words.

"That's why you hired me," he said, turning her face toward him with gentle fingertips, letting emotion back into his voice for the first time since he had seen his visions reflected in her eyes. "I won't waste your money drilling where there isn't any chance of water."

His words and his touch took away the fear that had chilled her. She put her hand over his fingers briefly in silent thanks for his reassurance.

"I know," she said in a husky voice, but her eyes said even more. She trusted him with her dreams and

First Class Romance

Delivered to your door by

Silhouette Intimate Moments®

(See inside for special 4 FREE book offer)

Find romance at your door with 4 FREE Silhouette Intimate Moments novels!

Now you can have the intense romances you crave without searching for them. You can receive Silhouette Intimate Moments novels, each month, to read in your own home.

Silhouette Intimate Moments is a series written for women—not for girls. These are stories about our times, when men and women's lives are ablaze with passion and explosive desires.

You can share in the power and abandon of their love, every month, beginning with 4 new Silhouette Intimate Moments novels. Worth $10.00, these romances are yours FREE, along with a Cameo Tote Bag.

By filling out and mailing the attached postage-paid order card, you'll also receive an extra bonus: our monthly Silhouette Books Newsletter.

Approximately every 4 weeks, we'll send you four more Silhouette Intimate Moments novels to examine FREE for 15 days. If you decide to keep them, you'll pay just $9.00—with no extra charge for home delivery and at no risk! You'll also have the option of cancelling at anytime. Just drop us a note. Your first 4 books and the Tote Bag are yours to keep in any case.

Silhouette Intimate Moments®

EXTRA BONUS
A Free Cameo Tote

You'll receive brand-new
novels as they're published!

FILL OUT THIS POSTPAID CARD AND MAIL TODAY!

NO POSTAGE
NECESSARY
IF MAILED
IN THE
UNITED STATES

BUSINESS REPLY CARD
FIRST CLASS PERMIT NO. 194 CLIFTON, N.J.

Postage will be paid by addressee

**Silhouette Books
120 Brighton Road
P.O. BOX 5084
Clifton, NJ 07015-9956**

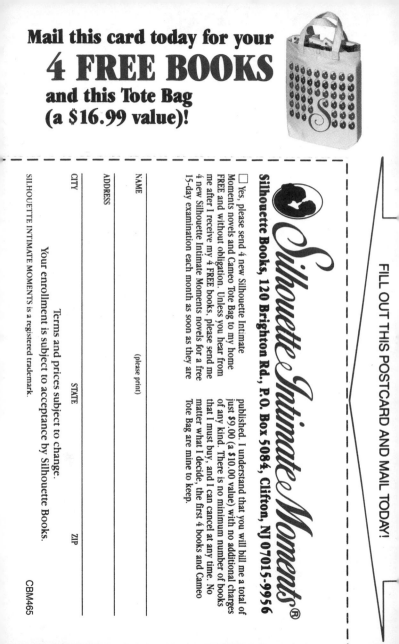

she was quickly, inevitably, coming to the point where
she would trust him with herself. That was something she had never done with any man. She had held
herself in reserve, knowing from the example of her
parents' lives and her sister's life that loving someone
wasn't enough to ensure peace, much less a dream of
love returned. So Hope had held herself aloof, loving
only the land.

With Rio such reserve was becoming impossible.
He was sliding through the hard, impermeable layers
that had formed around the life-giving core of her.
Each day with Rio, each conversation, each touch,
sank more deeply into her, coming closer to the
instant when he would break through the layer of
reserve and touch the flowing wealth of love concealed deeply within her.

The thought terrified her.

And the thought that he might not break through,
might not touch her, might not release her love, was
also terrifying.

"Are there other benches like this farther south
toward the ranch house?" asked Rio as he reined
Storm Walker toward the edge of Piñon Camp.

For a moment Hope didn't answer, lost in her own
thoughts. Then she visibly shook free of her conflict-
ing fears and focused on him again. His fingers no
longer touched her skin. She was surprised by the loss
she felt at such a simple thing as the absence of his
touch.

"No," she said. "Piñon Camp is a landmark around
here simply because it's different."

"How about cliffs? Old mining or timber roads?
Deep canyons or ravines? I'm looking for places
where I can see rock strata that are buried out of sight
in other areas."

Hope frowned, remembering details of the land
that she had ridden over since she was old enough to

sit upright in a saddle. "Just on the ranch land, or on the lease lands, too?"

"If the lease is above your watershed, I'll be glad to look at it, although I've already seen most of the government land. Whatever you have on your own property should come first."

Hope urged Aces to the edge of the bench until she could see the country falling away below. Storm Walker came up alongside, standing so close that her stirrup rubbed against Rio's.

"Over there," she said, touching Rio's sleeve to get his attention. Even that light brush of her fingertips against cloth reminded her of his vitality. The heat of him demanded a deeper touch, a longer sharing. "See that bald spot just beyond the ranch house?"

"Yes."

"Straight up from there, hidden behind the shoulder of mountain, is an old road. A hundred years ago there was some kind of mining operation up there. Silver or gold, I forget which. It didn't amount to a hill of beans, but they cut a wagon road up above Wind Canyon, into the high country where there was another mine. The mine caved in long ago, but some of the road is still there. It's a scary piece of real estate," she added bluntly. "It hangs by its toenails to the edge of Wind Canyon. The canyon is thousands of feet deep. The land is different there. Crumbly rather than solid. Even sagebrush has a hard time clinging to the mountainside."

"Perfect," said Rio, satisfaction obvious in his tone.

"If you say so," Hope retorted. "I remember that road scaring the hell out of me."

"You don't have to go."

She gave him a level look. He smiled slightly, knowing that she wouldn't stay behind.

"There are a few other places between here and there that have bare rock," said Hope.

"We'll see them on the way."

She smiled and shook her head. "Not unless we plan to be gone for a few days. Each one of them is up a blind canyon."

Rio's eyes narrowed as he considered the possibilities. "Any signs of water?"

"Springs?" asked Hope in disbelief.

"Nothing that obvious. I'm looking for unusually big brush, grass that stays greener longer than in other places at the same elevation, that sort of thing."

"Oh. Well, maybe in Stirrup Canyon. Dead Man's Boot might be a possibility. Then there's always Silver Rock Basin," she added, gesturing toward the lower part of the ranch. "Jackass Leap, too. That's up above the head of Wind Canyon."

"Hold it." Rio opened out the map fully. It was a USGS survey, showing each contour of the thirty sections of land that comprised the Valley of the Sun. The map was nearly four feet by four feet, more suited to a kitchen table than to a saddle. The paper showed deep creases and frayed edges from being handled. "Silver Rock Basin is no problem, but where is Dead Man's Boot?"

Hope laughed. "That's a family name, not an official one."

Rio smiled as he refolded the map. "Where do you think most of the names on maps came from? Place names are one of the richest oral traditions in the West." He handed her the pencil and the map. "Mark them in."

She took the pencil, unfolded a panel of the unwieldy map, and was promptly lost. The amount of detail already on the paper was both staggering and utterly unfamiliar. In addition to contour lines showing the changing elevations of the land, there were many other lines whose purpose wasn't readily apparent. Most of those lines had been drawn in by Rio.

Cryptic symbols both printed and handwritten appeared in odd places. Even more enigmatic notes appeared in the margin. Hope had only to look at the map to realize that Rio had put in a lot of time studying her land already, much more than he could have in the few weeks since she had hired him. She looked up, puzzled.

"Lost?" he asked sympathetically.

"Yes, but it's not just the map."

Rio looked as confused as Hope.

"It's you," she said quietly. "Nothing adds up. You're a drifting horse-breaker who knows more about this land than the highly educated, highly recommended hydrologist who was out here six weeks ago. You've worked for me for only two weeks, but this map is worn thin in the creases and has enough notes on it for a geological textbook."

She wanted to go on, to say, *You have only one name, and it's neither Scandinavian nor Zuni nor Scots. Nobody knows where you came from or where you're going, but Mason trusts you more than he trusts anybody but me. You have a reputation as a bad man to cross, but you've been so gentle with me that it's all I can do not to crawl into your arms and never let go.*

Hope wanted to say those things, but she did not, for Rio was already talking, answering the questions she had asked and a few that she had not.

"I heard about you all over the West," said Rio simply. "A drifter in Idaho told me that there was a woman who needed help in a place called Valley of the Sun, Nevada. In Utah a farmer I helped said that his wife's sister had heard from her brother that a woman called Hope needed a well and nobody would dig it for her. A cattle breeder I once found water for said he'd sold one of his best Angus to a woman with beautiful eyes and a mind like a steel trap, and that she was going to lose her ranch unless the rains came."

Hope listened and felt her throat close with tears she fought not to shed. But the thought of other people knowing her need, and caring enough to help in the only way they could, made it impossible to hold back the tears. She wanted to tell Rio to stop talking, that he was making her cry and she did not want to cry, but she could not get any words past the emotion filling her throat.

"So I drifted south, and I listened. Every time the wind blew it whispered your name and your need and your dreams," said Rio quietly, watching Hope with eyes that saw everything, the vulnerability and the tears, the determination and the strength. "The closer I came to the Valley of the Sun, the more people talked about you. People I had found water for left messages for me about you in every country store and café in the West. They all said the same thing: *This is a good woman, Rio. Can you help her the way you helped us?*"

The blue of Rio's eyes was so intense that it was like crystal burning in the sun. Hope watched him with an equal intensity, feeling his words sinking into her deeply, penetrating the protective layers she had built up to guard the vulnerable woman beneath.

"I didn't know if I could help you, and I wasn't going to come to you until I did know. This country isn't a stranger to me," continued Rio, looking out over the land again, freeing her from the blue blaze of his eyes. "I've found water in some damned unlikely places. And I've seen a few places where there is no water to be found by anyone. I didn't know if Valley of the Sun was one of those places. I went over all the USGS maps, got the latest Landsat photos, talked to university experts, and to Indians whose ancestors had hunted along the shores of long-ago lakes. I flew over the steep parts of your ranch with a photo recon camera and a pilot who wasn't afraid of God, the devil—or gravity." Rio's mouth turned up wryly. "Hell of a flyer, though. He saved me weeks of rough-country riding and hiking."

Hope looked toward Rio, but tears prevented her from seeing more than the powerful outline of his body against the sky. "Why?" she asked huskily. "Why did you go to all that trouble for someone you didn't even know?"

It was a question that no one had ever asked Rio. In the past, people had been more than happy to take what he offered. They had never stopped to wonder why he wanted to help. But Rio had asked himself that question for as many years as he had drifted through people's lives, through their dreams. He didn't have an answer. He had helped many people, touched the edges of their dreams, and moved on. Those people remembered him with gratitude and sometimes even affection. They always had a meal and a roof and a handshake for him whenever he went back. But they didn't know him. Not really. He was as much an enigma to them as their ability to dream in the face of brutal odds was an enigma to him. He found water for those special dreamers. And each time, each place, each well, he wondered if he would also find the ability to put down roots and dream for himself.

He had not found any dream to equal the whispering seduction of the wind moving over the face of the land. He doubted that such a dream existed.

"I admire people who are strong enough to dream," said Rio finally. His long fingers caressed her face, feeling the warmth of her tears sliding beneath his fingertips. "Like you."

"You're strong, Rio," she whispered. Then, even more softly, "What are your dreams?"

"I don't have any. I stopped dreaming the day I really understood what *half-breed* meant."

Hope's eyes darkened and she shook her head slowly, silently denying both the pain of Rio's long-ago discovery and the pain of her own realization that she was falling in love with a man who had no dreams. She closed her eyes and tried not to cry. He bent slowly toward her, brushed his lips over her eyelashes, tasted the warmth and salt of her tears. He wanted to do more, much more. She called to his senses and his soul in a way that nothing ever had, even the wind.

"It's all right, Hope," he murmured soothingly, kissing her softly, aching to turn the world inside out and make everything right for her, the past and the present and the future rich with water and dreams. But he could not do that, and unless he stopped touching her he wouldn't be able to remember why he should not touch her at all. He was the wrong man for her. It was that simple and that inescapable. Slowly, feeling as though he were pulling off his own skin, he straightened in the saddle again until he no longer touched her. "I'll help you find your well, your dream," he said.

It was the only promise he could give to her. The only promise he could keep.

"But what about you?" she asked, opening her eyes, seeing the shine of her tears on his lips. The sight went deeply into her, coming so close to her core that she almost cried out in fear and hope.

"I'll share your dream for a while," said Rio quietly. "And then the wind will blow and I'll be gone."

Hope looked away from Rio. For a few moments she fought her impulse to deny the truth of his words, to deny the pain stabbing through her as his need reached down past her barriers to the reservoir of love that she had protected so long and so well. She blinked slowly, releasing tears, and knew that it was Rio she cried for, not herself. It was too late to protect herself. He had touched her too deeply.

At that moment she knew that whether or not Rio found water on the Valley of the Sun, she would love the man who had no dreams.

"I'll dream for you, Rio," she promised in a soft, husky voice. "I'll dream for you until you can dream for yourself."

Hope brushed her arm over her eyes, clearing them of tears. After a moment she calmly began to puzzle out the intricacies of the map that Rio had given her, matching place names with contour lines until she could locate herself on the map. Slowly, then with increasing confidence, she began to fill in the old family names that Rio had asked for.

Motionless but for the occasional small stirrings of his horse, Rio watched Hope work over the map. He would have leaned closer, pointing out contour lines and explaining symbols to her, but he didn't trust his hand not to reveal the aftershocks of the emotion that had gone through him when he had heard her husky voice promising to dream for him. Sometimes women had cried over him in the past, when the wind blew and they knew he would be going soon; but Hope was the first woman to look deeply within him and cry when she saw the void where his dreams had been. She had wept then, knowing his emptiness and pain. She had wept for him rather than for herself.

And she would dream for him.

"I'll put in the rest of the names tonight," said Hope, refolding the map along its telltale creases. "Dead Man's Boot is closest to us. It has a clump of big sage that has to be seen to be believed. Nothing else like it on the ranch."

Hope didn't look at Rio when she spoke. She didn't trust herself to. If she saw again the soul-deep hunger in his eyes when he talked of dreams, she would not be able to control her tears. With a touch of the reins she sent Aces over the lip of the bench and onto the steep trail.

Holding Storm Walker in check, Rio watched until Hope disappeared into a steep fold in the mountainside. He had never felt so alone as he did at that instant, with her words still echoing through him. *I'll dream for you until you can dream for yourself. I'll dream for you. I'll dream. For you.*

The echoes were like the wind blowing through emptiness, defining it.

"Don't, Hope," said Rio softly, achingly, her husky words echoing through him, defining him. "You'll waste your dreams until the mountains are nothing but sand at the bottom of a nameless sea. I've forgotten how to dream. Don't dream for me."

Yet Hope's promise kept resonating in Rio's mind, sending fine tremors of emotion through him. He could not have been more shocked if she had said she loved him.

And then he realized that she had said just that.

Rio bowed his head, staring sightlessly at his fingers wrapped around the reins. Storm Walker tugged at the bit, wanting to follow the other horse. Rio didn't notice. After a long moment he finally yielded his iron grip on the reins, allowing the stallion to plunge over the edge onto the narrow trail. The shrill cry of a hawk followed him, carried by the wind.

Chapter 8

"Now you sure, honey?" asked Mason, his faded green eyes taking in the lines of worry on Hope's face. "I ain't all in a lather to drive to Salt Lake just to eat turkey and trimmings. We got real fine turkey right here in Nevada."

"Mason," said Hope, "go. I won't be alone here, and even if I were, it wouldn't be any big deal."

"I don't like it. Rio's out poking around most of the time. You'll be lonely."

The wind gusted suddenly, stirring up dust. The sky was blue and cold, devoid of clouds.

"Mason, if you don't go to Utah, I swear I'll saddle Aces and ride to Piñon Camp and not come back until Thanksgiving is over."

"You sure?" he persisted, watching her with anxious eyes.

"You can set your watch by it," she said firmly.

Mason sighed, shifted his battered suitcase to his

other hand, and followed her out to the tan pickup. "I don't feel right taking the truck."

"Rio said I could use his truck if I needed to go to town," said Hope patiently, getting ready to go over every argument one more time. "In fact, he insisted."

Mason hesitated before he opened the truck door and tossed in his suitcase. "All right, no need to put your hand on my back and shove. I know when I ain't wanted."

"Mason!" said Hope, shocked. Then she saw the mischief in his eyes as he turned away and understood that he was teasing her. "That's right," she said quickly, putting her hand on his back and shoving gently, "you're not wanted. Go away."

Then she spoiled it by throwing her arms around him and hugging him. He turned around and hugged her for a long moment before releasing her and climbing into the truck. The wind flexed again, pushing against him as though hurrying him on his way. Hope's hair flew up, tickling Mason's nose. He smoothed her hair with a gnarled hand, holding the soft strands away from the wind's insistent tugs.

"I'll be home by the end of the month," said Mason, resting his gray-stubbled chin on her dark hair. "Sooner, if Rio finds a place to start drilling. Keep that rifle handy. The bit of rain we been getting ain't put all the snakes down."

Hope agreed without arguing, not wanting to open up the subject of Turner. Other than a few calls at odd times of the night, Turner hadn't bothered her. Perhaps he had thought over the scene at his well and had finally gotten the message that she wasn't interested in him.

"Take care, Mason," she called, waving as he pulled out of the ranch yard.

"You too, honey. Don't be lonely, now."

"Sure," she said, smiling.

Her smile contained a sadness that she wasn't aware of. Even with Rio around, she was lonely. That was new. Before Rio came she had been alone but not lonely. He had changed that. Despite her efforts to withdraw from any emotional entanglement with him, despite his own elusiveness since their ride up to Piñon Camp, she longed to spend time with Rio, to talk with him, to touch him. She could not, though. He was like a rain-sweet wind blowing through her life, washing away the dust of years, revealing the living spirit beneath. But she was the land, unmoving; and the wind was always moving, always leaving the land behind.

The wind would come again, in time. And so would Rio. He would come every few years to claim his colts. She couldn't help wondering how many women around the West waited in an agony of hope for Rio to return, aching for him, holding their breath as they watched the road like ranchers scanning the desert sky for the first signs of life-giving rain. She didn't want to be one of those women.

Yet she was, and Rio hadn't even touched her.

Hope was both sad and grateful that Rio had left her alone since Piñon Camp. He had talked with her on the water runs, but his talk had all been of weather and cattle, feed prices and the cost of fuel. Ranch talk. His voice was no longer rich with visions, nor were his eyes dark with a hunger that went as deep as the night, as deep as his soul. He had not touched her at all in the nine days since Piñon Camp. Not even in the most casual way. Not once.

Mason had been right. Rio had too much respect for himself and for her to begin something that would inevitably finish with his leaving and her crying.

There were times when Hope didn't know whether

to laugh or to lash out at the irony of life. As a child she had heard her parents argue about whether to live on the ranch with its endless, brutal demands or to sell it. She had assumed that if they just loved each other everything would work out. Love was all that mattered. And then she had watched her mother and her father tear each other apart in the name of love. She swore that she would never love a man. The cost was too high. The destruction too great. The grief too endless. It was all there in her parents' lives, in their arguments, in their letters, the words and phrases burned into Hope's mind, a warning of love's limitations that was branded on Hope's soul:

I love you, Debbie. Come home to me. I need you. I need you with me at the end of the day when I'm so tired that nothing seems worth it.

And the reply, always the same.

Sell the ranch. I can't bear watching you kill yourself for that damned land. For nothing. I love you too much. Wayne, I love you.

In the end, the Valley of the Sun had killed Hope's father, just as her mother had predicted. It had killed Hope's mother, too. She had lived less than a year after burying the man she loved. Yes, her parents had loved each other. Passionately, bitterly, hopelessly, helplessly.

It hadn't been enough.

Hope had learned the hard way that there were practical limitations on the thing called love. She had watched her mother, her father, and her poor broken sister try to make love carry more burden than it could. Love didn't mystically change people. Hope knew that. She had seen it demonstrated time and again. Her mother had loved her father with every bit of passion in her soul. It had been the same for him. It didn't change him, though. Or her. She still could not live with the land and he still could not live without it. Love hadn't been able to overcome that fundamental difference between her parents.

Hope wasn't fool enough to forget love's limitations. She accepted the fact that she was falling in love with Rio. She also accepted the fact that it didn't make a damn bit of difference. Rio would leave her. He was rootless. Like the wind. And she had put down roots in the Valley of the Sun. Even if she could tear out those roots and survive, it wouldn't be enough. Rio was what he was—a rain-sweet wind moving alone over the face of the land. That was Rio. Alone. As inevitably and as finally as the wild wind was alone. It was the life he had chosen. It was the life he had lived. It had made him what he was.

And she loved what he was, for better or for worse.

The knowledge expanded through Hope like the shock waves of an earthquake focused deep within her. She swayed, wrapping her arms around herself as old certainties shattered and fell away, leaving her vulnerable and alone in a new world. Was that how her mother had felt when she realized that she had to leave the man she loved? Was that how her father had felt when he knew that the woman he loved would leave him? Had they seen the future coming down on them like a terrible desert storm, seen it and known that there was nothing to do but to hang on and hope to survive until the storm had passed?

They could not change each other. They could not stop loving each other.

And they had not survived the storm.

"Hope? What's wrong? Is it Mason? Is he sick?"

The voice was Rio's, deep and worried. Hope opened her eyes and saw his concern in the intensity of his glance, the hard line of his mouth, his hands reaching for her in the instant before he controlled them. She knew then that he cared for her as much as he could, and that he was protecting her in the only way he could; he was leaving her alone. She knew that he, too, saw clouds massing on their personal horizon. He was trying to protect her from that future storm, to keep her from being consumed. He was doing all that he could for her short of turning and walking away. That he could not do, for it would be even more cruel to her than staying. She had a ranch that was dying for lack of water, and he was a man who could find water in hell itself.

"Hope?" Rio's voice was soft yet harsh. "What is it? Is there anything I can do? How long have you been standing here?"

She answered the only question she could, for she didn't know how long she had been standing in the yard. Long enough for her skin to feel dry and for a fine shimmer of dust to coat her arms. Long enough to learn more about love than she wanted to know.

"Mason's fine. He's on his way to Salt Lake," she said, watching Rio with eyes that were dark with understanding and regret. Her voice was soft, as shattered as her former certainty that she could never love a man the way she had come to love Rio. Passionately. Helplessly. Hopelessly. But not bitterly. Not that. There was no room in her soul for bitterness, because she had accepted what she was, and what he was. "How did it go today? Did you find a place to drill?"

"Tell me what's wrong," demanded Rio.

"Nothing that can be changed," said Hope quietly, understanding her own limitations and his without reservation or evasion. If she were different, he would not care about her. If he were different, she would not love him as she did. "Nothing that I would change even if I could. I am who I am, and . . . you're Rio. I wouldn't change what you are even if it meant a river flowing forever through the Valley of the Sun."

Her sad, accepting smile made the small lines at either edge of Rio's mouth deepen into brackets of pain.

"Hope, I didn't want this." He breathed in sharply and said no more. His fingertips touched her cheek in the instant before he balled up his hand into a fist and stepped back. "I'm going into town. Some of my equipment just came in. Don't wait dinner for me. I'll get a room and stay over."

She nodded as the wind swirled around her, blowing over the land with a long low wail that was so familiar she didn't even hear it. The same wind curled around him, pressing his shirt against his chest, riffling through his hair like a lover's fingers.

Abruptly she turned away. As she closed the front door behind her, she admitted that it was just as well that Rio was leaving. She was too vulnerable right now, still caught in the aftershocks of realization. She didn't know if she could sit across from Rio in the intimacy of the kitchen and not tell him the simple truths that she had just discovered: *I love you. I wish you loved me. But it doesn't matter. Even if you loved me, you'd still have to leave. I understand you, Rio. I know that you'll hate yourself if you hurt me. And I'm already hurting. Hell of a mess, isn't it?*

The wind paused, allowing Hope to hear Rio's pickup truck leave the ranch yard in a rush of gravel and grit. Then the wind resumed, blotting out all noise but its own. Feeling too tired for eight o'clock in the morning, Hope sat in the straight-backed chair that was paired with the old oak desk her father had used. The first thing she saw was the note she had written to herself a year ago and pinned to the cubbyhole: *Second mortgage due 1/15.* For a moment she stared at the note, but it didn't worry her. She hadn't touched the money she had set aside for the balloon payment. Selling half of her remaining range cattle had been an emotional wrench, but it had given her enough cash to keep the ranch going for a while longer without nibbling away at the money she had set aside for the bank and for drilling a well. Sighing, Hope pulled out the ranch account books and began to catch up on the bills.

After a few hours of book work, the water run actually looked appealing. She left the house eagerly and drove to Turner's well. No other vehicle was in sight. Turner hadn't come there since the day she had locked herself in the cab to avoid him. Squinting against the strong wind, Hope jumped out of the cab and set up the hose. The job wasn't as difficult as it had once been. Rio had replaced the worn coupling and Mason had done something to the generator that made it start more easily. She wasn't as tired as she had been before Rio came to the Valley of the Sun, either. Without making any fuss about it, he had quietly, inexorably, taken much of the hard physical work from her shoulders.

When she reached her own land and her forlorn wells, her cattle stood hunched against the brash wind. They lowed a welcome as Behemoth trundled up to a trough. Enough rain had fallen so that all of the range animals weren't solely dependent on the various wells. Which was good. The wells weren't dependable at all. The rains hadn't been enough to bring up the natural feed, either. If the minor seeps and holes dried up again, forcing all the cattle back to the area around the wells, Hope would have to start hauling food as well as water—or sell more cattle.

She made one more round trip for water and was grateful that she didn't have to do a third. She hesitated, then treated herself to the luxury of a bath, hoping it would soak away the weariness that she had felt since she understood more than she wanted to about herself and Rio and love. The steaming bath made her feel better, less ragged. She toweled dry her hair and her body with slow movements. She smoothed a perfumed cream into her skin and walked with dragging feet to her room. She didn't want to put on jeans and a work shirt and boots again. She wanted to feel soft fabric caressing her skin, to look down and see her long legs bare of anything except a light golden tan. She wanted to look like a woman, to feel like one.

And why not? Mason wouldn't be here to smile at the first instant of seeing her, and then sigh sadly when he realized that there was so little opportunity for Hope to laugh and dance and flirt with admiring men. Nor would Rio be here to look and wonder whether she was trying to seduce him with feminine clothes and a perfume that could be sensed only by a man who was close enough to brush against her skin. Tonight she was a woman alone. She could dress to appease her own hungers.

Defiantly Hope put on delicate touches of makeup that brought out the beauty of her slightly tilted eyes and generous mouth. She went to her closet and pulled out a floor-length caftan made of a French velvet so fine and soft that it was almost indistinguishable from silk. The rich forest green of the cloth brought out the elusive green of her eyes. She hesitated, then put her hair up in one of the sophisticated styles that had once been a daily part of her life. The golden nugget earrings she wore belonged to her mother's mother, a present from a man who had come home from the Klondike. Her slippers were very high-heeled mules, made to accent the long, elegantly curved legs that had been her fortune. The legs themselves were revealed by a tantalizing slit that was just off-center of the deceptively casual lines of the caftan. It had been one of the most successful outfits she had ever worn in her modeling career, and it had cost her a fortune to buy it after the shoot. She had never regretted it. More than once the caressing velvet had picked up her sagging spirits.

Hope looked at herself in the mirror. She saw someone who had almost become a stranger to her, an elegant woman who would be at home anywhere in the world but had chosen to live in the Valley of the Sun and had never regretted it. Not even now.

"I hope my dinner appreciates me," she said, smiling wryly at herself in the mirror. "Not every meal is eaten by someone in pajamas as fancy as mine!"

Feeling almost lighthearted and definitely pleased with herself, Hope went downstairs. It was madness even to think of fixing dinner in the elegant caftan, but she was feeling a little mad at the moment. She opened the bottle of Chardonnay that she had put in the refrigerator for the day that Rio found a place to drill for water, poured herself a glass, and inhaled the heady scent of fine wine. She breathed in again, savoring the moment with the intensity that was as much a part of her as the love waiting deep within her for the exquisite instant of release.

Humming in quiet counterpoint to the long wail of the wind, Hope pulled a chicken out of the refrigerator. She cut away the breast and boned it with quick, smooth strokes, using a knife that Rio had honed to a glittering edge. Even Mason had been impressed, and had threatened to use the knife in place of his usual straight razor. She smiled slightly, remembering Rio's offer to shave Mason with a butter knife instead.

Hope set the knife aside, rinsed off her hands, and reached for the crystal wineglass. The wind's cry ascended the scale a few notes, then dropped into a temporary silence. As the wine touched her lips she heard the muffled sound of a vehicle pulling up outside.

Rio. He must have come back early.

The glass dipped alarmingly in her hand, almost spilling the golden wine onto the velvet caftan. She heard a door slam, heard booted feet coming up the front steps, heard the front door opening. She held her breath against the wave of longing that swept through her.

And then Hope saw John Turner walk through the living room into the kitchen as though he owned the house and everything in it.

Hope's first reaction was anger and a disappointment so deep that it made her dizzy. "Haven't you ever heard of knocking on doors?" she asked coldly.

The wind gusted back up to its full strength, making the house tremble with its endless power. It whispered grittily against windows and walls in a long exhalation that became a low wail masking all sounds from the outside, increasing the isolation of the ranch house.

"Is that any way to welcome your fiancé?" asked Turner, smiling with an anticipation that he didn't bother to conceal. The smile faded abruptly as he took in her elegant clothes. "Who are you waiting for?"

"No one," said Hope.

"The hell you aren't," snarled Turner. "No woman dresses up like that except for a man."

"I do."

She went to the refrigerator, pulled out a ham, and sliced off a chunk. Swiss cheese was next. Deliberately ignoring Turner, she cut the ham and cheese into neat strips. Turner watched her every motion with brooding eyes.

"It's Rio," said Turner, his voice flat, ugly, threatening. "They were right. He's gotten into your jeans."

Hope's fingers tightened around the knife handle. Very carefully, because her hands wanted to shake with anger and the first stirrings of fear, she made small pockets in the chicken breast with the knife's gleaming tip. She tucked strips of ham and cheese into the pockets, along with a sprinkling of herbs. There was no sound in the kitchen but the thin cry of the wind until she spoke curtly.

"Nobody's in my jeans." Then, with a precision that equaled the cutting edge of the knife, Hope added, "And if someone were, it wouldn't be any of your business."

Turner listened to her, measured the anger in the stiff line of her shoulders, and accepted the only part of her words that he wanted to hear.

"I told you that if you hired Rio, people would talk."

She shrugged with a casual ease she was far from feeling. Mason was gone. Rio was gone. John Turner was here, standing between her and the nearest door. "People talk all the time."

"Not about my future wife," he said bluntly.

The wind's keening rose in volume until it was just short of a scream. Hope wanted to scream with it, to curse Turner's thick indifference to anything but his own desires. Julie had been like that, totally self-absorbed. But her sister hadn't been cruel. Her selfishness had puzzled and saddened Hope; Turner's self-absorption frightened her. She took a slow, inconspicuous breath, knowing that if she showed fear, Turner would be all over her in an instant, dragging her down to the hard floor.

"What makes you think I'm going to marry you?" she asked in a tone of simple curiosity.

"Because I'm the only one who will have you. I made sure of it, babe," he said with calm satisfaction.

"Every man within a hundred miles in every direction knows that if he comes near you, I'll hammer him right into the ground with my bare fists. So nobody's been near you. Getting hungry, babe? I sure as hell am."

She wanted to point out that Rio had been the exception to Turner's rule, but she held her tongue. She sensed that making Turner angry would change a frightening situation into a desperate one.

"See," he continued, "I knew when you ignored me two years ago, when you came back here to live, that you were still mad at me for that hundred-dollar bill. You'd gone away to the big city and turned into a real classy piece. You looked better than ever, babe. And you wouldn't look at me." He shrugged massively. "Hey, fine. I had lots of time and lots of women to play with. I could wait." He smiled widely. "You know, I kind of liked waiting. Most women bore me after I screw them. But with you I could lie in bed and think of how many ways I'd do it to you. I never got bored."

The shudder of revulsion that went through Hope didn't escape Turner. He smiled, misreading her now as he had always misunderstood her in the past.

"Turns you on, huh?" he said, hooking his thumbs through his belt loops. "Yeah, me too. Come here, babe. I've got something for you."

"No."

"Hey," he said, smiling widely and holding up his hands as though she had a gun on him. "My intentions are strictly honorable. I won't touch you until we're married, if that's the way you want it."

"That's the way I want it," she said grimly.

"Then let's go, babe. There's a man in town who'll have us married before you can say—"

"No."

"What do you mean, no?" he said, exasperated.

"Just that. N.O. No." Hope looked at Turner and spoke calmly despite the fear prowling through her, shaking her as the wind shook the house, howling. "Don't you understand yet?" she asked with a calmness that was just short of desperation. "You want me only because you can't have me. You said it yourself. Women bore you. I'll bore you, too."

"No, you won't. You're the only woman who ever said no to me and made it stick. C'mon," he said impatiently, holding out his thick hand to her. "Let's go to town."

"No."

The hand became a fist. "Listen, I'm getting real goddam tired of hearing *no* from you. The game is over. Rio's sniffing around, and he's got too damn many women hot for him. He'll get in your pants, too. I've thought it over real carefully. I was going to come here tonight and beat that son of a bitch within an inch of his life. But I saw him in town, so he'll have to wait. You're here, though. I'm going to screw you until you can't even think of saying no. Got that, babe?"

Hope looked from Turner's flushed face to the fist he had unconsciously made of the hand he had held out to her. She wondered if he had been drinking, and decided it didn't matter. He hadn't had enough alcohol to slow down his reflexes, which was all that mattered to her. For a moment she thought of the rifle in the water truck. Who would have guessed that she would be cornered by a snake in her own kitchen?

The back door had never looked farther away. For an instant Hope considered going along with Turner's "offer" of marriage until she got to town and then running for the first shelter she saw. She measured the flat light in his eyes and realized that he wouldn't wait until town to rape her. He had been content with his

coarse fantasies as long as he knew that she wasn't
interested in any man. But now Rio was around.
Turner wasn't going to let her get away. Not tonight.

Hope's hazel glance flickered again to the back
door.

"You start running and you aren't going to like it
when I catch you," promised Turner. "I'll like it,
though. I'll like it a whole lot."

The chill wind moaned and blew over the land,
buffeting the house. For an instant Hope wanted
nothing more than to be as wild and free as the wind.
And as safe.

"I—I'll need to change my clothes if we're going to
be married in town," said Hope, mentally measuring
the drop from her bedroom window to the sloping
roof of the back porch and from there to the ground.
The wind would cover any sounds she made. She
could be in the pasture, up on Aces, and over the back
fence before Turner caught on. She was sure of it.

Turner cocked his head as though listening to the
wind. His blunt brown eyes looked Hope over, seeing
through the soft caftan to the softer flesh beneath.
"Sure thing, babe. I'll just come along and watch.
Sort of an appetizer. I'll even get in a bite or two," he
added, moving forward, extending his hand, "right
about *here.*"

With a twist of her body Hope evaded his grasping
hand. She wasn't quite fast enough, though. His
fingers grabbed the caftan below her waist. The lush
green material bunched in his fist. She stood very still,
her hands braced on the counter behind her. If she
moved, she knew that she would arouse his predatory
instincts even more. He liked women to fight him.
They were so easy to defeat, so soft, and their smooth
skin showed every mark.

"Is this what your word is worth?" asked Hope with
a calmness that went no deeper than her cold skin.

"You said you wouldn't touch me until we were married."

"Does that mean you finally decided to marry me?" he asked carelessly.

Slowly, as though in a dream, Hope felt the black wood handle of the boning knife pressing against the edge of her palm.

"It's about time," continued Turner. Almost absently his huge fist crushed the velvet fabric, tugging on it, trying to bring her closer. "I'm tired of jumping through hoops for you. First the mortgage, then the water, and you still keep saying no."

"I borrowed the money from the bank," said Hope evenly, trying to bring rationality to a situation that was degenerating into terror. "One year, interest only, the land and buildings as collateral. Nothing was said about sleeping with you."

"The bank is owned by my aunt, and I'm her favorite nephew. If it hadn't been for me, you'd have been turned down flat." The big fist twisted slowly, wrapping the green velvet more tightly around his fingers, inexorably dragging Hope closer. "I didn't figure you'd make more than one or two payments before you went belly-up. I was going to step in and buy your ranch. Then you were going to earn it back one night at a time, like any other whore."

"I've made every payment," Hope said, her voice so controlled that it was almost toneless.

"Yeah," he said in disgust. His fist twisted, tightening more fabric around his fingers, pulling her closer. "You sure as hell have. Hear you've got money saved up for the balloon, too."

She nodded, unable to force sound past the fear closing her throat. The wind spoke for her in a low, endless cry of despair.

"Well, hell, babe. You don't leave a man much room, do you?" he asked in exasperation. "You won't even put out for the water you've been taking. So I'm going to collect what's coming to me, starting now!"

Turner yanked the fabric, throwing Hope off balance. Her hand jerked away from the knife as she fell against him. His mouth came down on hers cruelly. His arms pinned hers against her side while his teeth ground against her lips. He backed up, dragging her with him until the kitchen table pressed against his thighs. He lifted his head and grinned, rotating his hips against her.

"How about right here, babe. Just you and me and the big hard table."

Nausea turned over in Hope's stomach. Her mind raced with frantic speed. She wanted nothing but to be free of Turner's touch, his smell, his obscene strength. With an effort of will that left her shaking, she smiled and lowered her eyelashes to keep him from seeing her revulsion.

"How about in my bed?" she asked, her voice hoarse as she deliberately kicked off her fragile mules, getting ready to run at her first chance. "I'd hate to get your fancy jeans all greasy."

Turner hesitated, surprised and a little disappointed by her unexpected capitulation. His arms loosened. "Well—"

Hope threw herself away from him with a strength that came from desperation. Turner staggered against the table, off balance for an instant. Her right hand closed over the boning knife as she sprinted alongside the counter, trying to reach the back door. Turner moved with surprising speed for a big man, cutting her off without quite catching her. She backed up rapidly, retreating from him. He stood with his legs braced far apart, admiring her flushed face and dark hair. He smiled with anticipation.

"This is more like it, babe," said Turner. And then he spotted the boning knife glittering in her hand.

"Put it down," he rasped. "Fun's fun, but I'm not into knives."

"Then get the hell out of my kitchen." Hope's voice was cold and empty, like the wind wrapping around the house in a sustained wail.

Turner hesitated before he smiled again, an ugly smile. "You won't do it," he said, closing the distance between them with small movements of his body. "And when I catch you, you'll wish to God you'd never even thought of it."

The sound of the wind masked the heavy sound of Turner's boots against the floor as he closed in on Hope.

Chapter 9

A VOICE SPOKE FROM THE LIVING ROOM, A VOICE AS COLD as the winter wind. "I really should let her skewer you."

Rio was just beyond the kitchen doorway, watching Turner with measuring eyes. "But Hope isn't used to drawing blood. I am, Turner. I'm going to see what color your blood is. Yellow, I'll bet."

He walked forward smoothly, stalking Turner, silence and strength and control in each clean movement. And violence. That was there, too, implicit in the coiled perfection of each stride.

Rio's presence was so unexpected, so stunning, that Turner simply stood for a moment and then shook his head like a dog coming out of a cold rain. Hope backed away from Turner in a rush that took her beyond Rio to the living room.

"Go outside," said Rio calmly, not looking at her, watching Turner with eyes that were both feral and utterly controlled. "I'll be out in a minute."

Before Hope could answer, Turner charged into the living room with his arms spread wide to drag everyone down. Hope threw herself to one side even as Rio's hand gave her a hard shove, removing her from Turner's reach. Ensuring her safety put Rio at a disadvantage. He went down beneath Turner's attack. Hope sprawled on the couch as the two men crashed to the floor with a force that shook the room.

As he had in so many bar brawls with smaller men, Turner used his superior weight and muscle to flatten his opponent. Then he straddled Rio, cocked a huge fist and prepared to beat the man beneath him into a bloody rag. Turner's descending blow was deflected by an upward sweep of Rio's left arm. His right hand made an unusual fist, middle knuckle slightly extended. He rammed a blow to Turner's heart with a twisting motion at the instant of impact. Even as Turner blanched at the pain exploding through his chest, the callused edge of Rio's open left hand connected with Turner's neck in a swift, brutal chop. With a sighing sound Turner slipped sideways and sprawled facedown across the living room floor.

Rio came to his feet in a single catlike movement. "Hope? Are you all right?"

"I—Rio?" she asked, disbelief in her voice. He had moved so quickly, so lethally. It had happened so fast, no more than a handful of seconds from the moment Turner had tackled him. Even with what Mason had told her, she hadn't expected Rio to be so deadly against Turner, who had earned a brutal reputation for boots-and-bare-knuckle brawling.

Rio took the knife from her slack fingers and set it on the lamp table as he knelt in front of her. "Are you all right?" he asked urgently, searching her face with blue eyes so dark they were almost black. "He didn't hurt you, did he?"

Abruptly the reaction hit Hope. She began to

tremble violently as tears spilled out of her eyes. Her skin went pale and her breath came in short gasps that couldn't get enough oxygen into her lungs. Rio saw blood welling from a cut on her lip and knew that Turner had caused it. Hope saw the change in Rio's eyes, saw the blackness of violence wholly unleashed in the sudden dilation of his pupils. With a guttural sound Rio turned toward the man lying unconscious on the floor.

"N-no!" Hope said quickly, her cold fingers closing over Rio's arm. The bunched hardness of his muscles shocked her. It was like grabbing a steel fencepost. "H-he d-didn't—"

Rio searched her face, hearing both the truth and the desperation in her broken words. He looked away from the tiny drops of blood on her trembling lips. A fierce emotion went through him, cutting him, making him bleed even as she bled.

"Hope," he said softly, wanting to touch her, knowing he must not. If he touched her, he would make love to her, kissing away even the memory of brutality, caressing her with his lips and tongue and body until she trembled and wept with ecstasy instead of fear.

Turner's low groan echoed the sound of the wind, rough and empty of meaning.

Rio slanted the man a single feral look—and then Rio closed his eyes and fought to keep himself from easing his long fingers around Turner's throat and squeezing until there was nothing left of him but an ugly memory. Rio looked away, flexing his fingers, willing himself back into control. It had never been so hard before, not even when he was young and as wild as a winter storm.

"R-Rio?"

"It's all right, Hope," he said, forcing calmness into his voice instead of the violence that prowled within him, hurting to be free. "I won't kill him." *Yet,* Rio amended silently.

Turner groaned again. Rio moved with predatory speed. His fingers clamped around Turner's thick arm. With an impatient jerk Rio rolled the rancher over onto his back.

"Can you hear me?" asked Rio coolly.

Turner's groan didn't tell Rio anything new. His palm smacked across the rancher's face with measured force. Turner's eyes opened. He saw Rio and lunged at him. Rio wrapped his fingers around Turner's arms just above the elbows and used the rancher's momentum to yank him to his feet. Turner sagged as waves of pain spread out from his elbows. The next time he looked at Rio, it was with dawning fear instead of rage. Rio saw the change and nodded slowly.

"We're going to reach an understanding, you and me," drawled Rio mildly, but his eyes were cold and his fingers dug deeply into Turner's thick flesh, grinding nerve against bone in a gesture that was punishment, warning, and promise in one. "You touch Hope again and I'll hurt you. Hear me?"

"All I hear is the wind, *drifter,*" grated Turner.

He said no more. He didn't have to. The knowledge that Rio wouldn't always be around to protect Hope was there in Turner's eyes. It was there in Hope's, too, raw fear and regret.

"That's right," agreed Rio softly. "I'm the wind. I'm everywhere. I see everything. I hear everything. I know everything. You touch Hope and you better start looking over your shoulder, living in your rearview mirror, locking your doors at night and checking the locks again before you go to sleep. You better start going to church every Sunday and praying to God that you never see me again."

Rio smiled in a travesty of sympathy. "It won't do

you a damn bit of good. One day you'll hear the wind and you'll turn around and I'll be there. And then I'll kill you."

The unlatched front door banged open, pushed by a cold shout of wind. Rio pivoted and released Turner with a hard motion that sent the rancher smashing into the door frame. He pulled himself upright, took one look at Rio's face, and stumbled down the front steps into his Jeep.

The wind's cold fingers raked through Rio's hair. He didn't notice. He stood in the doorway, watching while headlights made a sweep of the yard and accelerated down the road until there was nothing left but a pinpoint of brightness. The wind hummed around and through the house, making the walls shiver.

Rio shut the door, turned, and saw Hope shivering, too. She came to her feet slowly, looking at him with eyes that were wide and very dark.

"I know you d-don't—" Her voice broke and she tried again. "I know you don't w-want to, but would you hold me, p-please?" She swayed, holding on to herself because there was no one else. "Please," she said desperately, scrubbing her face and arms with her hands. "I can't s-stand the feel of him on my skin any longer!"

With a hoarse sound Rio came to Hope, wrapped his arms around her, rocked her gently against his body. He held her for long, long minutes, until her skin was warm beneath his hands and her body no longer shuddered with ugly memories. He felt her take a deep, ragged breath, and then felt her lean against his strength with a trust that made him want to cry out in protest.

"I would have used the knife," she said bleakly, her voice shaking slightly. "I would have tried to—"

"I know," he murmured, his voice utterly certain as

he smoothed his cheek against the dark satin of her hair.

"How do you know?" she asked curiously, tilting her face up to his.

"Because you're a one-man woman," said Rio, bending down to Hope. "And God help us both, *I'm that man.*"

He lowered his mouth to her trembling lips. He touched her with melting gentleness, cherishing her. The tip of his tongue caressed the cut on her lip. She made a low sound and swayed against him.

"Does that hurt?" he asked softly against her mouth, not lifting his head at all.

"No," she sighed, watching him through half-closed eyes. "It feels—"

Her voice died. She shivered and moved her head very slowly from side to side, offering more of her lips to him in a silent plea. Rio understood. With tiny, hot movements of his tongue he caressed her lips, licking away every last vestige of Turner's ugly embrace. Hope moaned and clung to Rio, letting his warmth and his tenderness fill her senses. Her lips parted in a helpless invitation that he accepted with a deep sound of pleasure and need. His tongue stroked the inner softness of her mouth, tasting her as tiny shudders of desire rippled through his powerful body, desire flowing hotly, threatening to erode his control. He shouldn't be holding her, touching her, tasting her on his tongue like a wild, sweet rain.

"Hope," he breathed against her mouth. And then again, urgently, "Hope! Tell me to stop!"

Her eyes opened, luminous with emotion. "I love you," she whispered, and her breath flowed warmly over his lips.

"*God*—" groaned Rio as he buried his face against her neck, unable to bear the radiant truth of her eyes. "I didn't want to hurt you," he said harshly.

"I know." Her voice was serene, certain, like her eyes.

"I don't have any past, any future, any present. I am the wind."

"Yes," she said, turning to caress his cheek with her lips, "I know."

Rio straightened and confronted the extraordinary beauty of Hope's eyes. His hard, warm hands shaped her face. "Then tell me to go," he said in a hoarse voice.

She smiled sadly. "Never, my love."

"Hope—"

"Kiss me," she said, standing on tiptoe.

"Hope, I don't—"

The soft heat of her lips, her tongue, drove every word from Rio's mind. He groaned deeply and took her mouth even as she took his. The gliding pressure of tongue over tongue was a wildness shaking him. He could not hold her close enough, taste her deeply enough, or control the passion exploding through him like a violent desert storm. Before the kiss ended he was fully aroused, needing her as he had never needed a woman before.

With an effort that left him shaking, Rio lifted his mouth from hers. "No more," he said hoarsely.

"Why?" she asked, her luminous eyes searching his.

His laugh was short. He felt her over every inch of his body, and each of his heartbeats was hotly echoed in the rigid flesh straining against his jeans, against her. He moved his hips once, slowly. The unmistakable hardness of male passion caressed her.

"That's why," he said, his voice rough.

Hope's smile was like her body, invitation and incitement at once. "That's the best reason I can think of *not* to stop," she murmured, kissing the corners of his mouth, moving against him in return.

"Hope—"

"I'm not asking you to stay with me forever," she breathed into his mouth. "I'm not even asking you to say you love me. All I'm asking is to feel your life inside me. That's all, Rio. Just that. You. Inside me."

Her words wrenched from him a cry that was both harsh and infinitely sweet. He could no more resist the outpouring of her love than the land could resist a silver fall of rain. Without stopping to think or to argue or to deny, he bent and lifted her into his arms.

"You don't have to carry me off to the bedroom," she said, smiling. "I won't change my mind or run away." She rubbed the palm of her hand over the hard muscles of his chest, the line of his jaw. His head turned suddenly and his teeth lovingly captured the flesh at the base of her thumb. She cried out as desire lanced through her. "I don't think I could run if I tried," she admitted, her voice ragged. "You make me weak, Rio."

He heard the surprise in her voice, felt the quivers of need that coursed through her body. He smiled rather grimly as he started up the stairs.

"I know you're not going to run away," he said. He stopped without warning and looked down at Hope. His pupils were fully dilated, leaving only a crystal rim of midnight blue. He took her mouth with a hard thrust of his tongue and laughed to feel the passion shaking her. "Little dreamer," he breathed huskily, and thrust into her again. *"God how I want you!"* He lifted his head finally, all but crying out in protest at having to end the kiss. "I'm carrying you because I'm trying to slow myself down."

"Is it working?" she asked, searching his face, reading his hunger in every taut line, every harshly drawn breath.

"What do you think?"

Hope smiled slowly. "I think your bedroom is closer than mine," she murmured, tracing the line of his jaw with the tip of her tongue.

Rio's eyes closed for an instant as desire shuddered through him. "I think you're right."

He stopped and kissed her again, searching the hot textures of her mouth with slow strokes of his tongue. He heard the sounds welling from deep in her throat, from his, and he wondered if he would be able to get enough of her even when he was buried within her.

And then he wondered if he would be able to wait to find out, or if he would take her right here, right now, on the stairs. He knew that she wouldn't protest if he turned her in his arms and fitted her body over his, sheathing himself in her passionate heat. It was there in her dark eyes dazed with hunger, in the way she opened beneath his kiss, wanting his tongue deep within her mouth.

With a hoarse sound that could have been her name, Rio pulled his lips away from hers and went up the stairway with long, powerful strides. The door to his room was open. He kicked it shut behind him and carried Hope over to the bed. There he stopped, still holding her, neither looking at nor kissing her.

"What's wrong?" asked Hope, sliding her fingers between the snaps on his shirt, feeling the surprising heat of his body.

Rio gave her a crooked smile that made her ache. "You've driven me crazy. I can't even let go of you long enough to undress you."

Hope would have smiled in return, but the desire she felt for Rio was too close to pain. Her fingers shook as she reached for the long zipper that was concealed beneath a front fold of the caftan. Green fabric fell away from skin that was both softer and hotter than velvet. One breast was revealed in creamy curves and a dark rose peak that grew tighter even as he watched, begging for his tongue, his teeth, his mouth.

Rio shifted Hope in his arms, allowing her legs to slide down over his. He didn't let go of her. He couldn't. He lifted her until her breast was level with his mouth. With small, slow movements of his head, he brushed his lips over her nipple and felt the passionate shivering of her response. Even as she cried out his name, asking for him, he drew her deeply into his mouth, caressing her as though he were drawing life itself from her.

It was a long time before he released her, long enough for her to be shuddering, long enough for her skin to become as hot as his, as misted with desire. He put her swiftly on the bed. One slender leg was revealed between green velvet folds. Her breast quivered as she breathed, its tip still taut and glistening with the evidence of his passionate caress. She smiled up at him with lips still hot from his kisses, wanting him.

IIe had never seen anything more beautiful, not even the land itself.

With hands that wanted to touch her he tore impatiently at his own shirt, undoing the steel snaps in a single ripping sound. The leather belt hissed as he jerked it through the loops. The rest of his clothes quickly fell to the floor and he stood naked before her, fighting to control himself, unable to conceal the hunger that made his breath short and his body pulse hotly with every rapid heartbeat. He saw her look at him, all of him, accepting him without shyness or fear. Her trembling fingers traced a line from his waist to his thigh. Hesitantly she touched the rigid evidence of his desire. He clenched his hands and groaned with pleasure. When her hands curled softly, sweetly around him, he thought he would lose control.

He lifted her hands to his mouth, biting them,

rubbing them across his chest, then lifting and biting
them again. He had just enough restraint not to leave
more than fleeting marks of passion on her skin, but
he wanted to. And she wanted him to. She wanted
him with an intensity that made her twist and tremble
and utter small, wild sounds that ate at the boundaries
of his control.

Green velvet folds melted away at his touch. She
wore nothing beneath but a flush of desire spreading
across her smooth, pale skin. His dark hands moved
from her lips to her toes, wanting all of her, shaking
with the wanting. His fingers tangled in the bittersweet curls between her thighs and then gently caressed her, silently asking if she was as ready for him
as he was for her. Her liquid heat closed tightly
around him. He knew then that she wanted him—and
that it had been a long, long time since she had been
with a man. The knowledge both excited and chas-
tened him. He withdrew his touch and swiftly bent
over his jeans, retrieving his wallet.

"Rio?" asked Hope, opening her eyes, afraid that
he had changed his mind and would leave her lonely
and aching.

He saw her fear, her hunger. He kissed her in swift,
hot reassurance. "It's all right, dreamer," he said,
biting her lips softly while he tore open the tiny
package he had found in his wallet.

"What are you—?" she began, then realized what
he was unwrapping. She didn't want that. She wanted
him. All of him, everything that he could give. "No,"
she said quickly, covering his fingers with her own. "I
don't want anything between us," she breathed.
"Nothing."

Rio was both surprised and hotly pleased, assuming
that she had wanted him enough to protect herself in
advance, freeing both of them from the sensual re-
strictions inherent in his only means of protecting her.

He watched as she leaned down until her lips could brush over the hard, aching flesh between his thighs. His fingers shook, spilling the packet to the floor. He uncoiled with a powerful movement that pressed Hope back onto the bed.

"Woman," he said thickly, "so much woman."

His whole body was rigid with the force of restraining the hunger that raged wildly through him with every echo of her words, every motion of her lips brushing over him. He felt his need of her like lightning raging through his body in a sensual storm. She trembled and opened to him, yielding a hot rain of pleasure as his fingers again found the secrets hidden within her softness. He had never wanted anything half so much as he wanted to take her in that searing, endless instant when pleasure melted her.

And he was sure he would hurt her if he did.

Rio rolled over onto his back. He brought Hope with him, lifting her until her beautiful legs were pressed alongside his. Hard hands caressed from her shoulders down her back, cupping around her hips, rubbing her softly against him. He groaned in a sudden, white-hot agony of need.

"Take me, Hope," he gritted, easing their bodies together. "Take as much or as little as you want. It's the only way I won't hurt you."

She looked down at him as pleasure swept through her. She shared it with him, moving against his hard length. "I can't imagine anything hurting with you," she murmured, watching him with eyes that knew only love.

"Dreamer," he said hoarsely, "beautiful dreamer." His breath caught as she caressed him again. Involuntarily he closed his eyes, losing himself in the passionate instant. Then he moved in return, and watched her with eyes that had no blue, only the dark glitter of desire. He felt her begin to ease her warmth over him.

And then he realized that he had been wrong. It hadn't been a long time since Hope had been with a man. She had never given herself before, to any man.

Ecstasy washed over Rio in a hot silver rain. "My God," he groaned, "I wonder which one of us is dreaming now?"

The only answer to his question was her warmth closing over him by soft increments, retreating, then advancing again. He wanted to put his hands on her hips and thrust into her, burying himself completely in her satin heat, ending the exquisite torment. All that prevented him was the intense pleasure that had transformed Hope's face as she moved over him. Eyes closed, generous mouth taut, she came to him with the abandoned grace he had seen when she arched herself to the sky and let water pour from her cupped hands.

"I want all of you," she whispered against his lips, straining to be as close to him as a woman could be to a man. "Help me."

Rio looked at Hope's flushed face and saw no fear. The simple truth of her words broke over him, shaking him. He felt her softness straining against the last barrier between them.

"Gently," he murmured, "gently, my woman." His long fingers caught her hard nipples, caressing her, sending exquisite lightning through her. He let the storm build until he felt pleasure burst inside her. At that instant he thrust once, smoothly, sweeping away the barrier between them before he retreated again, fearful of hurting her.

Hope followed his retreat, sliding over him, sheathing him deeply in her body as they both cried out in fierce pleasure, wanting it to last forever, to live and die feeling only the sweet instant when she first measured his full power. He was no longer the wind. He was as hard and as hot and as hungry for rain as the desert itself. He could feel the storm coming now, feel it sweeping out from him, feel himself on the brink of—

His hands clamped over her hips, holding her absolutely still. "Don't move," he groaned, fighting for control of the storm they had created. "It's too soon. You aren't ready."

Slowly Hope opened her eyes and looked down at the man she loved. Every muscle in his body was rigid, hot, gleaming with sweat. He filled her mind, her heart, her body, and she wanted nothing more than to bring him a pleasure as wild and as true as her love for him.

Rio could hold Hope's hips immobile, but there was nothing he could do about the deep, involuntary movements of her body as she looked down at him with love in her eyes.

"Oh, God—" he gritted. "Don't—"

And then he could say no more. Hope was all around him, tugging at him, and he gave himself to her as though she were the wind calling his name. She closed her eyes, savoring his release, feeling the most intense pleasure of her life as the man she loved moved within her. She kissed his hot skin, breathed in his unique male scent, tasted the saltiness of him. With a smile she lay along his chest, content to listen to his heart beating wildly beneath her cheek.

When Rio could breathe again his hands slowly traveled from Hope's tangled hair down her spine to the warm curve of her hips. His fingertips brushed over her intimately, making her breath catch. The sensitivity of her own flesh surprised her. She lifted her head and looked into Rio's indigo eyes. He moved against her, within her, smiling up at her with male intent.

"Rio?" she asked, not understanding. She knew that he had no reason to be hungry now.

"Did you think I would leave you unsatisfied?"

Hope could only shake her head. "You haven't," she said simply, still not understanding. "I've never felt more pleasure than I did with you just now."

A hot shudder of desire went down the length of Rio's body as the implication of Hope's words sank in. She had never had more pleasure—and he had not even begun to make love to her. The thought tore at him with the honeyed claws of ecstasy barely restrained. "I've never lost control with a woman before," he said in a gritty, rueful voice, "and damned if you aren't taking me right up to the edge all over again."

"I don't understand," she whispered.

"You will," he promised, rolling onto his side and fitting his mouth to hers in a single powerful motion.

It was like being caught in a warm, gentle whirlwind. Hope felt his tongue thrusting sensually into her mouth even as his hand found the satin weight of her breast. He caught the tip between his fingers and tugged. Lightning streaked through her. She moaned as her body moved reflexively, tightening around him, and he laughed in pure satisfaction. The sound was another stroke of lightning taking her body by storm. He drank the sounds that rippled from her. His fingertips closed on her hard nipple as he felt the hot waves of pleasure take her, giving her to him. He shifted his hand to the lush curve of her bottom, flexing his fingers against her resilient flesh, and his words were a dark wind surrounding her, telling her more than she had ever dreamed about sensual hunger and response.

"Rio," she said breathlessly, "I—"

The word became a cry as his hand slid between their joined bodies, finding and caressing the most sensitive part of her. He felt her sudden trembling, her breath stopping within her, her nails digging suddenly into his back, and he laughed again softly, teasingly, confidently, like his fingers stroking her, taking her to the edge and then holding her there poised and shivering on the brink of release.

"Rio—?"

It was a ragged sound, question and surprise and something close to fear as Hope felt her own body taken from her control, a thunderstorm at the instant of breaking, her nerves' an incandescent network of lightning straining to be free. Instinctively she held back, uncertain.

"Dreamer," he said huskily, caressing her, "come to me."

Hope cried aloud as she gave herself to the storm, to him, holding nothing back, knowing ecstasy for the first time in her life. It swept through her like a wild wind, shaking her to her soul. She held on to Rio, crying, and he held her, kissing away the sweet rain of tears. Blindly she clung to him as her lips caressed his neck, his chest, the hard nubs of his nipples. She was drowning in the ecstasy, in him, and she whispered her love with each breath she took.

He heard her words, felt the tiny wild movements of her body, and control began slipping away from him once more. He fought the whirlwind of desire spiraling up from their joined bodies, making him fill her until each of her breaths was a separate caress over him. He wanted to hold himself back, to protest that he wasn't like this, that no woman had ever aroused him until he wanted to scream with it, but even that primitive release was denied because his throat was as tight around his words as she was around him.

"I wondered on the stairway if I could get enough of you," said Rio finally, his voice low and gritty, as intimate as his slow, deep movements within her body. "I don't think I can. Have you had enough of

me?" he asked, biting her shoulder with fierce restraint.

Her only answer was a sharp cry as anticipation
coiled impossibly, hotly, within her again. Lightning
strokes of new pleasure ripped through her before the
aftershocks of her first ecstasy had fully stilled. She
tried to say his name but could not. He filled her, all
of her, leaving room for nothing except the hot silver
rains sweeping over her once again. This time she
didn't hesitate in surprise or fear. She knew that he
was waiting for her within that torrential storm.

And then he was there with her, holding her
powerfully as ecstasy broke around them, consuming
them.

It was a long time before the sensual storm passed,
leaving them spent, gleaming with moisture, their
bodies tightly intertwined. Rio kissed and caressed
Hope gently, cherishing her. He had never known
such a wild, sweet pleasure with a woman. He hadn't
even believed it was possible. The excitements and
satisfactions of Hope were like a new land opening
before him, a new wind calling his name.

He said her name softly as his mouth opened on her
lips, asking for a greater intimacy. When she answered with a gliding pressure of her tongue, he
caught it almost hungrily. He didn't understand that,
for it wasn't sexual need driving him. He felt like a
man racing to catch the wind, to hold it, to absorb it so
completely into himself that he would never be separate again. He held her, surrounding her, letting her
drift asleep within the cradle of his arms.

Rio did not sleep. He lay and watched moonlight
bathe Hope in unearthly silver beauty. And when he
could control himself no longer, he began touching
her with his hands and his lips and his tongue. She
woke slowly, languidly, murmuring Rio's name and
her love as his mouth caressed her lips, her neck, her

breasts, her body, moving over her like his brother the wind, learning each of her soft secrets. Long before he came to her she was crying and twisting against his unbearably knowing mouth, lost in the ecstasy shaking her. Even then he did not take her, but instead began all over again, memorizing her, leaving none of her hot skin untasted, knowing all of her, cherishing her with a primal sensuality that shattered her.

He took her then, when his name was a wild cry on her lips. It was her name, too, his broken cry against her mouth, their voices intertwined as deeply as their moonlit bodies.

Chapter 10

HOPE WOKE TO THE FRAGRANCE OF RAIN FLOWERS SPILL-
ing softly over her. She opened her eyes and saw
bright yellow blossoms drifting from Rio's hand. His
smile was as warm as the sunrise flooding the room
with shades of gold and rose. He kissed her lips
gently, then pulled the blankets up to her neck,
concealing the womanly curves of her body.

"Last night taught me that I have no willpower
where you're concerned," Rio whispered as his hand
rested on the blanket over her breast, "so I'm going to
put your temptations out of my sight."

"Why?" she asked sleepily, winding her arms
around his neck. "If you give in, I won't be nearly so
tempting to you afterward, will I?"

He laughed almost roughly as he disentangled her
arms. He bit her palms and touched the sensitive skin
between her fingers with the tip of his tongue.

"The more I have you," he admitted, closing his
teeth over each of her fingertips in turn, "the more I

want you. And if I give in, the only explorations that get done on the ranch today will get done in this bed."

Hope's hazel eyes kindled. "What a lovely thought," she murmured, curling her fingers around his, tugging him down toward her.

"Does that mean you don't want to go riding with me?" asked Rio. He saw amusement curve her lips. "Let me rephrase that," he said hastily. "I've got a very interesting prospect for a well. Do you want to go over it with me?"

The implications of Rio's words evaporated Hope's sleepy, sensual humor. "Do you mean that? Have you really found a place to drill for water?"

"I don't know. So far, things look good. I was going to check it out yesterday, but went into town instead." He looked at her with intense eyes, wondering how she felt toward him in the clear light of another day.

Hope's smile faded as she remembered why Rio had left yesterday. He had wanted to avoid becoming her lover.

"Hope—" he began, seeing the memory of his leaving darken the color of her eyes.

"No," she said, putting her fingers over his lips. "I know you didn't want this. But it happened. I don't expect you to change. Don't expect me to change, either. I love you, Rio. Nothing will change that."

He gave her a swift, fierce kiss, then stood and left the room quickly. It was as though he didn't trust himself to touch her without sweeping away the blankets and knowing again the wild sweetness of her body joined with his.

"Your bath is two feet deep and steaming," called Rio as he went down the stairs. "By the time you're dressed, breakfast will be ready."

"Where are we going today?" Hope asked as she got out of bed. She shivered when her warm bare feet hit the cold bare floor.

"Ain't telling," came Rio's fading voice.

She smiled at his laconic imitation of Mason. Then she raced for the bathroom and the hot welcome of a bath. She lingered, soaking out every small ache, until the smell of food cooking drifted upstairs and into the bathroom. Reluctantly she stood and looked around for a towel. The rack was empty, and the nearest towel supply was in the linen closet down the hall. The cold hall.

Just as Hope had nerved herself up for the dash to the closet, the bathroom door opened and Rio's hand appeared. A thick, soft towel dangled from his fist.

"Missing something?" he drawled, stepping through the door and closing it behind him so that the steamy warmth couldn't escape. He held the towel wide in silent invitation. She stepped into it, and his arms. He kissed her until it was impossible to know whether her flushed skin came from the hot bath or from the even hotter passion that he called from her. "That's what *I* was missing," he said huskily. Then he lifted his head and put her away from his body. "If I don't stop right now, neither one of us is going to be in any shape to get on a horse."

"Especially if the horse is Storm Walker," she said, smiling at him with trembling lips.

"I think I'll leave that tough old son in the corral today," admitted Rio. "I suspect he has more hard in him this morning than I do."

Hope closed her eyes and shivered, remembering very clearly the hardness of Rio's beautiful body beneath her hands. "Rio?" she murmured, half-opening her eyes.

"Yes?"

"Get out of here," she said in a husky voice, standing on tiptoe, brushing her mouth over the pulse beating rapidly in his neck, "before I drag you fully dressed into that tub."

For an instant Hope thought he was going to take off his clothes—and so did he. With a wrench that was almost painful he forced himself not to touch her. He started to say something, shook his head ruefully, and removed himself from the steamy intimacy of the bathroom.

"Breakfast is ready," he said from the safety of the hallway. *And so am I,* he added silently. His response to Hope kept taking him by surprise, like finding an artesian spring in the middle of a vast desert waste. The spring shouldn't be there. All logic and experience was against it. But there the spring was, pure and sweet and inexhaustible, pulsing with rhythms that were deeper than logic and experience, as deep as life itself.

By the time Hope was dressed Rio had served both of them a mound of hotcakes, ham, and eggs. She took one look at the huge breakfast and then glanced at him in silent protest.

"You'll be glad for every bite by lunchtime," he said.

Hope ate without arguing. She knew he was right. Besides, she was uncommonly hungry. When she tucked the last morsel of hotcake neatly into her mouth and looked up from her plate, Rio was smiling at her.

He touched the fullness of her lower lip, licked his fingertip, and said, "Sweet."

"Syrup always is," she pointed out reasonably, smiling at him with love in her eyes.

He shook his head slowly. "Not syrup. You." He sighed and pushed his chair back from the table. "Let's go before my good intentions hitch a ride on the wind."

"Where are we going?" asked Hope for the second time that morning.

This time he answered. "Wind Canyon."

Rio poured the rest of the coffee into a canteen, tossed a paper bag full of sandwiches to her, put his arm around her, and walked out into the morning. She slid her arm around his waist and leaned lightly against him. Her long legs kept pace with clean, graceful movements. He watched her with something close to fascination as she ducked through the fence, caught Aces, and began grooming the horse.

"You have beautiful legs," said Rio, firmly putting out of his mind how it felt when they had wrapped around him, holding him against her straining warmth.

She looked up, startled. Then she smiled. "That's how I got the money to keep the ranch alive. Shoes, hosiery, and slit-to-the-thigh bedroom stuff was my specialty. That's where the green caftan came from. One of my last modeling assignments."

"So you take it out and wear it when nobody is around," he said, remembering the silky beauty of her body glowing up through the deep green velvet.

"Except for last night." Hope shuddered. "Turner knew I'd be alone. He saw you in town."

"I know. One of the clerks in the hardware store told me that Turner had taken one look at me through the window, turned on his heel, and took off out of town like the hounds of hell were after him." Rio's eyes changed, becoming as hard as blue-black stone. "I came back as fast as I could."

"I'm glad," she said simply.

"Not half so glad as I am."

Emotions vibrated in Rio's voice, a volatile mixture of rage at Turner, anger at himself, and a hunger for Hope so intense that it still could shake him.

Rio went into the barn. He emerged in a few minutes, leading Dusk. The mare started to walk toward the horse trailer that had been unhitched from Rio's pickup and parked beside the barn. It was the action of a horse accustomed to being trailered all over the West as her owner went from town to town, ranch to ranch, horizon to horizon.

"Not yet, girl," he said, draping a rein over the corral railing. "We've got a well to find first."

Hope had seen the horse turn toward the trailer, had heard Rio's casual words, and now she felt a cold wind keening through her soul.

Not yet.

She leaned against her horse and fought to control herself, shocked by the storm of grief shaking her. *You knew he was going to leave,* she told herself harshly. *Last night didn't change that. Tonight won't change it. Nothing will change it. You've fallen in love with the wind, and you knew it even while you were falling. You have no complaints. Not one. He has given you all he can, more than any other man has ever given you—and from what he's said, he's given you more than he has ever given to any woman. Are you going to throw it in his face and say it's not enough? Are you cruel enough to make him hate himself? Is that your idea of love?*

After a moment Hope straightened her shoulders and resumed grooming Aces with smooth motions of her arm. A few minutes later she saddled the mare and led her out of the corral. She mounted swiftly, before Rio could help her, touch her. Side by side the two horses loped along the dirt road. The wind blew fitfully, tearing puffs of dust from the land.

Rio glanced over at Hope occasionally, quick looks that were hidden within the shadow of his hat brim. He had seen intense unhappiness on her face for a moment back at the corral. He had wanted to go to her, to hold her, to assure her that everything would be all right, that he would protect her. And then he had seen her gather herself, shaking off whatever had clawed her. He didn't know what had happened, or why. He only knew that for a moment Hope had been torn to her soul. He knew what that kind of pain was like, how unexpected it could be, almost overwhelming. So he watched her covertly, reassuring himself that she was all right.

Hope caught the indigo flash of Rio's glance and turned, smiling at him for a moment before she looked back over the velvet-shadowed hills glowing in the early sun. The peace of the morning and the rhythmic beat of hooves were like a benediction. Rio was accustomed to such sunrises, such silence—but this time Hope was with him, sharing the quiet and the compelling land. Like the dawn itself, she had an aspect of stillness that pleasured him. Other women he had known were hurt or frightened by silence. They had demanded that he take their emotional temperature with constant conversation. He had hated that, hated being with someone so shallow that she changed temperature with every one of his silences.

Rio leaned over and ran his fingertip down the line of Hope's jaw. She looked at him and smiled, her eyes almost golden in the rich morning light. He felt hunger and something more move through him, something indescribable, as though a spring welled up from his soul and lapped gently outward, sweet water bringing life to everything it touched. He touched Hope again as though to reassure himself that she was real and he was real and the moment itself was real.

Finally the two horses moved into the thick shadows slanting from Wind Canyon's broad mouth. There was a long exhalation of air, an almost subliminal stirring of the atmosphere that was always more pronounced at this location than at any other canyon mouth on the ranch. Hope looked up the canyon where the old wagon road began to snake into the heights. She shuddered and looked away, grateful that

Rio hadn't wanted to go all the way to the abandoned mine.

"What are we looking for?" asked Hope.

"Nothing we can see."

She gave him a sideways glance. "That's going to make it a wee bit difficult, isn't it?"

Rio tugged his hat more firmly around his head and smiled slightly. "Look at Eagle."

Dutifully Hope looked at the ragged peak that had dominated the skyline of all her childhood mornings.

"What do you see?" asked Rio.

"Rock. Lots of it."

"Close your eyes. You'll see more that way."

Hope looked at him for a second and then closed her eyes.

"Remember that sandwich we talked about?"

"The one with waterproof bread?" asked Hope whimsically.

"That's the one. Now, imagine the sandwich not being broken. Imagine it just being slanted up to the sky at a fairly shallow angle." Rio looked at Hope's intent face. Her lashes were almost black against her golden skin. He remembered the intriguing softness of the lashes against his lips, and the scent of her when he rested his cheek between her breasts. Then he yanked his wandering thoughts back to aquifers and Eagle Mountain. "Now, that peak is like a party sandwich with all kinds of fancy layers. Rocks like granite, quartzite, and slate are the waterproof strata. The meat of the sandwich is limestone laid down in ancient seas. The limestone doesn't vary much in thickness here. But the surrounding strata do. Granite intrusions can be only a few inches thick in some places, hundreds or thousands of feet in others."

Hope frowned, eyes still closed as she visualized a rather lumpy, disorganized sandwich. "Then how do you know where to sink the well? If you start where granite is thousands of feet thick, you'll never get anything but worn-out drill bits and dry holes."

"That's why you go to the Colorado School of Mines and get a master's degree in hydrology," said Rio dryly. "That way you're supposed to have a fighting chance of guessing right."

Her eyes flew open as realized what Rio had said—at some time in his past he had earned a master's degree from one of the foremost centers for the study of applied geology in the United States. She watched him intently, wondering if he would tell her more about himself, but he was looking at Eagle Peak with trained eyes that saw through the mixed strata to the chance of water beneath.

"Not much limestone shows through on this side of the mountains," he continued. "That's probably why your geologist gave up." To himself Rio added wryly, *That, and the fact that his grandfather wasn't a Zuni shaman who taught a wild kid to be so still that he could feel clouds condensing around distant peaks and water flowing in the earth far beneath his feet.*

"But there is limestone in those mountains," he continued. "It shows high up in the most deeply eroded peaks over on the dry side of the Perdidas. Because it weathers away faster than other strata, undermining the surrounding layers, the exposed limestone is all but buried by slides of harder rocks." Though Rio was looking up at the rugged mountains, his focus was inward where knowledge, experience, and instinct arranged and rearranged the possibilities of the strata. "The limestone I saw could be simply fragments of a stratum that has long since dissolved away. Or it could be the tip of an aquifer that's thousands of feet thick and has been soaking up water for millions of years."

Hope's breath came in quickly and caught, filling

her until she ached. The thought of so much water waiting beneath her feet was almost unbearable. "Is it filled with water?" she asked, her voice husky.

"That's why we're here," said Rio, dismounting. "To decide if it's worth the gamble of drilling."

"How will you do that?"

Rio hesitated, unable to explain that he had done everything he could by all conventional measures. He had narrowed the search to three possible sites, of which Wind Canyon was by far the most likely. Now he would walk the land, letting its silent messages seep into him. He would wait deep within himself for the rippling echo of water flowing beneath his feet. It was like tiny currents of electricity whispering through him, an intimation of *something different*. Often it was a feeling so subtle that it was all but impossible to describe and quite easy to overlook. Silence was crucial—silence and a stillness that had to come from his whole mind. White men called what he was doing water-witching or dowsing, and claimed not to believe in it despite the fact that many Western wells had been found by men carrying peeled forked sticks that quivered and dipped in the presence of hidden water. His grandfather had called Rio's gift the breath of the Great Spirit. Rio didn't call it anything at all. He accepted it, just as he accepted the color of his hair and the number of his fingers.

"Experience," said Rio finally, handing Dusk's rein to Hope. "That's how I decide. If the land feels right, I drill."

"And if it doesn't?"

"I move on," he said in an absent voice as he dismounted and unbuckled the deep saddlebags he always brought with him. He rummaged for a moment, brought out a pair of rock-scarred hiking boots, and put them on in place of the cowboy boots he had used for riding. "I learned when I was young to trust my instincts," he said quietly, lacing up the boots. "My grandfather was a good teacher."

Hope wanted to ask more questions. All that prevented her was the feeling that Rio's mind was elsewhere. He began to walk slowly over the rocky canyon floor, almost like a man looking for a faded trail, but she sensed that it wasn't the dry surface of the ground he was concentrating on. She dismounted and loosened the cinch on her saddle and then on Rio's. After a short search she found a flat, sunwashed rock to sit on. In the cool hours of early morning the sun felt good. Knees tucked under her chin, arms wrapped around her legs, Hope watched the man she loved move over the land like a tangible, intelligent wind.

Rio quartered the mouth of the canyon with slow strides. The ground he walked over was more the lip of an outwash plain than a true canyon. Several miles wide, jumbled at the center with debris from thousands of flash floods, Wind Canyon's alluvial soil was so coarse that little grew here. It was also so porous that water coming down from the heights simply sank between the rocks and vanished. Her father had tried drilling a well in a canyon mouth similar to this one. He had drilled down hundreds of feet farther than his deepest well before he decided that there was no end to the dry, rocky alluvium. That was when he had decided to drill where the Hope was now. He had struck groundwater and had prayed that his worries were over.

With a weary gesture Hope readjusted her hat. Thinking about her father was difficult, yet every time she thought of water she would think of him. She loved the land. She had loved him. And the land had killed him. He had worked himself to death trying to get around the ineluctable reality of a retreating water table. It was as though he believed if he just worked hard enough, long enough, faithfully enough, water would return to the land. With each summer's visit to the ranch she had seen her father grow older, more tired, more unbending in his determination to make the ranch become what it once had been—alive.

Within a year after her eighteenth birthday her father had had a stroke. They had visited him in the small hospital, sitting beside his bed, listening to him fight for breath. At least Hope and her mother had sat and listened; Julie had been terrified of the broken, white-haired old man who had taken the place of the strong father of her memories. His death had solidi-fied that terror, and her mother's hatred of the land. Only the fact that her father had willed his half of the ranch to Hope had prevented her mother from selling it.

Instead, her mother had abandoned it, leaving Mason to live amid the wreckage of so many dreams. Hope had come back as often as she could, but the demands of providing for her mother, her sister, herself, and the Valley of the Sun had meant long hours of modeling. Rarely could she afford to leave Los Angeles to come home to the land that she missed with an intensity that would have shocked the people she worked with. They thought her passionless be-cause she did not share their weekend romances and transient lovers.

Before Hope was twenty her mother died. She had lost control of her car and crashed into a cement overpass. At least that was what the accident report had said. Hope knew that it wasn't that easy. Her mother hadn't wanted to live. Even Julie's iridescent smile and feverish pursuit of the perfect lover hadn't been able to penetrate her mother's grief. In the end

only Hope's silent, unbreakable love of the land had
touched her mother. She had left the ranch to Hope,
requiring only that Julie receive half of the profits.

There had been no profits. Not during the two years
that it took for Julie to kill herself with drugs and
despair, nor in the two years since then. The only
money that had come to the Valley of the Sun had
come via Los Angeles and the Sharen Morningstar
Modeling Agency. Hope had lived in L.A. until she
could not stand it any longer. Then she had returned
to the land she loved more than anything else in life.
She had told herself that she had enough money to do
everything—meet daily expenses, pay off back taxes,
and drill a new well in the bargain if it came to that.
She didn't think it would come to that. There had
been dry years before. They had always passed before
the well failed. It would be the same this time.

It hadn't been the same.

She had been forced to take out a second mortgage
at punitive interest rates. She had told herself that it
would be all right, that once a good well was found,
the second could be renegotiated on the basis of the
ranch's greatly enhanced production. But no one had
found a well. She had spent thousands of dollars on
surveys only to be told that there was no water to be
had on the Valley of the Sun.

Hope shifted on the rock's unyielding surface and
wondered how long she had sat there, thinking of a
past she couldn't change. She was all but numb.
Gingerly she slid off the rock and stretched. Dusk
flicked an ear in her direction, snorted softly, and
returned to her three-legged doze. Aces had her head
up, ears pricked forward in an attitude of attention.
Hope followed the direction of the mare's interest and
saw Rio walking along the southern margin of the
canyon, where rock crumbled and rattled down the
sloping foothills onto the dry, furrowed land below.

Hope saw Rio begin yet another zigzag across the miles-wide canyon. Soon a small fold in the land hid him as he worked his way up the broad canyon floor. She tightened the cinch on Aces, mounted, and grabbed Dusk's trailing rein. She went farther into the canyon, passing Rio far enough away not to disturb him, and chose a piece of higher ground to wait on. There her view of Rio would be unimpeded as he zigzagged slowly toward her, searching for water hidden deep beneath the dry land.

She shifted position many times in the next hours, riding Aces and leading the patient Dusk on a slow retreat up the canyon. Rio followed silently, quartering the land with extraordinary patience. The climbing sun brought first warmth, then a gentle autumn heat to the canyon floor. Congratulating herself on her foresight, Hope found a wide, shallow bowl of land set apart from the canyon floor. She weeded out the obvious rocks, spread an old quilt on the ground, and fell asleep beneath the sun's golden caress. She dreamed of Rio, a river flowing through the landscape of her love. She awoke to a kiss as sweet as spring water, as warm as sunlight.

"Wake up, little dreamer," murmured Rio against her lips.

"But the dream was so lovely," she whispered.

"Was it?" he asked, smiling.

"It was you, Rio. You and a well and water flowing. All of life in a single dream."

Rio held her between his hands, unable to speak. She watched as sunlight struck his eyes, turning them into deep blue gems. His eyelashes were thick, utterly black, like his hair burning darkly beneath the sun. She looked up at him and knew beyond any doubt that he had been right—she was a one-man woman, and Rio was that man. Whether he was here or thousands of miles away, that would not change. When he left he would take her love. While he was here she would take from him what he could give.

And she would pray that part of what he gave her was his child.

Rio kissed her very gently, as though she were a dream he was afraid to awaken. "You are so beautiful to me," he said when he reluctantly lifted his head. "Even more beautiful than your name. Hope."

Sunlight brought out both the gold and the green in Hope's hazel eyes, and the love. He kissed her dark, soft lashes and then stood up swiftly, not trusting himself to touch her any more. Since he had seen her asleep on the faded quilt he had thought of nothing but the ecstasy that waited for him deep within her body.

"Lunchtime," he said. He went to Aces, pulled the sandwiches and canteen from the saddlebags, and returned to Hope. "Ham or roast beef?" he asked.

"Yes," said Hope, stretching.

Rio paused, then smiled crookedly. "You *are* a dreamer if you think you get both sandwiches."

"Two?" she yelped. "You mean you only made two sandwiches?"

"Well, after all that breakfast—" Rio shrugged.

She looked at him in a silence that was broken by her rumbling stomach. He glanced sideways at her, chuckled, and put two sandwiches in front of her.

"No, you need it more than I do," she said hastily, trying to shove the lunch back toward him. "You're the one who's doing all the walking."

Rio pulled two more sandwiches out of the lunch bag and looked at her innocently. She snatched back the food she had been handing over to him. Muttering about men who had been out in the sun too long, Hope bit into a sandwich. They ate quickly, sharing sips of coffee from the canteen. In the end Hope could eat only half of what he had given to her. Smiling to himself, Rio wrapped up the remaining sandwich and put it back into the bag.

Despite the coffee, Hope felt sleepy. She yawned and stretched again.

"Bored?" asked Rio.

Startled, Hope blinked. Bored? With Rio so close and the ranch she loved all around her? "Just content," she said softly.

"Sure?"

"Have I missed something?" she asked, puzzled.

"It seems like every time you come with me, either I talk your ear off about geology or I don't say much at all about anything." He watched her intently. "I just thought you might be bored."

Hope stared at Rio for a long moment before she realized that he was serious. "Up at Piñon Camp you shared your visions of this land with me," she said in a low voice. "I saw miracles. Continents moved and range after range of mountains rose from the sea. There was water everywhere, good water, lakes gleaming beneath the sea, forests growing tall and thick against the mountains, snowfields and glaciers blazing on the rocky heights." She smiled helplessly, unable to explain what she was feeling. He was so silent, watching her. Didn't he believe her? Hadn't he heard when she said that she loved him?

"Rio," she said, framing his tanned face with her hands. "I've never been more excited and yet at peace with anyone or anything, not even the land itself. Today I've watched you move over the land. You—" She hesitated and then continued softly, sadly. "You're a brother to the wind. You know things about the land that no one else does."

Brother-to-the-wind.

The words struck Rio with the force of an explosion, shaking him. Somehow she knew the name that no one else had ever spoken aloud but his grandfa-

ther, a name given to Rio during a ceremony conducted in a place few white men had ever seen.

"You see—too much!" said Rio, standing abruptly,
feeling naked before the clarity of Hope's vision.

He strode away from her, farther up the canyon.
Then he realized the unfairness of what he had done
and struggled to control the emotions that were
reducing him to reflex and irrationality. His grandfather had always told him to *listen*, to hold himself
utterly still and *listen* with every bit of himself. So Rio
stood unmoving, *listening* as he never had before. He
heard only Hope's love for him in every word, every
gesture, every look. There was nothing else, no desire
to chain the wind, to break him like a wild horse, to
change him into a man who would be more comfort-
able to love. Like the wind itself, she asked nothing of
him.

And like the land itself, she gave everything in
return.

Tension flowed out of Rio, leaving him both at
peace and alive in a way that was new to him. He
turned and walked back toward Hope, sensing the
warm fall of sunlight, the subtle murmuring of the
wind, the power of his own body and the gritty
whisper of the land beneath his feet. It was a hard
land, an honest land, a miraculous land with a million
million yesterdays and more tomorrows than a man
could count, a land where rains came and sank into
stone until strange rivers flowed by tiny increments
through the fossil remains of ancient seas.

Rio closed his eyes, feeling the years peel away until
he was thirteen again, lightheaded from ceremonial
fasting and shivering with cold. It hadn't mattered.
Nothing had been real to him but the presence of
buried water like electric shocks against the soles of
his bare feet.

It was the same here, now. There was water within

the stone, water's ghostly presence tingling up
through him with each step until he stood transfixed.
Incredible currents sang through him, making him
want to throw back his head to the sky and shout, but
he had no voice. He had only the certainty of ancient
water running black and sweet and deep beneath his
feet.

Hope had seen Rio turn and walk back toward her,
had seen him slow, then stop. The absolute stillness of
his body told her that something was wrong.

"Rio?" she called, scrambling to her feet.

If he heard, he didn't answer.

She ran across the canyon bottom toward him. As
she came closer, she saw his face. She stopped as
though she had stepped into quicksand.

"Rio?" she said softly.

His eyes opened. They were almost as black as the
water buried deep beneath the earth. She walked
toward him, touched him, and shivered suddenly. It
was as though the ground had shifted. He saw her
knees buckle. His arms swept out, pulling her close,
supporting her.

"My true name is Brother-to-the-wind," he said,
giving to her what he had given to no other person.

And then he kissed her while the land whispered its
secrets to him, to her, water singing to both of them
from deep within the earth.

Chapter 11

"HONEY, YOU SHOULD HAVE CALLED ME SOONER," chided Mason as he slammed the truck door and held out his arms to Hope.

She ran down the front steps and hugged him. "I wanted you to have a real Thanksgiving vacation," she said, her words muffled against his red flannel shirt.

"But the well—"

"You got back in time to help me set up the rig," said Rio.

Mason looked over Hope's shoulder at the tall dark man filling the doorway to the house. As Mason and Hope climbed up the steps, he gave Rio a sideways look. "Heard in town you had some trouble with Turner."

Hope stiffened, remembering the ugly look on Turner's face as he had stalked her through the kitchen.

Rio's hand stroked gently over her hair, reassuring

her with his touch. Without thinking she turned her head so that her lips brushed against his palm. Mason saw the gesture, understood the ramifications, and frowned. Deliberately Rio put his arm around Hope and drew her against his side.

"Turner won't be back," said Rio. "He knows that Hope is my woman."

"Is that true?" asked Mason, his faded green eyes focused on Hope.

"Yes," she said, searching Mason's eyes, remembering what he had said about Rio. *Temporary man.* "Don't be angry."

"Angry? Shoot!" Mason smiled and held out his hand to Rio. "Welcome home, Rio. It's about time you found a good woman and settled down. And God never made no better woman than Hope!"

Hope started to protest, to explain that Rio hadn't meant that at all. Rio tilted her face up to his and kissed her lightly on the lips, stilling the protest he saw forming.

"I know," he said softly.

Rio's words could have been an answer to Mason's declaration or to Hope's unspoken protest.

"This calls for a drink," said Mason happily, striding into the house. He went directly to the old-fashioned walnut bar cabinet that stood at one end of the living room. "And none of that city bubbly, neither. Rye," he announced, bringing a bottle out of the bar. He pulled out three cut-crystal whiskey glasses, examined them critically, and poured a splash of amber liquid into each. He handed out two glasses, held the third high, and said, "To the both of you."

Hope smiled and touched her glass against Mason's, making crystal ring triumphantly. She turned to Rio—and the searching intensity of his look made her knees buckle as they had in Wind Canyon when she had sensed the certainty of water coursing through

him. Her hand trembled, sending tiny shivers through
the potent whiskey. Rio's glass rang sweetly against
hers, then against Mason's. She wanted to reassure
Rio that he need not worry about her, that what had
happened between them was her choice, her joy, her
dream; but Mason was there, smiling like a man who
had just stumbled onto the golden end of a rainbow.
So she simply looked at Rio, telling him silently what
she could not say in front of Mason.

Brother-to-the-wind, I love you. All of you. The
easy and the difficult and everything in between.

She sipped the aromatic, potent whiskey, watching
Rio over the brilliant crystal rim of her glass. He
watched her in turn, open to every shift of emotion
across her face. The taste of rye swept across his
tongue, exploded in his mouth; but it wasn't half so
potent as the love he saw in Hope's eyes. He touched
his glass to hers again, then bent and kissed her
slowly, *listening* to her as though she were an undiscovered country whose secrets he was only beginning
to understand.

"Guess I better dust off my go-to-town suit," said
Mason smugly. "How much time I got?"

Hope smiled up at him from within the curve of
Rio's arm. "For what?" she asked.

"To git geared up for your wedding," he said as
though he thought she had better sense than to ask
such a question.

"There's no rush," said Hope, her tone both calm
and very final.

It was an unmistakable verbal No Trespassing sign,
but Mason had considered himself Hope's honorary
father for too long to heed the warning.

"What do you mean?" he said, his heavy gray
eyebrows lifted high. "Gal, I want my grandkids born
proper!"

Hope felt Rio's tension in the sudden hardness of

his arm around her shoulders. "Mason," he said in a soft, inflexible voice, "leave it alone."

Mason's mouth opened, then closed tightly. He saw the narrowing of Rio's eyes and the flat line of his mouth. Only a foolish man would ignore the warning signals of Rio's anger, and Mason was not a fool.

For a moment there was an electric tension in the room. Mason looked at Hope with swift concern as it dawned on him that being Rio's woman was not the same as being Rio's future wife. A surge of anger shook Mason—Hope had given herself to a man who didn't appreciate her. On the heels of anger came a tumble of confused thoughts: *It don't make sense. Rio ain't a drunken buck who can't keep his pants zipped. Rio wouldn't touch a woman like Hope unless he cared about her in a permanent sort of way.*

Mason sighed. "You be right careful of Hope," he said quietly, looking Rio straight in the eye. "That there woman's worth more than you and me put together."

In silence Mason tossed back the rest of his rye, put the bottle away, and went out to the truck to bring in the supplies he had picked up in town. Rio and Hope followed, helping to carry in the sacks and boxes of food. The hardware for the drilling rig was left in the truck.

Hope soon discovered that in this, as in any other heavy work around the ranch, Rio calmly assumed that he would do the majority of the labor. Without hampering Hope in any way, he made it clear that she wasn't to lift, drag, shove, or otherwise disturb the heavy burlap bags of potatoes and rice, flour and beans, sugar and dried apples.

"I'll get it," he said, lifting the slithery weight of the rice bag to his shoulder. Then, as she reached for the potatoes, he added, "Mason's going to drop one of those bags."

She looked up, saw that Mason was indeed teetering on the edge of losing a grocery bag of fresh vegetables, and snatched it from him. The next time she was reaching for something heavy, Rio picked it up before she could, even though he already had one bulging sack riding on his shoulder.

"Rio," she said in a reasonable tone, "I've been playing tug-of-war with fifty- and hundred-pound bags of food since I was twelve."

"Bet you lost, too."

She smiled reluctantly. "Well, my style leaves something to be desired but," she added pointedly, "the job gets done just the same."

Rio grinned and shifted the heavy bags so that their weight was comfortably balanced on his shoulders. "Stand on tiptoe so I can kiss you."

As soon as Hope's lips brushed his, he murmured, "We have a deal, woman. You dream for me and I'll haul mountains into the pantry for you."

Mason cleared his throat loudly from the doorway. "You know," he said, "them that don't work don't eat."

Rio laughed and stole another kiss from Hope. Mason tried not to smile, then gave in and grinned as broadly as a kid. He had never seen Rio so open, so . . . free. And Hope, well, Hope looked like she had swallowed the sun. Mason decided that he'd stop worrying about wedding dates and Rio's wandering past and Hope's generous, vulnerable heart. A man would have to be stump dumb and mule stubborn to walk away from Hope. Rio was neither.

Hope sorted out vegetables at the kitchen counter, listening to the good-natured chaffing Mason was giving Rio over some incident from his past. For a moment Hope simply bowed her head and let relief sweep through her. She had been afraid that Mason wouldn't accept the fact that she was Rio's woman, period. No rings, no ceremony, no 'til-death-do-us-part. But she could give Mason one of his heart's desires. She could have a baby for him to fuss and worry over, a child who would call him Grandfather and pester him with endless questions about the past.

If she were lucky. She hadn't been lucky this month. After two weeks with Rio, her period had come with the regularity of the moon's own cycle. Next month would be different. It had to be. She wouldn't get many more chances. When the well came in, Rio would leave. She knew it as certainly as she knew that she wanted his child.

Yet deep within her mind a voice cried, *Why must he go? What can he find out there that he can't find on the Valley of the Sun?* The question had no answer, and no end to the asking. It was still quivering in her mind when Rio shut the bedroom door behind him that night and took her in his arms.

"I'm sorry, little dreamer," he said, stroking his hands down the line of her back.

For a moment she stiffened, wondering if he had read her mind. Then he continued and she let her breath sigh out against his shirt as she realized what he was talking about.

"Mason won't lean on you again. He understands now."

How can he? asked Hope silently. *I don't understand myself.*

But all she said aloud was, "I'm glad. Maybe he can explain it to me."

"What?"

"You."

"What don't you understand?" he asked.

"Why you'll leave." Before Rio could speak she kissed him, filling herself with his taste. "Never mind," she whispered against his lips. "It doesn't matter. Understanding you won't change anything,

not really. I'll still love you and you'll still leave me."
As she spoke, her hands moved over his arms, his
shoulders, his chest, and she shook with a sudden
hunger for him. "Love me while you're here, Brother-
to-the-wind. Love me now."

Rio's hands tangled in Hope's dark hair, tilting her
head back so that she had to meet his eyes. What he
saw shook him to his soul; grief and acceptance,
passion and love. Most of all, love. She loved him as
no one ever had, more than he had believed anyone
could love.

"Hope," he said hoarsely, "I don't want to hurt
you. Please, don't let me hurt you."

Her hands moved over his body, savoring the heat
and power and hardness of him. "I'm hurting now. I
want you so much I'm shaking. Can't you feel it? I—"

The rest of Hope's words were lost as Rio's mouth
came down on hers with a power that would have
been painful if she hadn't wanted him so badly. She
shivered as his salt-sweet taste filled her mouth. Her
hands kneaded down his back to his waist and then his
hips, loving the lithe, flexed strength of him, wanting
to feel the smooth heat of his skin beneath her palms.
Her fingers slid inside the waistband of his jeans. He
said something hot and dark as she found the silver
belt buckle and tugged. It didn't come free. She made
a broken sound of frustration and he laughed low in
his throat.

"Is this what you want?" he asked, stepping back,
peeling away his clothes until he stood naked before
her. "Is this—"

His words ended abruptly as she came to him,
licking his lips with tiny strokes of her tongue, teasing
him when he tried to capture her mouth. She moved
against him, gently pushing him backward, inciting
him with her provocative caresses and elusive re-
treats. He felt the bed against his legs and sank back,

pulling her after him. She slipped from his arms and her hands and mouth moved over his face, his shoulders, his chest. He tried to unbutton her blouse but she evaded him again.

"No," she murmured, biting his nipple with exquisite care. She sat up and her hands moved quickly, taking off her clothes, throwing them aside. "Let me dream you," she whispered, coming down beside him in a warm rush. "Let me. Dream."

For a moment Rio didn't understand. Then she began to move over him like sunrise, warming everything she touched; and like sunrise, she touched everything. The pleasure of her hands was extraordinary. The pleasure of her mouth was an ecstasy so great he could not breathe. And still she dreamed him, creating him with each hot touch of her tongue, each shivering instant when she held him, dreaming and loving him equally, suspending both of them in a timeless sensuality that ended only when he looked at her and knew that he had to share both the dreaming and the dream or he would die.

"Hope," he said, reaching for her, his voice as harsh as his breathing.

Her only answer was the hot, intimate glide of her tongue over his aching flesh. In the next instant the world spun and she found herself flattened beneath his weight. Her smile was a blaze of sensual anticipation. His smile was narrow and taut as he felt her elegant legs move caressingly against his in demand.

But it was his turn to dream, and hers to be dreamed, and he would not be denied one single instant of it. He moved over her like the wind, wrapping her in a sensual storm, taking her to the edge of breaking and holding her there, shaking, holding himself there with her, dreaming with exquisite passion. When he finally came to her, he drank her scream of pleasure with a consuming kiss. They moved together as one, dream and dreamer, and neither knew who was dreamer or dream.

They fell asleep with Hope locked tightly in Rio's arms, her question abandoned because the answer no longer mattered. She was the land and he was a rain-bearing wind. Against the reality of that truth, no question or retreat was possible. She would stay, he would go, and love would be the empty sky stretched between them.

"Wake up, dreamer," murmured Rio, nuzzling against the smoothness of Hope's breast. "We've got a well to dig."

Her eyes opened slowly. The first pale radiance of dawn was filling the room. She smiled at the hard-faced man whose hair was wonderfully tousled from her loving fingers. With a sigh she eased her hands into his thick black hair, loving the feel of it against her sensitive skin. He moved his head slowly, increasing the pressure of her caress, responding to her touch with a frank sensuality that never failed to send frissons of heat through her. With a contented sound he kissed the dark rose tip of her breast.

For a moment there was only silence and dawn and the gentle warmth of their pleasure in being together. Then Rio sighed and reluctantly got up and went down the hall. After a few lazy minutes of wishing that he were still in bed with her, Hope followed, still half-asleep, lured by the sound of running water. When she stepped into the bathroom he leaned out of the bathtub shower while she wrapped her hair in a towel. He kissed her nose, nibbled on her lips, and pulled her into the shower.

The water had just barely begun to warm the pipes.

"How can you stand it?" she asked, shivering.

"Keeps me out of trouble."

"Are you calling me trouble?"

"Real quick this morning, aren't you?"

He gave her a kiss that made her forget the temperature of the water, handed her the soap, and left her before he started something that they didn't have time to finish properly.

Hope didn't linger even though the water was getting hotter with each passing second. She knew how eager Mason was to get out to the well site. And so was she. Today would be the first day of drilling. Part of her was like a kid at Christmas, half-wild to unwrap the biggest present and end the suspense. The rest of her was adult, though. She wanted the well. She must have it in order for the Valley of the Sun to survive.

But when the well was dug, Rio would leave.

The smell of bacon and coffee greeted Hope as she walked down the stairs. Mason was hovering over the former and Rio handed her a steaming cup of the latter. Automatically she went to the screened porch and looked out at the dawn sky. Pure, shimmering with light and color—and absolutely devoid of clouds. It was cold, too, the kind of dry cold that made the air shine like polished crystal.

"No rain," said Mason without looking up from the bacon. "This here drought is shaping up to be a real doozy." He dragged a few crisp strips of bacon onto a paper plate to drain. "How are the troughs holding out?"

"Filled them yesterday," Rio said, sneaking a piece of bacon while Mason's back was turned. He took a big bite and fed the remaining half to Hope.

"Saw that," Mason said complacently. "May be old but I ain't blind. You doing the eggs this morning, gal, or are you gonna eat whatever I take a notion to fry?"

Hastily Hope put down her cup of coffee and began cracking eggs into a pan. Within minutes everyone was sitting down to breakfast. Silence reigned until the last bit of food was eaten. While Mason and Rio loaded lengths of pipe and plastic five-gallon cans of water and fuel into the pickup, Hope raced through the kitchen, setting up everything for dinner. The three of them climbed into the truck and started for Wind Canyon.

As soon as they turned off the main ranch road, the surface deteriorated into twin ruts snaking over and around natural obstacles. It was a road better suited to horses than to vehicles, but as long as it didn't rain, the four-wheel-drive pickup would be able to cope. Hope sat quietly between the two men. From time to time she would look covertly at Rio's profile, admiring the blunt male lines of his face and the indigo clarity of his eyes. He caught her look, took his hand off the wheel long enough to trace the line of her cheek with a gentle knuckle, then concentrated on the rugged road again.

Wind Canyon looked different to Hope now. Instead of being a dry, nearly useless piece of the ranch's history, it had become the leading edge of the Valley of the Sun's future. To Hope the air was cleaner, the sun brighter, the sage more silver, and the mountains a beautiful, jumbled treasure-trove whose riddle Rio had solved.

Rio saw the excitement on Hope's face and wanted to warn her once again that he couldn't guarantee a successful well. There was water here, no doubt about it. Water that had fallen on the mountaintops and transformed limestone into a solid, improbable sponge. Water that had sunk into the aquifer gradually and then moved through it at a pace that made a glacier look swift. Water pulled by gravity and pushed by the increasing weight of each season's rain sinking down until the aquifer became a solid river under tremendous pressure, millions upon millions of acre feet of pure cold liquid waiting to pour forth once the

impermeable stratum over it had been breached.
Water that had flowed for a million years and would
flow for a million years more.

Yes, the water was here. He could still remember its
presence rippling up through his body. But how far
down was the aquifer? And how much hard rock was
between the aquifer and the surface of the earth?
How much hard *luck* waited, too? Broken drill bits
and tools dropped into the drilling hole, injury due to
carelessness or exhaustion, water found but far too
little to do any good, too much rain making it all but
impossible to supply the drilling site.

Wryly Rio acknowledged to himself that rain didn't
seem to be a problem for a while. The rest of the list
wasn't so easily dismissed. The only way to find out
how far down the water lay was to drill until you hit it.
If you ran out of time, money, luck, or guts before
you brought in a well, you had your answer—the
water was too damned far down.

It was the time factor that ate most deeply into
Rio's confidence. He had worked as little as a week
drilling a successful well and he had worked for
months on hard luck, hard rock holes. Though Hope
hadn't said anything herself, Mason had quietly
passed on the information that the second mortgage
was due in seven weeks. She insisted that she had the
money to pay off the second and still keep the ranch
alive, but Rio knew that Hope's resources were not
infinite. He didn't want her to pour everything she
had into a useless hole in the ground.

He hoped that the aquifer was close to the surface.
But every bit of his education and instinct told him
that the water was down, way down, right at the
breaking point of money, luck, and nerve.

The pickup bucked and slithered and crabbed up
Wind Canyon's rocky bottom. In the two weeks that
Mason had been gone, Rio had used the pickup's

winch to pull out inconvenient sage clumps and taken
an axe to the piñon and juniper that were in the way.
The result was a rough track that would turn to glue
and quicksand with the first real rains. There was
neither time nor money for a better road. If it came
down to it, Rio would camp out here and bring
supplies in on horseback. He'd slept in worse places in
the past. He'd sleep in worse places in the future.
When you were drilling wells, comfort wasn't on the
list of necessary supplies.

Rio parked the pickup beside the bleak geometrics
of the old derrick he would use. Small, battered,
rusted, the derrick was nonetheless sturdy. It had
been set up in some godawful places, places where
even a professional optimist would have laughed at
the thought of water; and that ugly old derrick had
brought in well after well. The drilling machinery
itself wasn't any more impressive. It was comprised of
cannibalized parts of rigs tossed away and forgotten in
Hope's barn, plus equipment Rio had garnered in a
hundred other barns around the West. The new pieces
Hope had bought to make it all fit together stood out
like dimes dropped on a dirt floor, making everything
else look even more shabby by comparison.

"Good thing this ain't no beauty contest," said
Mason, climbing down out of the truck. "We'd lose
sure as God made little green apples."

Rio's only answer was a grunt as he shouldered
supplies out of the truck and over to the drill site.
Even though the three of them worked quickly, it
seemed like forever to Hope before everything was in
place and Rio was ready to go to work. She all but
danced with impatience as he started up the engine
that would drive the drill. The sudden thrust of sound
was appalling in the pristine silence.

Rio saw Hope's reaction, smiled, and said loudly,
"You get used to it after a while."

"Yes," she retorted. "It's called going deaf!"

Rio laughed as his long arms snaked out and lifted her up to his height. "Give me a kiss and then go over to the board and throw the number-one switch."

Eyes alight with excitement, Hope wrapped her arms around Rio and gave him a kiss that made every bit of him yearn to be alone with her. Everything about her called out to him—her sensual riches, her serene silences, her determination, and her intelligence. It was the same for Hope. She loved being close to Rio, talking with him, being silent with him. He was a river flowing through her, bringing life to everything he touched.

Rio let Hope slide down his body with an aching slowness. When he released her, she felt almost disoriented. She shook herself and went to the board attached to the derrick. Lights, dials, switches, gauges, and a tangle of wires took the pulse and temperature of the drilling equipment. She located the number-one switch and looked over her shoulder at Rio. He was standing braced, leather-gloved hands steadying the mechanism that controlled the alloy drill bit. He looked up at her and nodded.

Hope's hand swept down. Power flowed into the drill. The bit turned rapidly, making an odd, high noise. Then it touched the ground, biting into it with a grating sound. The soil was loose, alluvial. It wasn't long before the drill vanished, pulling pipe after it. Rio looked up from the drill, smiled quickly, then gave the board a single casual glance. Nothing was lit up that shouldn't be, and nothing was dark that should be glowing. He didn't really need to look at the board to know that everything was working properly. He went by the sound of the engine, the vibrations of the drill, the feel of the equipment.

He knew that the first part was going to be the fastest, the easiest, and the most rewarding time of drilling up until the instant water was struck. Other than the occasional massive boulder, the bit wouldn't have to chew through anything substantial until hard rock was reached. Out on the plains that could be thousands of feet down, for debris had been washing out of the highlands for millions of years. But here, gravity and regular flash floods had scoured the alluvial soil down to a minimum.

The well itself would be beyond the reach of those seasonal floods, because it was situated in a shallow bowl above the canyon floor. Forty extra feet of digging was a small price to pay for a well that would survive the winter floods.

After an hour or two Hope told herself that it was foolish for her to stand around and watch pipe disappear by inches. She should go back to the ranch, get on Aces, and check on the range cattle that were depending on natural water instead of the wells. There was also Sweet Dreams, another of Sweetheart's calves. Hope thought she had detected a slight hesitation in the heifer's gait, but it had been too dark to be certain. She should check on that, plus wire up the hole a coyote had dug to get to the chickens. Then there were the bills to pay and the latest tax assessment to protest.

And the drill bits—she couldn't forget them. She had to send some old ones in to be sharpened and order two special hard rock models. The expense involved had shocked her, but she hadn't protested. If Rio needed titanium alloy drills with diamond-studded teeth, that's what he would get.

Uneasiness moved through Hope as she remembered Rio's face when he had asked for the special drill bits. He had said that he might be able to get the job done with the bits he had, but it would take much too long. Though he had said nothing more, the implication was that he didn't have much more time to spend on the Valley of the Sun.

The thought made her ache, even though she had to admit that she didn't have a lot of time, either. Not when it came to the well. It was proving much more expensive to drill than she had expected. She had based her estimates on what it had cost to drill the Hope, and then had doubled it, adding a margin for error. The margin hadn't been big enough. A lot had changed since the Hope had been drilled nearly a quarter of a century ago. A combination of inflation and advanced technology had made the cost of drilling a well soar. Just buying the parts to make the used equipment work had cost more than she had budgeted to buy a whole second-hand rig. The endless bags of "mud" used to lubricate the drill hole cost nearly as much as an equal weight of grain. As for pipe—you would think from the price of it that pipe, like the bits, was made of a gem-studded space-age alloy rather than plain old-fashioned steel.

Though Hope had said nothing to Rio, she would have to dip into the money she had set aside to pay off the second mortgage in order to buy the new drill bits and the extra pipe he had ordered.

"Hope? Hope! You gone deaf, gal?" yelled Mason. He had an oil can in his hand and was poking at the engine. "I asked you three times if you're gonna check on the water out at the west end of Silver Basin."

Hope pulled herself out of her worries and answered Mason with a nod. He immediately resumed nursing the noisy engine. Hope wished she had something as useful to do here, but she didn't. All she could do for now was to brood over what the invisible drill bit was finding. It hadn't even gotten down as far as the roots of hardy desert plants. If water were that close to the surface, she wouldn't need to dig a new well here or anywhere else on the Valley of the Sun.

"Need anything?" asked Hope loudly, catching Rio's eye.

To her surprise he nodded and gestured her over to him. Wondering what they could have forgotten at the ranch, Hope stepped up to the drilling area. Rio took off his leather gloves, framed her face with his strong hands, and kissed her gently.

"You, Hope," he said against her ear, holding her close. "I need you."

Sudden tears burned in Hope's eyes. She buried her face against his neck and hung onto him with all her strength.

"I'm here," she said fiercely. "I'll always be here for you, Rio."

She felt his arms tighten until she could hardly breathe.

"Watch that third turn on the way out," he said, finally releasing her. "The wheel will buck like a steer halfway through." Then, quickly, he added, "Be careful, little dreamer. Keep that snake gun loaded."

Hope's eyes widened. "Do you think Turner will—"

"No," interrupted Rio, his voice harsh. "If I thought that he'd touch you again, ever, I'd take him up in the mountains and lose him. It's just that—" Rio made a helpless, almost angry sound and kissed her suddenly, searchingly, before he lifted his head and looked at her with eyes the color and radiance of indigo twilight. "You're so damned precious to me. The thought of anything happening to you—" He took her hand, peeled back her work glove, and saw again the bruise that he had noticed this morning. "Even such a small thing as this." His lips and tongue gently touched the bruise which was no bigger than his fingertip. "I can't explain it. I don't even understand it. I just know that the thought of you being hurt makes me bleed."

Hope saw the intensity of Rio's emotion in his eyes and felt it in the powerful, taut muscles beneath her hands. For the first time she had the tiniest stirring of hope that perhaps he wouldn't leave after the well was drilled. The possibility shivered through her, making her tremble. It was like the possibility of an artesian well, an endless upwelling of life itself transforming everything it touched. She and Rio could live on a revitalized Valley of the Sun, raising children and loving each other until the last sun had set—and still the land would go on, the water would flow, and their children would sow their own crop of dreams and know the bittersweet joys of harvest time.

Rio's breath caught at the emotion radiating from Hope's face. She had never been more beautiful to him, more alive, almost incandescent in her love for him. The thought of anything dimming that joy was a tearing agony deep within him.

Hope—my beautiful dreamer—don't let anything hurt you. Even me.

Especially me.

Chapter 12

THE DRILLING WENT SLOWLY. ONE PIECE OF EQUIPMENT after another gave out, protesting its burden and its ill-matched mates. The delays ranged from hours to days, depending on how soon a replacement part could be brought in. When the bit finally reached hard rock, the pace of the drilling slowed to inches, then to fractions of inches, despite the special bits. The engine that drove the drill was too old to push for long hours at top speed.

The stratum of hard rock was thick and unyielding. No water hid within it, for there was no place within the dense crystalline stone for liquid. Everything soft had been cooked out when the rock was deep within the earth's mantle, where the heat and pressure were so great that solid rock strata melted and deformed like great layers of wax. Rio changed bits, drilled, changed bits again, and drilled again. The unvarying work and the noise were numbing. Progress slowed to increments that were measured in frustration and increasing incidents of mechanical breakdown.

Hope stopped asking how the work was coming. The lines on Rio's face, and on Mason's, told her all she needed to know. She drove the men to Wind Canyon at dawn, picked them up at dark, and ran the ranch in between. The rains still hadn't come in enough quantity so that the cattle were free of the troughs. She hauled water from the Turner ranch, and she did it with a rifle for company. Turner hadn't shown up again. She hoped he wouldn't. Just the thought of his thick arrogance made anger run like molten rock in her veins.

People from town and from Turner's ranch began to show up at the Gardener ranch house. They always had an excuse—a saddle to sell or to buy, a mare to be bred, invitations to Christmas barbecues. Invariably the conversation circled around to what was really on the visitor's mind. *How's the well doing, Hope? Strike anything promising yet? Hell of a place to drill, clear up in a canyon. Everybody knows that water goes down, not up. You lookin' for artesian water? Ain't never heard of no artesian well around here, and my grandaddy was born just the other side of your ranch. Don't envy you none. Drilling wells is expensive as hell these days, and the price of beef just ain't worth mentioning.*

Those were the most tactful people. The others, including a few of Turner's men, began looking at Hope as if by becoming Rio's woman she had declared herself available to every male within a hundred miles. None of them said or did anything out of line, because none of them wanted to take on the kind of grief Rio would give them. But they looked at her with a lecherous speculation that made her angry. *Hear Mason went up to Salt Lake for Thanksgiving.*

Musta been lonely for you, huh? Oh, yeah, Rio was here, wasn't he? Gotta hand it to him. That drifter has a good eye for how the land lays. Hear he tried to buy a ranch around here a time back. Didn't have no money, though. Bet your little ranch looks real good to him.

Hope ignored their insinuations and sideways looks, staring them coolly in the eye until the men shifted uneasily and allowed as how it was time for them to be getting back to town or to Turner's ranch or to whatever hole they had crawled out of. She turned down all invitations and issued none herself, having neither the time nor the inclination for holiday parties.

The hard stratum had finally given way to softer rock. There had been a moment of breathless anticipation when Rio had brought up a core sample. The stone was dry, as dry as the hardest quartzite. There was no aquifer at this level. The drilling went faster, though, expensive pipe and lubricant vanishing down the hole in the earth as though there were no end short of China. Rio said nothing, simply drilled and kept on drilling through compacted soils older than man, strata that had been laid down long before true mammals walked the earth, drilling down and down and down, pouring money and dreams into the dry land and getting nothing back but dulled or broken drill bits and blistered hands.

Then Mason's hands got too bad for him to work. Hope saw it one morning, when he could hardly pick up the pot of coffee. She looked at Rio and saw the same knowledge in his dark eyes. Mason's hands wouldn't heal unless he rested them—and he was too proud and too stubborn to admit it. His pain showed in the tight lines of his face and the dark circles beneath his eyes.

"I have to go into town this morning," said Hope

quietly. "Mason, I want you to stay at the house. There have been too many people coming through here lately, and some of them I've never seen before." She looked up at Rio. "You can get along without him for a day, can't you?"

"I'll manage," said Rio with just the right mix of reluctance and acceptance in his voice.

Hope thanked him with her eyes. "Do you need anything up at the well?" she continued, ignoring Mason's mutterings to the effect that he didn't want to "baby-sit no damn house" when there was work to be done.

Rio handed over a list. Just before Hope's fingers closed over it he pulled back. "We've barely got enough pipe and mud left to cover the normal lead time in ordering. There's only one hard rock bit that's still sharp for when we hit another solid stratum. The other bits are in the pickup."

Hope nodded and took the list, trying not to show her dismay. She had already taken part of the money that had been earmarked for the second mortgage. Now she would have to go take even more. She had been prepared for that, however. That was the reason for her trip into town today. She was going to try to renegotiate the second mortgage for another year. Or six months. Two months. One. Enough time for Rio to drill down to the artesian water that lay beneath the dry land, waiting for the silver moment of release.

She knew that the water was there. She knew that Rio wanted to find it with the same intensity that she did, perhaps even more. He called himself a man without dreams, yet she sensed that this well was Rio's dream in everything but name. No matter how many people had told her it was impossible, she had not flinched in the face of her own dream of living on the Valley of the Sun. She would not flinch in the face of Rio's dream, his need. She would give him all the time she had, all the pipe she could buy, all the drill bits, all of it.

"Aren't you even going to ask me how close we are to water?" asked Rio, looking at her with clear blue-black eyes.

"Do you know?"

"No."

"Then," said Hope with a gentle smile, "there's no point in asking, is there?"

Rio caught her hand, rubbed his cheek against her palm, kissed it in silent thanks. "After nearly four weeks of drilling and nothing to show but dry rock, most people would be all over me like a bad smell."

"Most people don't have enough sense to come in out of the rain," she retorted.

"Dreamer," he said huskily, kissing her palm again. "My beautiful dreamer."

The warmth of that moment stayed with Hope all through the long drive to town. She ordered the drilling supplies first, paying a hefty charge for a rush delivery. Then she went to the small brick building that had a freshly painted sign out front: RANCHERS TRUST AND SAVINGS. The loan officer was expecting her. He had been expecting her since checks had started coming through her money market account, eating into the funds that he knew she had reserved for the balloon payment on the second mortgage. He was a patient man. He let her go through her entire speech with barely a frown to wrinkle the loose skin of his forehead.

And then he said no.

He explained quite lucidly that she was basing her request for a loan extension on a fool's dream, a well being dug up a godforsaken canyon by a half-breed troublemaker who had nothing to his name but a

five-year-old pickup truck and a horse he said he'd
caught running loose. The loan officer concluded by
saying that the only way she could get an extension
would be to find a co-signer for the note. Then he
picked up the ringing telephone, listened, and excused
himself from the small office where loan interviews
were conducted.

Hope sat for a minute, gathering herself for the
long drive back to the ranch. She felt as though an icy
northern wind had blown over her, sapping her
strength. The refusal hadn't been unexpected, not
really. It had been very final, though. There was
nothing in the man's manner to give her any grounds
for hoping that he might change his mind in the few
weeks between now and the day that the note was
due.

The door opened and closed behind Hope. She
turned around, expecting to see the loan officer again.
What she saw was John Turner.

"Now, what kind of look is that for the man who's
going to save your ranch?" asked Turner, smiling.
"We're going to make a deal, you and me. I'll co-sign
that note and you come to heel when I snap my
fingers. No more giving away to drifters what I'm
paying good money for, either. You cross your legs
and you cross them tight or I'll beat—" He stopped
abruptly and pulled a sheaf of papers out of his
pocket. "Take your choice, babe. Me and your ranch
or nothing. And don't kid yourself," he said, tossing
down the papers in front of her. "That blankethead
won't hang around once we foreclose on the Valley of
the Sun."

All the pressures Hope had been under exploded in
her mind. All the disappointments, the fears, the
endless quest for water, the knowledge that Rio
would leave when water was found—everything.

Rage swept through her, evaporating the despair she had felt, replacing it with a storm of adrenaline. She stood up suddenly, her eyes narrow.

"Get out of my way," she said. Her voice was soft, low, vibrating with anger.

Turner walked toward her, stopping just short of her, so close that he could smell the subtle perfume she used.

"Need a pen?" he asked, almost brushing the back of his arm over her breast as he reached inside his suitcoat pocket.

"What kind of flowers do you want?" asked Hope.

"Flowers?" Turner frowned, nonplussed.

"For your funeral."

He flushed angrily. "I haven't laid a finger on you, and if you tell Rio any different, you're lying!"

"You won't have to wait for Rio," she said, her voice brittle with contempt. "I'm not your victim to bully or to crawl all over in your bathroom fantasies. If you touch me, I'll come after you myself. And I won't use a kitchen knife this time. I'll use a rifle."

For a moment there was only silence cut by the thick sound of air being drawn into Turner's lungs through nostrils pinched by rage. His lips twisted into a cruel smile.

"I'll see you on January sixteenth, at your ranch house, and the sheriff will be right with me," said Turner in an ugly voice. "That's the day you'll beg to crawl into my pants. I'm going to enjoy hearing every word of it."

"It won't happen," Hope said, certainty in every syllable. "I'm not like the other women you've hounded and bought and bullied into bed. I'm not like the men you've dangled money in front of and leaned on until it was easier for them to sell you their stock or real estate or mistress than it was to make you angry by continuing to say no." She paused, then asked with real curiosity, "Have you ever wanted something that didn't belong to someone else? Ever? Even once in your spoiled life?"

Turner's only answer was the red flush crawling up his face.

"That's what I thought," she said quietly. "You're still a baby. You're buried in toys, but the only one you want is the one you see someone else holding. You're obsessed with it—until you get it. Then you drop the new toy and look around to see what other people are playing with. You've never grown up. But that's your problem, Turner. Not mine. Not anymore. No matter what happens with the ranch, with Rio, with anything at all, *I will never be your toy.*"

Hope waited for several minutes after Turner slammed out of the room. Slowly the adrenaline seeped out of her, leaving her face pale and her muscles like sand. When her hands no longer trembled she picked up her purse and let herself out. Other than a few curious stares from tellers who knew her, no one seemed interested in what had happened in the tiny office. She took a detour a few miles out of town to a small house where a silversmith lived. There she picked up her presents for Mason and Rio. She couldn't believe that Christmas was only a few days away. She had never felt less like celebrating.

As soon as Hope pulled into the ranch yard she ran into the pasture to check on the Angus herd. Sweetheart came walking over, radiating muscular health with every stride. Her eyes were clear and deep, like pools of liquid darkness shining out from the midnight sea of her winter-thickened coat.

"Sweetheart, you're so beautiful that you make me feel like a frump," said Hope, rubbing the cow lovingly. She gave her a pan of grain, then shook the feed sack until the other cows became interested. Quickly she poured out a long, thin line of grain. As the black cattle lined up, she watched their movements critically. None of them appeared lame now.

For a few moments Hope simply stood and looked at her cattle, reassuring herself that everything was well with the Angus. Without realizing it she smiled, feeling better just for being among the healthy, handsome herd. The cows had a solid, earthy reality that had always made her believe in the possibility of her dream of a rejuvenated ranch. She was looking at more than beautiful animals. She was looking at the future of the Valley of the Sun.

"Good night, Sweetheart," she whispered. "And you, too, Sweet Dreams. Grow big and strong and gorgeous, just like your mom."

Humming quietly to herself, Hope unloaded the truck and began dinner. By the time Mason came back from picking up Rio, there was just enough time for him to shower before dinner. Hope called out a cheerful ranch greeting to Rio when she heard him coming down the stairs to dinner.

"Come and get it or I'll feed it to the pigs!"

Rio usually responded by grabbing her and kissing her soundly. This time, however, he simply held her as though she were in need of comfort—or he himself was.

"Long day?" she asked softly.

His arms simply tightened around her. "Hit more stone," he said. "Finally got through it." Then, "It's dry on the other side, too."

Hope felt cold spreading through her. She put her lips against his neck and counted the beats of his heart for a long, silent moment. Then she stirred and smiled up at him. "Come on, you'll feel better after you eat."

Rio moved his thumbs gently over her cheekbones and lips. He started to speak, then kissed her with a tenderness that brought a sheen of tears to her eyes.

"There is no one like you," he said simply.

That night Rio told her again, differently, wordlessly, taking her and being taken in turn, giving himself to the endless passion and shattering release that only Hope had ever called from him. He no longer questioned the urgent upwellings of her need and his own, the hot perfection of their fused bodies, the sense of rightness he felt all the way to his soul when he held her asleep in his arms. There were times when he wished that he could drill for water in Wind Canyon forever, finding nothing but the unbelievable joys of this woman's love.

Yet Rio knew he must find water, ending this dream and beginning another, Hope's dream of a Valley of the Sun that lived again. He must find it soon, for he knew that the longer he stayed the more he would hurt her when he left. And the thought of hurting her was like hot metal drilling through his flesh and bone to his soul.

The next morning Rio told Hope that he would start drilling around the clock.

"We're running out of time," he said. "The well has to be in by January fifteenth. Otherwise you'll never get the bank to extend your loan."

She looked at him and shook her head slowly. The darkness in Rio's eyes was more than she could bear. "I can pay off the second mortgage, Rio. There's no need for you to kill yourself working double and triple shifts. We have as much time as you need."

He gave her a look that shook her to her soul, as though he sensed that she was talking about more than the well being drilled through layers of rock and time into an undiscovered past and an even more enigmatic future.

"One of Mason's grandnephews is coming in after Christmas," said Rio. "I won't start until then."

Hope didn't object again. If Rio saw the pain beneath her silent agreement, he said nothing.

They spent Christmas Eve out at the well site. Hope strung lights on the derrick, hung popcorn and cranberry strings over nearby sagebrush, and cooked the turkey over a spit that Rio and Mason had rigged. They sang all the old carols, Hope's true alto mixing with Rio's bass while Mason played a scarred harmonica with surprising skill. Tears ran down both Hope's and Mason's cheeks as the music brought back people and Christmases past. When there were no more carols to sing, they toasted Christmas and the well and one another with cut-crystal glasses of rye that caught and multiplied every colorful light strung from the derrick.

For a time there was only silence and the wind and the special peace that came with the season. Finally Mason stood, stretched, and went to the truck. He returned quickly, two gifts in hand. For Rio there was a hatband tanned from a rattlesnake that had made the mistake of taking up residence near the pasture trough. For Hope there was a strip of the same foolish snake made into a belt. Rio gave Mason a new pair of leather work gloves that were tough and yet flexible enough not to bind knuckles sore from arthritis.

Hope went over to the box of kitchen supplies that she had brought up for dinner. Inside she had concealed two small presents. She gave Mason his package first. The silver buckle she had bought for him was a hammered oval with a running horse inset in mother-of-pearl. Mason held the buckle in his gnarled hands, admiring the play of firelight across the silver and pearl surface. Then he chuckled, went over to the bright work light in the shed on the far side of the derrick, pulled off his belt, and began replacing his old brass buckle with the new silver.

While Mason worked, Hope handed Rio his present. He looked at her for a long moment, holding the small package in his hands before he began unwrapping it. Inside the box, nested within layers of tissue paper, was a bracelet made of a single piece of cast silver. There was just enough of a gap in the oval circlet that it could be fitted over a man's wrist. The curved surface of the bracelet was inlaid with pieces of polished turquoise in a rippling-wave pattern that was the Indian symbol for Rio's name. Inside the solid band the silversmith had inscribed the phrase: *For as long as the water flows.*

Rio felt the cool perfection of the silver with his fingertips, read the phrase, and felt emotion wrench through him. He fitted the bracelet on his arm with a smooth twist of his hand. The silver glowed against his dark skin. The wavy lines of the river symbol seemed to flow with each shift of wind and flames. He looked up at Hope, firelight and emotion reflected in his eyes. He could not remember the last time that someone had given him a present, much less something so perfectly suited to him.

"Thank you," he whispered, pulling her down into his lap, kissing her gently, repeatedly, as though he were afraid that she would slide through his fingers like the wind if he tried to hold her tightly. "It's like you. Unexpected. Perfect."

For a moment he pulled away from her. He opened his collar and moved his hands to his neck.

"There's no fancy wrapping on your gift. I wanted to give it to you the same way I got it long ago, warm with the giver's own life," he said, lifting an Indian necklace from its concealment beneath his shirt. "This was my great-grandmother's, my grandmother's, and my mother's. Mother gave it to me when she left me with my grandfather and went back to the city."

The necklace shimmering in Rio's hands was in the

traditional squash-blossom pattern, but instead of hammered silver crescents and turquoise stones, the blossoms were made from dimes more than a century old. It was a riveting synthesis of white and Indian culture, with a stately beauty and history that made chills move over Hope.

"Rio, I can't take—"

He silenced her with a kiss. His fingers unbuttoned her blouse and then his hands circled her neck. She felt the smooth, oddly reassuring weight of the necklace against her breasts. The silver was like a caress as it radiated back the heat of Rio's body.

"Rio—" began Hope helplessly.

"My grandmother told me that one day I would find the right woman to wear this necklace. I never believed her until I saw you by Turner's well with water running like liquid silver from your cupped hands." He kissed her lips softly. "Perhaps some day your daughter will wear this necklace and you'll tell her about the man who gave it to you. I can think of no greater gift than that this silver be warmed by a child born of your body."

"What—what about your children?" she asked, her throat aching.

Rio's smile was like a knife turning in Hope. It was just as painful for him. "I wanted a woman to have my baby once. It was in the city, before I'd accepted that I was what my grandfather had named me. Brother-to-the-wind. The woman loved me but she wasn't Indian. She didn't want to have mixed children."

"Then she didn't love you," said Hope flatly.

He shook his head slowly. "No, she was just being honest. I've always been grateful to her for that. Another kind of woman wouldn't have told me until we were married. It happened like that to my cousin."

"I'm not like that," said Hope, her voice shaking. "I want—"

But Rio was still speaking, refusing to hear her, and his words were like knives turning in Hope. *"I'll never again ask a woman to bear my child."*

Hope bowed her head and fought the tears that threatened to overwhelm her, hearing Rio's lifetime of isolation summarized in his relentless words. She wondered if she were carrying his baby now, if after he was gone she would one day give a warm silver necklace to a child he had never known.

For a long time there was only silence and the keening of the wind as it blew down the canyon and poured transparently into the basin below. As Rio's hand moved slowly, repeatedly, over Hope's hair, the silver band on his wrist glowed with reflections of the firelight. Even more brilliant were the cascading stars and the glittering, ghostly river of the Milky Way overhead.

Mason returned to the campfire, proudly wearing his new buckle. If he saw the gleam of tears on Hope's face, he said nothing. As the fire burned low the coyotes came out and sang their own carols. Ancient harmonies shivered through the darkness with an eerie beauty that made it easy to believe in spirits and gods walking across the face of the night.

"My grandfather loved Christmas," said Rio quietly. He sensed Hope's surprise in the sudden turning of her head against his shoulder. "It's true. It was the only time that the white-eyes gathered in family clans and sang the songs of power with their souls in their voices. He said he could feel the Great Spirit flowing through the churches like a rain wind, sweeping away the dust of the previous year."

"Then why didn't he become a Christian?" asked Hope softly.

"He did."

"But I thought he was a shaman."

"He was." Rio pulled Hope even closer between

his knees, brushed his lips over her sage-scented hair, and tried to explain. "Oh, he knew there were other gods, lesser gods, Indian gods, but he was convinced that the white man's God was superior. For Indians the proof of power is in day-to-day living. His children spoke a European language, learned European history, and worshipped a European god. That was power."

Rio hesitated, then added softly, "But the coyotes still sing harmonies older than man, the rains still can be called from a cloudless sky, and the wind still is brother to a few men. For Grandfather that, too, was power." There was a pause and then Rio's chest moved against Hope's back in silent laughter. "He had a devil of a time convincing Grandmother, though. She prayed for his half-heathen soul until the day she died."

"Is he still alive?" asked Hope softly.

"Yes," said Rio, brushing his lips over Hope's hair. "He's part of the coyote's song and the long cry of the wind. He's a phrase from a white man's carol and a breath of the power pouring through a Christmas church. There was room in his soul for all of them. I like to think there's room for him now in all of them."

Mason's soft "amen" came from across the campfire.

The wind gusted, sending a shower of sparks upward in an incandescent spiral.

Mason stretched wearily and stood. "Well, I'm gonna take these old bones back to a soft bed."

"I'll bring Hope back in a while," said Rio.

"Suit yourself." Mason walked beyond the range of the campfire and climbed stiffly into Hope's truck.

"What about you?" she asked Rio. "Aren't you going to stay at the house?"

"I brought up a bedroll and mattress earlier."

"Big enough for two?" asked Hope, sliding her

fingers beneath his denim jacket, seeking the warm flesh between the snaps on his shirt.

Rio's body tightened at Hope's touch, as though her fingers were molten silver instead of flesh. He stood up, pulling her with him, and led her to the bed he had made in the lee of a big clump of sage. There he made exquisite, consuming love to her. Like a passionate wind he whispered her beauty and her sensuality, sang of his own need to fill every hollow of her, and then came to her and moved within her, telling her with his touch those secrets that only the wind knew. Again and again he brought her to shivering completion, knowing her with an intimacy that was greater with each touch, each instant, each movement of his powerful body over hers. When she wept his name in her ecstasy, he gave himself to her and to the silver rains he had called from the desert of his own need.

Long before dawn the drill was turning again, chewing down through solid rock, dragging a long steel straw behind. As the days passed, softer rock gave way to harder and then to softer again, a layer of sandstone that was damp but not wet, as though the years had leached all but a shadow of water from the rock. No matter how many times the engine broke down or how many cores came up dry, Rio said nothing; but his eyes were black and his mouth was bracketed with grim lines of exhaustion and determination. The teenager who had come from Salt Lake to help him worked with the tireless strength of youth. Mason worked with the unflinching endurance of a man who knew his own limits and had not yet reached them.

Every afternoon Hope came to them, bringing supplies and a smile. Except once. One day she didn't come to the drilling site because she knew she could not smile, not then. She had just sold every last head of stock on the Valley of the Sun except Storm Walker. The stallion was spared because he had been promised to Rio as a sire for as long as the water flowed.

The second mortgage was paid off that afternoon, as was the shipment of drilling supplies. Hope drove back to a ranch empty of cattle, and to Storm Walker's endless, resonating whinnies as he searched for the four mares that had been loaded up and shipped out that morning. The stallion's desolate calls were echoed in Hope's emotions as she looked out over a pasture empty of black Angus. She stood and watched the sunset mirrored in the half-full, utterly useless trough.

When she turned around, Rio was there.

"Where are they?" he demanded, but there was no real question in his voice. He knew what had happened just as surely as he knew the date: January 15.

"McNally in Utah bought them." She smiled sadly. "He was delighted when I called. Said he'd regretted selling Sweetheart to me ever since he heard about her calves."

"And Storm Walker's mares," said Rio harshly. "Did you sell them, too?"

"Yes."

"Christ." Rio closed his eyes like a man who had seen too much. His hands clenched into fists that strained the leather of his work gloves. "Hope, my degree in hydrology doesn't guarantee a well! The money from the cattle should have gone for a new life for you somewhere else, not for a goddamned useless hole in the ground!"

Hope went to him and put her hands on the coiled strength of his shoulders. "I didn't sell my cattle out of faith in your degree, Rio. I've seen you move over the land. I've seen your uncanny communication with it. I've seen you feel the presence of water beneath your feet. Your gift is as mysterious, as intangible, and as real as my love for you."

Hope watched Rio's eyes open. Her breath caught at the dark tumult of emotions reflected in them. "Rio, I know the water is there. If it's possible to drill down to it, you will. If it's possible to pay for the drilling, I will. And if it's impossible, then we'll at least live the rest of our lives knowing that we did everything we could, no bets hedged, nothing held back. There's no shame or regret in losing that way. There's only shame and regret in not trying!"

Rio stared at Hope with sudden raw intensity. He didn't know that he made a choked sound as he reached out and crushed her within his arms. He knew only that no one had understood and accepted so much of what was hidden beneath his rough surface.

And Rio also knew that he would find water for her if he had to drill down to hell itself.

First Mason and then his grandnephew succumbed to the exhaustion of working around the clock. Hope came to the drilling site and stayed, working alongside Rio, blistering her hands and scraping herself raw on the unfamiliar equipment. She lay down with him at night, falling asleep in his arms even as she felt their warmth and strength closing around her—and sometimes she awakened beneath a glittering canopy of stars and felt Rio's mouth and hands caressing her until she couldn't breathe for wanting him. It was then that she dreamed the search for water could go on forever, keeping Rio here with her on the Valley of the Sun.

And then one morning the sun came up with a rumble and a drawn-out groan of thunder. Between one instant and the next Rio snatched Hope from her station by the derrick board.

"Run!" he said, clamping his hand on her arm and all but yanking her out of her boots.

"What's wrong?" she gasped when Rio finally stopped running and turned back to look at the rig.

"It's going to rain, little dreamer," he said triumphantly, grinning down at her. "It's going to rain for a thousand years!"

She looked at the dry, cloudless sky and thought that he had gone mad.

Thunder rumbled and the derrick groaned.

"Rio? Is it—" She stopped speaking, almost afraid to believe.

"Yes!" he answered, laughing exultantly.

Water rushed up out of the drill hole like a bright silver spear, rising above the derrick before the flow fanned out into a jeweled curtain of water scintillating with every color of the dawn. After the initial, almost explosive release, the artesian fountain gradually diminished to half its former height and began dancing in graceful spurts and pulses that reflected the massive, hidden rhythms of the earth.

Hope turned and ran back down the canyon, not stopping until the brilliant, transparent drops of water rained down over her. She held out her arms as though she would embrace the dancing fountain. Then she turned and threw herself into Rio's arms. She licked silver drops from his eyebrow, his cheek, his lips.

"Sweet," she said, laughing and crying at once.

He kissed drops from her eyelashes and lips. "Very sweet," he murmured.

"The water," said Hope, nuzzling against him. "I was afraid it might be a saltwater well. But it's sweet, so sweet."

"Not as sweet as you," he whispered.

She threaded her fingers into his straight black hair, feeling the warmth of him welling up beneath the cool veneer of artesian water. "Thank you," she breathed.

She repeated it again and again and again until the words blended into kisses and she felt passion shimmer through her. But instead of responding as he always had, Rio gently lowered Hope until her feet were on the ground.

The dawn wind blew through the canyon, whispering the secrets of the land.

"We should tell Mason," said Rio.

He dipped his head for a kiss so fiercely yearning that Hope trembled even as she returned it. He released her quickly, yet his fingers slid down her arms as though he could not bear to end the contact. His eyes were as dark as a night with no stars, as empty as the wind curling through the canyon, calling his name.

"Rio?" she asked, sensing that something was wrong.

And then she heard the cry of the wind and knew. She started shaking and could not stop.

"N-no," she whispered, closing her eyes. "Not yet. Not now!"

Suddenly she turned away from him, jamming her fist against her mouth to stop the flow of words she had promised herself she would never speak. She fought to control her emotions, knowing that if she came apart now it would destroy everything that she and Rio had, even memories. She must not make him feel guilty for giving her what she had asked—demanded—of him. She had been strong so many times in her life. She had to be strong once more. Just for a few minutes. Just long enough to say good-bye to the man she loved.

"Hope," said Rio, trying to be gentle. His voice was held so tightly that it was unrecognizable. "I'm sorry," he said hoarsely. "Don't you see? If I don't go now, it will just be worse when I do leave." Then, with a self-hatred that clawed at both of them, he added bitterly, "I never should have touched you!"

After a long moment Hope turned back to him, her face desperately calm. "You gave me as much as you could," she said in a throaty voice, "and that was much more than I ever expected from any man. Don't be angry with yourself for that, Rio. I'm not. I love you—*and I know that my love isn't enough for you.* I knew it before I fell in love." Her voice softened as she held her hand out to the brilliant dance of water. "You gave me my dream. I would give you your dream, but you don't have one, and the one I dreamed for you wasn't strong enough. So I'll give you all I can, all you want. The freedom of the wind."

"Hope—" Rio's voice tightened into silence. His hands clenched again. "Oh, God, I wish I were a different man!"

"No!" She closed her eyes, not trusting herself to look at or touch him, hearing his anger at himself twisting destructively through every word. "Don't hate yourself, Rio. If you do that, you'll hate me, too. I couldn't bear that. If you think of me at all, remember that I loved you. All of you. Even the wind."

For an instant she thought she felt the warmth of his breath against her lips. Then the wind blew, taking everything away, the warmth and the man. When her eyes finally opened again, she was alone.

"I love you, Brother-to-the-wind," she whispered.

Nothing answered but the dance of artesian water.

Chapter 13

HOPE DROVE THE PICKUP OVER THE ROUGH ROAD LEAD-
ing into Wind Canyon. The man in the passenger seat
looked at the dry, harsh land expressionlessly. He
glanced up at the forbidding Perdidas and the steep,
eroded foothills. He shifted in the seat and sighed.

"If you'd told me there was water here, I'd have
said you were crazy," he said flatly.

Hope gave Bill Hunter a quick glance and concentrated again on the road, saying only, "A lot of people
thought I was. Including the Reno bank you work for.
That's why they're demanding a survey of the well
before they even consider a loan."

Silently Hope thought about the Turner bank. She
hadn't bothered to ask for another loan from them
even after the well had come in. She would never
again put herself in debt to anyone related to John
Turner.

"Who brought the well in for you?" Hunter asked
curiously.

"A man called Rio."

"Rio?" Hunter turned suddenly, his face alive with interest. "Tall man? Looks like an Indian except for his eyes?"

"Yes." Hope's voice was clipped, almost curt.

"Well, hell, if the bank had told me that, I'd have saved us all a trip. If Rio brought in your well, it's as good as gold. Better," he added, chuckling. "Cattle can't drink gold."

She tried not to ask, but her hunger for news of Rio was greater than her pride. Maybe Hunter had seen or heard from Rio. "Do you know Rio?" she asked as casually as she could.

Hunter shrugged. "Can't say as anyone really *knows* Rio. We went to school together."

Again Hope looked quickly at the hydrologist.

"Yeah, I know. I look older than him," said Hunter. "I am. Rio was barely sixteen when he started at the School of Mines. He had his master's before he was twenty. Most brilliant man I've ever met." Hunter braced himself as the truck lurched over a particularly rough patch of road. "Loneliest, too. Being an Indian is no treat in some parts of the West. A lot of men would have grown up real mean if they'd been treated like Rio. Not him, though. He'd just go out into the mountains for a while and then come back . . . soothed, I guess. Yeah. Soothed." Hunter smiled rather grimly. "Course, the fact that he beat the hell out of more than one redneck son of a bitch soothed him from time to time, too, I imagine."

Hope's hands tightened on the wheel until her knuckles were white. She couldn't bear the thought of Rio being hurt for no better reason than an accident of birth. Like the woman who was so blind and so stupid that she had refused to have Rio's child. The thought of that enraged Hope. She would have given up even the well if she could have had Rio's baby.

Maybe this time. Maybe this is the month my period won't come.

"How'd you meet him?" asked Hunter.

He had to repeat the question twice before Hope heard him.

"People told him I needed a well. Desperately."

Hunter nodded. "Yeah. That's Rio. Funny thing. He could have been rich ten times over. He could have taken that money and crammed it down the throats of every redneck he ever met. He didn't, though. He just drifted until he found someone that life had really dumped on. If they had the grit to fight, he'd help them. They paid him in crops or cattle or a place to sleep—whatever they could afford. Bet that he's got stock scattered all over the West. But never money. No way."

"They paid him in dreams," she said, thinking aloud.

"What?"

"Rio is a man without dreams," explained Hope softly, sadly. "When he finds people who can dream, he helps them."

There was a long silence during which Hunter reassessed the woman who sat beside him. "Never thought of it that way, but you're dead right," he said finally. "You must have got closer to him than most."

Hope said nothing.

"Damn shame someone didn't help Rio when he was still young enough to dream," continued Hunter, lighting up a cigarette and blowing smoke out the open window. "Hell of a childhood. Mother and father drank, and he ran loose in the streets. When he got too wild they dumped him on his grandparents and took off."

"How old was he?"

"Twelve, thirteen." Hunter took a hard drag on the cigarette and sighed. "Don't know what his grandfather did to straighten Rio out. That was one tough old Indian, from all I hear. Had about as much give in him as a rock."

Hope concentrated on the road, but it was Rio she saw, a younger Rio, defiant and lonely. "Are his parents still alive?"

"Not hardly. They wrapped their car around a telephone pole on the way home from a bar. Rio must have been about fifteen then."

She flinched.

"Rough road," commented Hunter, hanging on to the armrest as the truck jolted over a pile of rocks.

It wasn't the road that had brought the grim lines to Hope's face. She said nothing, though. She didn't trust her voice. She wanted Hunter to keep talking, to share with her his memories of Rio, every one of them. She felt that if she could collect enough memories, enough pieces of Rio, he would be whole again— and so would she.

"You must be a friend of Rio's," said Hope finally. "You know a lot about him."

Hunter smiled and drew on the cigarette again. "More like a fan. Rio's kind of a hobby with me."

Hope glanced at Hunter, her hazel eyes dark. "Why?"

"I did my thesis on dowsing. I thought it was a crock of stuff, no two ways about it. Rio heard about the thesis. Upshot of it was that he and I went head-to-head on a piece of desert west of here." Hunter smiled ruefully, remembering. "He was maybe seventeen, but you forgot that when you looked him in the eye. He was one tough hombre even then. He found water before I'd finished my preliminary survey." Hunter shifted on the bouncing seat and looked out the window at the unpromising land. "Finding water is my profession—and I'm damned if I can figure out how water-witching works. So I collect stories about dowsing while I'm out doing hydrological surveys. Rio's name comes up regular as the sun. He's been finding water since he was thirteen."

Hope made a startled sound.

"It's true," said Hunter, stubbing out his cigarette. "I know a lot of facts about him—his parents, grandparents, the wells he's found, the people he's helped, the horses he's tamed, the men he's fought, the women he could have had and didn't. But I don't know anything about him, not really. Not even his name. No one does. A real private kind of man. Never shared his secrets with anyone."

My true name is Brother-to-the-wind.

Rio's words echoed in Hope's mind, making her throat ache and her eyes burn with unshed tears. He had shared so much with her, given so much to her, taken so much less from her than she wanted to give.

The truck slithered over the last sandy patch in the road, breasted a small rise, and looked down into a rippling silver bowl of water where a small artesian fountain danced above the surface of the new pond. The hydrologist got out as though in a trance, never looking away from the silver transformations of the water. Hope stood next to him, feeling the wind caress her skin with restless, transparent fingers.

"I'll be damned," said Hunter reverently.

He shook himself and hauled out some forms, asking questions rapidly, filling in the blanks with a mechanical pencil as she answered. When she told him how deep Rio had gone to get water, the pencil paused. Hunter whistled soundlessly.

"You got guts, lady. Anyone else would have given up halfway down." Then, sighing, "No wonder you're broke." He paused. "Heard you sold everything but your stud to pay for the well."

Hope closed her eyes, haunted by memories of beautiful black Angus waiting patiently for grain. "Yes," she said curtly.

Hunter measured the height of the artesian fountain falling into the pond that had filled the hollow where the well had been drilled. "How much has the fountain gone down since it first came in?"

"It didn't diminish at all after the first few minutes."

Hunter hesitated. "Going to put a lid on that fountain?"

"Not right away. I know I should, but—" Her words stopped.

"Yeah, I know what you mean. It's something to see, isn't it? You know, you could put a small dam down in that crease." He pointed toward a dip in the rim of land surrounding the pond. There, water flowed out toward the canyon floor below, creating a stream where none had ever before flowed. "Drill a pipe through the base of the rim and let gravity do the rest. If that's not enough punch, install a wind-driven pump. That way you could have piped water and your artesian pond, too."

Hope smiled, pleased by the idea. Hunter looked startled for a moment. It was the first time she had smiled in the hours that he had been with her.

"Don't worry about your ranch, ma'am. When the bank gets my recommendations, they'll lend you enough to get started again. It won't be a quarter what you need," he added bluntly, "because wells are dicey things. But you've got plenty of guts. You'll make it."

"Thank you."

"Don't thank me," he said, watching the rippling water with something close to awe. "Thank Rio. For a man without dreams, he sure as hell has made a lot of them come true."

"Let 'er rip, honey!" said Mason, grinning as he put a final twist on the connection that would bring water from Rio's well into the old network that had been serviced by the Hope.

She opened the valve and heard water churn into the cistern buried beneath her feet. Behemoth had made its last run to Rio's well to bring water. The ancient truck had been replaced by a costly, gleaming pipeline snaking back along the old road starting from the ranch house and leading into Wind Canyon's shadowed depths. Soon the other pipelines would be finished, too, thick silver straws leading to troughs where range cattle could drink during the dry months of summer, and crops could be irrigated. But there was no hurry, for there were no cattle yet. It was the wrong season to buy just-weaned calves. That would come in autumn, after the alfalfa and oat hay crops had been brought in. If the crops were good, she would be able to afford to buy more than beef calves for the Valley of the Sun.

Autumn. Rio had come to her in the autumn, telling her that he would find water. It had been in autumn that he had first made love to her while a cold wind blew. The memory shook her even as wind had shaken the house that night. She had thought that with the passing days her memories would grow weaker. But they had not. They had grown even as the life in her womb grew, thriving in the secret places of her body, stronger with each hour. She could hardly wait until next autumn, when Rio's baby would be born. She ached to hold it to her breast and hear its tiny cries.

"Prettiest sound I ever did hear," said Mason with satisfaction, listening to the rush of water.

He looked at Hope, realizing that she wasn't listening. He frowned and bit back a curse. She hadn't been the same since Rio had left. It wasn't just that she didn't smile easily or laugh at all. She was different. A woman now, no girl left in her. The Valley of the Sun had always been important to her, but it was more than that now. It was everything. In the three months since Rio had left, other men had come to the ranch. They had asked Hope to church and to barbecues, to movies and to parties. Her answer was always the same, no matter how handsome or respectful the man was—no. Mason had chided her once. The look in her eye had been enough to make him want to run, but all she had said was, "I'm a one-man woman."

The sound of a heavy truck driving into the yard between the barn and the house pulled Hope out of her autumn dreams. She looked at Mason. He shook his head.

"Nope, I didn't order nothing."

Rio! He's come back!

The thought came and went like lightning—hot, blinding. She didn't know that there was a flash of raw hope on her face as she turned and ran toward the sound. Nor did she know that every bit of light faded from her eyes when she saw that a stranger drove the truck.

"Lost?" she asked as the driver rolled down his window.

The man was fifty, as weathered as the hills, and about as talkative. "Yer name Hope?"

"Yes," she answered, a question in her voice.

"Where ya want it?"

"What?"

"Seed." He jerked a grizzled chin toward the truck bed.

She peered around and saw the bags of oat hay and alfalfa seed. "I didn't order any seed."

He nodded and waited impatiently, wanting to know where to unload.

"If I didn't order any seed, then that's not my seed in the truck," said Hope reasonably.

"Rio sez bring it. I brung it." He stared at her, waiting to be told where to put the seed. A look of exasperation crossed his unshaven face. "Where ya want it?"

"I'll show you," said Mason, coming up behind Hope. "You say Rio sent it?"

The man grunted and revved the truck's engine, having exhausted his well of small talk. In utter bemusement Hope watched the man back up to one of the storage sheds and begin unloading bag after bag of seed. He answered no questions, asked none, and refused anything more than a cup of coffee.

After the man had gone, Mason silently slit a bag. Smooth, rich, plump, the satiny contents cascaded from his hands and whispered back into the sack. "Prime," he said softly. "Really prime seed."

Hope said nothing, simply thrust in her hands and let seeds pour from one hand to the other, seeing fields green with alfalfa and shimmering gold with oats. There were thousands of dollars worth of seed stacked neatly in the shed, sacks pregnant with future harvests. With Rio's seed she could begin to rebuild the Valley of the Sun.

When she slept that night she dreamed of Rio's child, her child, their child running through fields thick with grain and sweet with alfalfa flowers. The dream slowly changed, filled with the muted thunder of rain. She woke up in a rush only to find that it wasn't rain that had awakened her, but trucks—a convoy of cattle trucks pulling into her yard. Above the roar of diesels came the concerted bawling of yearling steers.

Rio?

Again, like lightning, the thought scored across Hope's emotions. She pulled on her clothes with fierce speed, kicking into her boots even as she yanked on her jacket. When she ran into the front yard the sun was barely more than an incandescent fingernail hooked over Eagle Peak.

"You Hope?" asked a broad, bluff-looking man as he climbed down out of the diesel's high cab.

"Yes," she said, looking up into his wind-roughened face.

"Name's Martin," he said, holding out his hand.

Hope shook it, feeling as though she were still asleep, still dreaming. The sound and the smell of cattle swirled around her on the April wind, stirring her. She had missed their earthy smells and plaintive bawls. She looked at them yearningly.

"Yeah, you're Hope all right," Martin said, smiling. "He said, 'Look for a woman with dreams in her eyes.' "

Hope's eyes widened, revealing hazel depths where both gold and shadows turned. "Rio sent you?"

"Sure did. Where do you want the calves?"

"But I didn't order—" Her voice broke. She started over again. "Mr. Martin—"

"Just Martin, ma'am."

"Martin," she amended somewhat desperately, wondering how to tell this man that she hadn't ordered cows because there wasn't enough money to pay for them. Not yet. Not until she harvested and sold a few crops. "I can't afford—"

Martin shook his head. "Nothing was said about money, ma'am. Didn't Rio tell you we were coming?"

She shook her head mutely.

"Yeah, well, that's Rio. He was edgy as hell when I saw him. Never saw a man so restless. He came four months early and didn't hardly even stay for a cup of coffee. Just gave me your name and told me to ship whatever I owed him down here."

"Down here?" said Hope, shaking her head, feeling as though she were drowning in the dawn and the bawl of cattle. "Where are you from?"

"Montana. Don't mind telling you, it was some trick to comb these yearling steers out of a late blizzard and ship them through a Montana spring." He smiled suddenly, his dark eyes alive with laughter. "Not that I mind. If Rio had said drive 'em to Hawaii, I'd have loaded 'em up and driven west until my hat floated." He glanced over at the pasture opposite the house. "That fence strong enough to hold back a few yearlings?"

Hope closed her eyes and took a deep breath. The earthy smell of cattle was like a homecoming. "Yes."

She turned and walked toward the big gate leading into the pasture. She didn't know where she was going to find food for all the cattle—there had to be hundreds of them, and even now another truck was pulling up to the ranch. Although the winter had been mild, there wasn't enough natural food yet for the cattle. Then she realized that she could buy hay with the money she had earmarked for seed.

Yearling Herefords crowded down the ramps and spread over the pasture like a rich russet tide. The bawling of cattle rose to meet the cataract of light spilling down from the Perdidas. Hope leaned on the fence and watched, hardly able to believe her eyes. She sensed Martin coming up beside her. She turned to him with a smile that made him wish she weren't Rio's woman. He had no doubt that she was, though. It had been in Rio's eyes when he spoke her name— and in hers when she spoke his.

"They're beautiful," she said, emotions resonating through her voice.

Martin laughed as he looked at the wild-eyed, winter-lean yearlings fanning across the pasture. "You're a rancher, all right. Nobody else would think those ragged steers were beautiful."

Hope hesitated, watching Martin, wanting to know how Rio had looked, if he was happy or sad, well or drawn out to a fine humming wire of tension. Like her. *Restless. Edgy as hell.* Like Rio.

"I didn't know they were short of water in Montana," said Hope, fishing delicately for information.

Martin gave her an amused look. "Not hardly. I met Rio a different way. I found three men driving about forty of my cattle into Canada. I should have gone for help, but I was so damn mad I just waded right in. You see, those cows were every penny I had in the world." Martin shook his head, remembering. "Well, to make a long story short, the men beat hell out of me and left for dead. I would have been, too, if Rio hadn't happened along. He patched me up, got me to a doctor, and disappeared. When I got home again a week later, every last one of my cows was back like nothing had ever happened."

With a quick jerk to his Stetson, Martin continued. "Rio stayed and ran things until I was on my feet again. I told him that half of everything I owned was his. He refused it, saying even God only took a tenth, and God was a hell of a lot more useful than one cross-breed Indian." Martin shook his head. "That was twelve years ago. Rio's never asked a thing from me, until now." With a smile the Montanan added, "And I've done right well for myself in those years."

Martin and his men left a few hours later. The rest of the day was relatively peaceful until Hope and Mason sat down to dinner. They had barely picked up their forks before two huge hay trucks rumbled up the road. She and Mason looked at each other and got up without a word. As soon as they reached the yard a familiar greeting rang out.

"Where you want it?"

The drivers of the two trucks were a husband-and-wife team. Four brawny teenage boys were with them. Mason directed them to the hay shelter, talked with them for a few minutes, and came back to Hope.

"Rio sent them. From New Mexico."

The Webster family stayed long enough to unload the hay, drink quarts of coffee, and shake hands all around. Both Websters assured Hope that this was just a small part of what they owed Rio, but it was all he would take. If Hope ever came up short of feed, though, she should give them a holler.

The next afternoon two more cattle trucks arrived. Hope thought she was beyond the ability to be surprised, but she was wrong. When she recognized the name on the truck cabs she felt hot and then cold. *McNally's Black Angus.* She had bought Sweetheart from McNally, and sold her back to him, too.

"Bob?" she asked in a dazed voice as the short, thick man climbed down out of the lead truck. "Bob McNally?"

"As ever was," he said, grinning. "Nice place you got here," he said, looking around at the ranch where late afternoon sunlight flowed like honey across the land. "Mite dry, but Rio said he solved that particular problem." Bob stretched like a man who had spent too many hours behind the wheel. As the other driver walked up, Bob said, "Well, honey, where do you want your Angus?"

Behind Hope, Mason laughed and swore softly. He gestured to the other driver, showing him the pasture gate. As the truck was backed into the opening and the ramp let down, Hope began to argue with Bob McNally.

"*My* Angus? If they belong to anyone, they belong to Rio!"

"That sure isn't what he said." Bob pulled on his Stetson's pale rim, steadying the hat against the playful tugs of the wind. He touched the side of the black metal truck. "These are yours, Hope. Every last hair on their shiny little hides."

"I can't take them. I haven't done anything to earn them."

Bob looked at Hope with pale blue eyes that saw through her carefully controlled voice to the woman beneath. "That's not what Rio said. He said you'd sold your cattle, your horses, your future—because you believed in him. When anyone else would have cut their losses and run, you stuck it out. And you did it knowing full well what the odds against you were." Bob smiled strangely. "That reached Rio down where nobody ever touched him before. Kind of opened him up and made him bleed. These cattle are yours, honey."

"But—"

"Watch you don't get trampled, ma'am," called the driver as he freed the cattle.

Mason and Bob gently crowded Hope back out of the way. She didn't object anymore. She couldn't. She had recognized the first of the sleek black cows to come down the ramp.

"Sweetheart!"

The cow's head came up at the familiar voice. She ambled down the ramp and nudged Hope with a damp muzzle, looking for grain. Her calves followed her, grown and half grown, dense black cattle walking down the ramp and drifting over the familiar pasture to pick at the sheen of new growth that winter rains had called from the land. The wind followed them, ruffling their thick, lustrous coats.

"I—I can't take them," said Hope, her eyes wide,

her hands clenched as she fought not to rub down Sweetheart's solid barrel. "These never were Rio's cattle."

Bob shrugged. "Without Rio I wouldn't have had a pot to piss in or a window to throw it out of. He was only fifteen when he found water for me. I gave him two heifers and the use of my best bull. He never came back for them or their calves until this year." Bob smiled. "Came time to sort out what was his, we both just kind of decided that these had his name on them. Now if you don't agree, you're just going to have to take it up with Rio. I sure as hell don't plan on crossing him."

Without making a conscious decision Hope found her hands rubbing through Sweetheart's warm coat. "They're Rio's," she said huskily. "As long as the water flows."

"There's a new one in here," said Bob, going to the back of his own truck. "I'd recommend the barn, but it's your choice."

The other driver pulled his truck out of the pasture, shutting the gate behind. Hope and Mason followed Bob to the first truck. They watched as a massive black bull walked down the ramp with ponderous grace. Every rippling muscle proclaimed the animal's extraordinary breeding. Though the bull could have easily crushed the humans, it stood quietly, waiting for the man's signal. Bob spoke softly to the bull. It watched him with calm, very dark eyes.

"I can't—" said Hope, her voice breaking. The bull was worth more than her whole herd of Angus put together. "I just can't take him!"

"You want me to tell Rio that you couldn't find room in your barn for his bull?" asked Bob blandly.

"Yes! No!" Then, despairingly, "Damn you, Rio! I didn't want you to feel guilty about me!"

Hope turned and ran to the house. Mason and Bob

exchanged a long look and led the bull to a huge stall in the barn.

When Hope went to bed that night her mind was a turmoil. The wind brought the random scents and sounds of cattle swirling through the darkness. The scents and sounds of her dream. They were Rio's cattle, Rio's hay, Rio's seed—but the dream was hers, dreamed for herself and for the man who had no dreams.

Just after dawn several pickup trucks rattled into the yard. The sound of a truck door slamming and a man's voice hailing the house brought Hope upright in bed, her heart hammering with a sudden wild hope. *Rio?* She pulled on her clothes, kicked into her boots, and raced down the stairs. The yard in front of the barn was alive with pickup trucks hauling horse trailers. Three, four, five trucks, each pulling a four- or six-horse trailer. And inside were sturdy cow ponies. Drivers climbed out, stretched, called back and forth among the trucks with the rough voices of men who have been up all night drinking coffee and smoking cigarettes.

"Mornin', ma'am. You be Hope?" asked one of the men. He was tall and thin with a Tennessee accent running like a warm river through his speech.

"Yes."

"Pleasure, ma'am," he said, touching the brim of his hat. Then he turned his head, whistled shrilly through his teeth, and called, "Yo! Jake! This here is Rio's woman!"

Jake came over, shook Hope's hand, and asked, "Where do you want us to put our gear?"

"What?"

"Our gear, ma'am. Rio said you needed help."

"I can't afford to pay you," said Hope bluntly.

Jake smiled gently. "Makes no never mind, ma'am.

We couldn't pay Rio, neither. Didn't stop him none. Won't stop us."

"But—"

"Ma'am, I sure do hope you're not going to put us crossways of Rio. He's got his heart set on us being here."

In the end Mason led everyone to the second bunkhouse. Other than Jake and the tall man from Tennessee, the rest of the "men" were hardly more than boys. They had handled cattle and horses all their lives, however, and it showed.

"Oh, ma'am?" called Jake.

"Yes?"

"This one's yours," he said, leading Dusk out of one of the trailers. "Rio said you liked to ride at night, and he was worried about you getting on a spooky horse."

"Thank you," she whispered helplessly. She hadn't ridden since she sold her mares, for she had been afraid to risk her pregnancy on one of Storm Walker's friendly bucking sessions.

In the days and weeks that followed, in twos and fives and tens, beef and breeding cattle arrived from every state west of the Rockies. Hope gave up objecting to the men who drove the trucks. Despite differences in age and wealth, the men all shared an absolute determination not to cross the man called Rio.

As the fifth month without Rio began, Hope thought she had accepted it all—the loss of Rio and the gain of the well, the loss of Rio and the gain of the cattle, the loss of Rio and the gain of his child. She thought she was strong enough to see him in every sunrise, hear his name in every wind, taste him in every silver drop of water from his well and not destroy herself in her endless longing for him.

And then one more afternoon came, one more truck pulled in the yard, and one more man asked her, "Where do you want them?"

In unnatural silence Hope watched horses led down the ramp into the corral. They were magnificent animals, long-legged mares with clear eyes and powerful haunches and life running through them like leashed lightning. Mares cake-walking across the yard, their heads raised high, nostrils flared to drink the scent of the wind sweeping down from the Perdidas. Wind ruffled silky manes and tails, whispered to pricked ears the secrets of the land, and then sped on.

Hope stood without moving, riveted by the mares' beauty. A dream burst within her, a vision of the future when Storm Walker's foals would grow sleek and strong, running through fields where grass never failed and water always flowed. Rio's stock and her land and their child, and the artesian fountain he had found hidden deep within rock, water flowing, an endless promise of life.

The Valley of the Sun was truly alive again.

Tears flowed silently, helplessly, down Hope's cheeks. She hadn't cried when Rio left or in all the long hours since then. But she couldn't stop crying now. To see her family's dream come true, her father's dream, her own dream, and yet to be alone within that dream . . .

Hope turned and blindly made her way to the barn. Jake and Mason saw her, saw her tears and her fumbling fingers, and gently took the bridle from her hands.

"Going for a ride?" asked Mason.

Hope nodded, unable to speak.

"Then you'll want Dusk," said Jake.

She nodded again.

The two men went off and quickly returned with Dusk. Though it was a very mild spring day, Jake had brought his own heavy jacket back with him. He wrapped it around Hope, Mason handed her the reins, and both men stepped aside while she rode into the yard.

"She going to be all right?" asked Jake in a low voice.

"She better be," growled Mason, "or I'm gonna skin that thickheaded son of a bitch and use his hide to wipe my boots."

Jake smiled a bit grimly. "Holler if you need help. Me and the boys—well," he said with a shrug, "we owe Rio, but that's one damned fine woman."

Dusk knew where to go without being told. She took to the road eagerly. Hope rode without thinking about it, still lost in the moment when she had realized that she wasn't as strong as she had thought she was. She wasn't as strong as she had to be to live on the Valley of the Sun alone within her dream. So she rode blindly, tears welling over her cheeks faster than the wind could dry them.

The mare stopped just beyond the rim of the artesian pond, where grass grew in startling, lush profusion, nourished by the water. Hope dismounted, leaving Dusk in the patch of grass, finding another for herself. She sat without moving, remembering how it had been to be fully alive within her dream and Rio's arms. With memories came tears the color of artesian water streaming down her face. Sunlight thickened into the rich orange and molten gold of late afternoon. The wind lifted, keening over the land. Hope neither saw the sun nor heard the wind. She was lost in her memories and her broken dream.

"Hope?"

The voice was from the broken dream, deep and warm, a richness that was like a caress. Rio's hand smoothed over Hope's hair, calling her from her memories. She blinked and saw Rio through her tears. For a moment her eyes blazed with returning life, a dream made whole again. But even as emotion swept through her, she realized that she was seeing just half of a dream. The wind had blown, bringing him back to her.

And it would blow again, taking him away.

The life that had blazed in Hope faded, taking the dreams from her eyes. Rio called her name in a raw voice and knelt beside her. She took his hand and cradled it against her cheek, wondering why half a dream took more strength to survive than a dream that was utterly broken. He gathered her against his body as though she were more fragile than the dreams that had faded from her eyes.

"I'm sorry, I never meant to hurt you," he whispered, rocking her, stroking the cool silk of her hair, repeating the words as though if he just said them often enough they would take away her tears and replace them with the incandescent dreams that had once been there.

She simply put her arms around him and let herself drift within half a dream, too emotionally spent to do more than fill her senses with his presence. He eased her down into the grass, cradling her against his warmth, talking to her softly, trying to explain the wind. His husky words wept over her like immaterial tears.

"I've spent my life roaming the land, looking for . . . something. Like the wind, I never found it. Then I came to the Valley of the Sun and saw you fighting for your dream. I wanted to help you as I had helped other people who dreamed. So I stayed.

"And then I began to dream, too," said Rio, brushing his lips over Hope's soft hair. "I dreamed of a woman who loved the land more than she loved anything—yet she risked everything she loved on a drifter's belief that he could find water where none had ever been found before. I dreamed of a woman strong enough to stand against drought and soft enough to set my body on fire. I dreamed of a woman who offered me herself and asked nothing in return. I dreamed of a woman who looked at a half-breed and saw a man, and loved what she saw."

Rio's arms tightened even as he felt the shudder of emotion that took Hope's body. He didn't know whether it was joy or rage, love or hate, that made her tremble against him. He knew only that he had taken the dreams from her eyes and had left the emptiness of the wind in their place.

"My dream and your love frightened me," he admitted huskily. "It was like a beautiful cage closing around me, demanding that I stay. So I ran and tried to find freedom in all the places I'd found it before. The land was there but it wasn't the same. It didn't dream. It didn't reach into my soul and make me want to dream with it. There was nothing but the wind mocking me, wind as empty as I was."

With a deep, yearning sound, Rio kissed Hope. Her hands crept beneath his jacket, feeling the tension of his muscles and his heat radiating through her. She tried to speak, to tell him that she loved him, but her throat was filled with tears. In the end she simply held him and watched him with eyes that accepted everything, even the wind.

"So I came back to the Valley of the Sun," said Rio, wanting to explain what he barely had begun to understand himself. "The ranch looked beautiful, more beautiful than my dreams—until I found out that you weren't there. No one would tell me where you were, when you would come back, *if* you would come back. Even Jake. He just looked me in the eye, said you'd cried for me, and I'd better not hurt you again." Rio's arms held Hope as though he were afraid he would wake and find her gone. "I came here, looking for memories, and I found you, my dream." He kissed her deeply, knowing again the sweetness of her mouth. "Marry me, dreamer," he whispered, "love me as much as I love you."

"Rio," she said, her voice shivering with tears even as she turned her lips to his, "I don't want to cage the wind. You'd hate me."

"Never," he said softly. "I've found out that the wind is empty, not free. Like me without you. You're my freedom." He straightened for a moment and looked into her eyes, golden with the setting sun. "Marry me. Be with me. You—" He hesitated, then kissed her with a gentleness that made tears run like molten gold over her cheeks, over his lips. "You don't have to have my children," he whispered. "I know that's too much to ask of any woman, even in my dreams."

Hope laughed and cried and whispered her love as she unfastened the heavy man's jacket she wore, and the jeans and blouse beneath. She took Rio's hands and moved them over the warm silver necklace and the woman beneath, over her swollen breasts, her thickened waist, and her stomach rounded with the promise of his child. She felt the sudden trembling of his hands, saw the disbelief and the incredible hope in his eyes as he looked at her.

"Yes," she whispered.

Rio bent his head and she felt his lips move over her skin, felt the warmth of his breath against her breasts and the unexpected, agonizing heat of his tears as he laid his cheek against her rounded womb and whispered his love for her. His words and his tears and his touch told her he would always be with her, as close as her heartbeat, as deeply a part of her as the water hidden far beneath them; and like that water, their love would well forth irresistibly, bringing life to everything it touched.

The wind ruffled the silver surface of the artesian pond, caressed the two lovers entwined on the grass, and then sang softly down the canyon, blowing over the land, blowing alone.

READERS' COMMENTS ON SILHOUETTE INTIMATE MOMENTS:

"About a month ago a friend loaned me my first Silhouette. I was thoroughly surprised as well as totally addicted. Last week I read a Silhouette Intimate Moments and I was even more pleased. They are the best romance series novels I have ever read. They give much more depth to the plot, characters, and the story is fundamentally realistic. They incorporate tasteful sex scenes, which is a must, especially in the 1980's. I only hope you can publish them fast enough."

S.B.*, Lees Summit, MO

"After noticing the attractive covers on the new line of Silhouette Intimate Moments, I decided to read the inside and discovered that this new line was more in the line of books that I like to read. I do want to say I enjoyed the books because they are so realistic and a lot more truthful than so many romance books today."

J.C., Onekama, MI

"I would like to compliment you on your books. I will continue to purchase all of the Silhouette Intimate Moments. They are your best line of books that I have had the pleasure of reading."

S.M., Billings, MT

*names available on request